TOMB SWEEPING

ALSO BY ALEXANDRA CHANG

Days of Distraction

TOMB SWEEPING

STORIES

ALEXANDRA CHANG

ecco
An Imprint of HarperCollins*Publishers*

This is a work of fiction. Names, characters, places, and incidents are products of the author's imagination or are used fictitiously and are not to be construed as real. Any resemblance to actual events, locales, organizations, or persons, living or dead, is entirely coincidental.

HarperCollins books may be purchased for educational, business, or sales promotional use. For information, please email the Special Markets Department at SPsales@harpercollins.com.

FIRST EDITION

Designed by Jennifer Chung

Library of Congress Cataloging-in-Publication Data has been applied for.

ISBN 978-0-06-295184-7

23 24 25 26 27 LBC 6 5 4 3 2

FOR IRVING AND AJ,

TO JEFF

CONTENTS

TOMB SWEEPING

UNKNOWN BY UNKNOWN

I

When I'd gotten laid off, the managers said it had nothing to do with my performance. They had purchased a piece of software that could do my job at a thousand times the speed. There was no way I could compete, and they were very sorry. They offered me a month of severance for every year I had been at the company. Seven months of pay.

I had joined when I was still considered a young woman, twenty-seven, at the cusp of my late twenties. Now I was very much in my thirties, jobless, with nothing tying me to the place where I lived besides the one-bedroom apartment I rented that still had ten months on the lease. I wasn't hurting for money yet, but I was bored and growing increasingly anxious. I suspected I should be doing more with my time than eating weed gummies and lying in bed binge-watching reality dating shows with heinous and hilarious names like *Simp Island* and *From Stalker to Lover*. The shows made me certain I would die alone. It wasn't necessarily the most frightening thought, since I liked being alone, but it was the first time in my life that I had the time to meditate on my mortality, on how everything I had spent the last seven years of my life doing—focusing on my career, developing my independence, saving my money for some future better life—had been, ultimately, meaningless, and it stirred inside me feelings I had difficulty understanding, let alone managing.

Two months into unemployed life, a former coworker took pity on me. He texted to ask if I would be open to a monthlong house- and pet-sitting job for friends of his family, who were having a hard time finding somebody they could trust (and, I assumed, had the free time in their schedule). The only requirement: a video interview with the owners of the house. The work acquaintance suspected it was more a formality—he had already told them I was a perfect fit. I had been perceived as competent at my previous job. I listened, I didn't fuss, I fixed other people's mistakes.

The proposal of escape into someone else's home, someone else's life, appealed to me.

Over video chat, I caught my first glimpses of the house's interior. A modernist chandelier hung in the background, there was a hint of a giant fiddle-leaf fig, a few large paintings on the walls. It was a pixelated and glitchy mess—the internet connection was weak at the house.

"We're up in the most beautiful, secluded hills," said the owners. They were a nice-looking white couple in their fifties, artists and art collectors with a dog named Georgia—"After Georgia O'Keeffe, of course"—and would be going on a "long-needed inspirational trip" to Portugal now that travel had reopened. They warned that not only did they have limited internet access, but phone service could be challenging, too. They had a landline I could use, thousands of satellite TV channels, and a vast collection of DVDs and records. "You won't be left wanting," they promised.

They went into great detail about the intricacies of the house, attempting to point their iPad's camera at the kitchen sink, the guest bedrooms (I could choose from three), the husband's recording studio full of instruments (hobbyist only, I was welcome to use), the wife's painting studio (please don't disturb), their meditation room, the deck hot tub, the backyard swimming pool, the indoor fireplace, the outdoor fire pit . . . I wasn't able to make out much beyond the outlines of items frozen on the screen, and the owners' voices often cut out. It was, however, clear how beautiful the place would be in person. How it would be an escape from my living situation, an escape from the stomping of the neighbors in the apartment upstairs, the sirens of passing ambulances and fire trucks, the strange smell emanating from beneath the kitchen sink, the persistent hum coming from some unknown part of the building.

I nodded and took notes while the owners talked. They liked that. I could see the digital jerks of their nodding heads, their disjointed smiles through the screen. They told me I was wonderful, something I hadn't heard in a long time. I was susceptible to praise. I felt a warmth rise up from my legs into my chest—the sense that my life was back on its intended path. They asked me to promise that I would take the very best care of their home and dog, and most of all, they hoped I would benefit from the space, which they called, euphemistically, "a beautiful retreat from the world's increasing chaos." I had never been on a retreat, let alone worked a job described as a retreat. I told Katherine and Erik—those were their names—that I would be most appreciative of the opportunity.

On the day of my arrival, I was late, and the couple had only fifteen minutes to show me around their home before their driver would arrive and take them to the nearest airport two hours away. The house was more secluded than I had realized, which was why it had taken me so long to get there, by train, then bus, then taxi for the last remote leg into the woods. Katherine and Eric were gracious and told me not to apologize. They hugged me on the porch and welcomed me in through a giant arched wooden door with matching arched windowpanes.

The house was a California Arts and Crafts revival, according to the owners. It had an open-concept layout—a long gigantic room where spaces flowed naturally from one to another based on the arrangement of furniture, all of which had an elegance and warmth that shocked me into silent appreciation. None of it was ostentatious, which made it all the more desirable. The floors were made of beautiful wide slats of blond wood, finished perfectly, not too shiny or too matte, the natural grain adding warmth to the space. There was an entire wall of floor-to-ceiling windows, framed in that same beautiful blond wood, which overlooked the forest. Two panels slid open onto a wraparound deck.

The house was high up in the hills of Northern California, where the redwoods reigned. Though the house technically fell within the borders of a nearby town, it was in one of those areas that had its own unofficial name used by everyone in the know who lived there, indicating it was far nicer than whatever was in the flats. From the deck, all I could see were the old trees cascading down, down, down. If I squinted, I could make out the blue of Monterey Bay in the beyond. There were no other houses in sight, though I knew from the drive up that a few were tucked away like this one, hidden along the hillside.

The couple's dog, Georgia, followed us wherever we went, panting and rubbing her body against our legs, especially mine. I scratched her from neck to butt, which made her pant harder and left my jeans covered in her white Lab hairs.

"She likes you," said Katherine. "What a wonderful sign."

The couple seemed to believe in signs.

"We'd just about given up on the trip when we heard about you," Katherine relayed as Erik *mmm*ed and *hmm*ed in agreement. "It was the most perfect timing. A wonderful sign that this was meant to be." Katherine said she and Erik had fallen in love with this house because of a sign—the previous owners were selling the house fully furnished, art, plants, and all. A few pieces of art matched the couple's taste, and as Katherine was a painter, she knew it was meant to be. She told Erik she absolutely had to have this house.

"And the view took my breath away!" said Katherine. "Of course, we replaced most of the furniture."

"Whatever Katherine wants," Erik said, smiling.

The couple's dynamic reminded me of something a friend once told me after her breakup: that the only healthy (hetero—though my friend hadn't specified this at the time) relationships are the ones where the woman is in charge. I could see that Katherine and Erik had a very healthy relationship. I was especially taken by Katherine, who moved with a grace and effortlessness that put me in mind of a heron I'd once seen preening itself in a creek. I wanted a life like hers.

The driver soon arrived, and Erik left to load their suitcases.

"One last thing," Katherine said, walking me to the back of the property. She pointed out the trail behind the house that led even higher up the hill. The trailhead started at the foot of a tall, blackened tree trunk. "The previous owners told us this tree burned two hundred years ago," Katherine said. "Isn't it stunning?" I nodded. We stared in reverence at the tree for a few seconds. "It's a lovely, relaxing hike up the trail," Katherine added. "But do avoid the shed up there. It's not structurally sound." She said that a construction crew would be there in a couple of weeks to tear the shed down and build another, bigger one, where Erik's music studio would be relocated. They required more space.

II

After the owners left, I walked around the house, looking at everything on the tall shelving units, noting the placement of each small item—fountain pens, slippers, candles, seashells, a golden bookmark in the shape of a sailboat, framed photographs—and opening drawers in the kitchen, in the office, in the bedrooms, to take in and memorize what exactly went where. The house and its contents held a power over me that was intoxicating. The entire home had a sublime lived-in quality that looked perfectly tidy, and I did not want to disturb each item's rightful place. I wanted to ensure that when the owners returned, I left behind no trace of myself.

Katherine had written extensive notes about the house, more than twenty pages typed out and left paper-clipped on the kitchen's marble island countertop. I looked over them, checking and rechecking the schedule of my tasks and the various numbers and codes for the driveway gate, front door, and help lines. The notes also included details on how to use and care for the house's various amenities.

I developed a routine. In the mornings, I did as the notes directed: fed Georgia her food along with two CBD chew treats, then let her out onto the property, where she could carry on with her morning activities of chasing lizards and sunbathing. Every Thursday, I followed this by watering the indoor and deck plants—a task that took a good twenty minutes, each huge pot requiring a full watering can. I walked back and forth from sink to plant, taking my time to ensure all life in the house was nourished.

Afterward, I carefully made cappuccinos with the mini La Marzocco espresso machine (from working in coffee shops during college, I knew these cost several thousand dollars) and sat at the sturdy wood breakfast table (not to be confused with the formal marble dining table beneath the modernist chandelier) as the morning light came in through the wall of windows that looked out onto the forest. Though I wanted to leave no trace of my presence in the house, I also wanted to inhabit the space as it was meant to be inhabited, to fully experience a life deserving of a home like this one. I rode the Peloton in the downstairs workout room, then used the hand weights to do a set of exercises pinned to a corkboard on the wall. I would occasionally sit on a pillow in the meditation room and turn on the Bose sound system, which played a CD of underwater whale sounds produced by a nearby aquarium. I took baths in the guest bathroom's jet tub, with lavender salts Katherine had specified in her notes that she'd bought for my use. Every other evening, I would dip test strips into the hot tub's water to check its pH levels, soak there for a bit when the weather cooled, then toss in the requisite scoops of chlorine, calcium, and pH increaser or decreaser to maintain the tub water's health. After every meal, I would clean the kitchen so that it looked as though nobody had cooked anything, ensuring that the stove and counter surfaces were not marred by even a droplet of water.

This is all to say that I took my time there very seriously.

The deck was my favorite feature, made of dark-stained wood and wrapped along two sides of the house that overlooked the hills. At noon each day, I ate a lunch of nuts, a salad, and a stove-grilled vegetarian sausage from the market a fifteen-minute drive down the hill and, afterward, went out on the deck to tan. I made sure to apply the owners' tanning oil each time. I'd lie flat and still as a corpse in a bikini, on the "chaise longue," as the owners had called it, sometimes topless, sometimes occupied with a book pulled from the home's shelves. I'd turn my body a dozen times, imagining myself slowly cooking like an animal on a spit. I pretended this would be my life forever. Sometimes as I lay there, I felt as though I were dissolving, what distinguished my body from its surroundings melting away. Occasionally, the sensation frightened me, but most of the time I was relieved. I wouldn't matter anymore. I would no longer be matter. Always the feeling would pass, and I would return to my body and its boundaries. When I was done each day, I would take a photo of myself against one of the house's exterior walls, lines of sweat visible on my face. The house was the color of my skin. Or close enough. A mauvy pink, with undertones of brown. I wanted to document my progress of blending in.

Below the deck, there was a lovely tiered garden with lavender and succulents and bamboo, along with wildflowers I couldn't name but which I photographed meticulously, as well as a small orchard of a few lemon and avocado and orange trees. The wildlife appeared happier up here. The bees clustered around the lavender bushes and never bothered me. Lizards lay out on sunbaked rocks with their eyes slitted, so at peace they wouldn't skitter away unless I reached out to touch them. The occasional deer wandered through the property, though they were often scared off by Georgia's barks. Besides the barking, the dog would spend most of the day sleeping, moving herself from deck to dirt to deck to dirt. When I tried to coax Georgia up the steep trail for her daily afternoon walk, she would go as far as one particular curve, then sit, immovable, unless I waved a treat for her to follow. Even then, she would take only a few steps until I offered her another bite. We never made it as far as the to-be-avoided shed, though I could see it not far off from the spot where Georgia stopped to chew on whatever wood chip or branch she could find. It was nothing of note, though it certainly looked run down, with faded green paint and a caving roof. Georgia would then whine to go back to the comfort of the house. She was the most stubborn and lazy and spoiled dog I had ever met, and I grew to love her for these qualities.

I had never felt more alive and purposeful than in that house. The quiet of the hills sharpened my senses. Before coming to the house, I couldn't recall the last time I had been thrilled or moved or excited by anything. I couldn't recall anything significant from the last seven years of working. And since I'd been laid off, I had grown increasingly numb scrolling through job listings with words that seemed to evaporate upon reading, their meaning emptied out, only unfamiliar shapes and sounds.

But here in the house, every moment contained meaning. The way the light came in through the bedroom window in the morning signaled the weather. The way Georgia nudged my hand for food spoke to her mood and attitude for the day. How my coffee tasted indicated my own mood and attitude, which was largely positive, grateful, openhearted. When I walked from one place to another, the bottoms of my feet were alert to the wood's cool touch; I could feel the arch of my sole and each toe pressing gently off the floor until landing again. I imagined being as elegant as a water bug skidding on the surface of a pond, or an ice-skater landing a jump, or the owners, who I was certain moved through the house with such grace and purpose.

I would often stop in front of the home's many paintings, gauging my reaction, whether I could see something new or different each time I looked. They were all nameless—it was not, after all, a museum—and I could not find any record of who had made them, each signature an illegible squiggle. They were by people who I assumed the current or previous owners knew personally, or were famous enough to be wanted in a home like this one. Some could have been Katherine's paintings, for all I knew.

My favorite one was a relatively small painting, maybe sixteen by twenty inches, that hung in the hallway outside the guest bedroom. It wasn't given one of the prime wall spaces, possibly because of its size, or because it was somewhat odd. It was an abstract painting, I think. The background looked like it could be a park of sorts, various greens in the lower two thirds in strokes that resembled grass and trees, then deep blues and purples and pinks in the upper third, a raucous sky. In the foreground, there were body parts of various shades strewn about—several hands and feet, four ears, three arms, five legs, two torsos, three noses, and five cylindrical shapes I assumed to be necks. If I were to describe it to somebody, I imagine it might sound like a creepy painting. I'm not an art person, and I don't know the language of painting, but whenever I looked at this one, it disoriented me in a way that made me happy to be alive. I felt reborn, like that past version of myself was only a cartoon of who I truly was.

III

I never felt lonely in the house. I hadn't realized how lonely I'd been previously until I arrived there, like a lifelong ache I'd understood as the norm had been relieved. In part, Georgia kept me company. There was also a constant rotation of people who would come up the long driveway throughout the week. The owners had a lot of help—landscapers, housecleaner, pool cleaner, septic experts—who, too, moved with purpose and expertise. I appreciated what each person did to maintain the glory of the house, but really, we didn't speak much, and we all stayed out of each other's ways to accomplish our tasks. The lack of loneliness came instead from the house itself, the way it held and protected me.

It wasn't until the beginning of my last week in the house that my routine was broken, when the construction crew finally arrived to tear down and rebuild the shed up the hill. They were a noisy group of three men who blasted sports talk radio from their giant truck as they pulled up the driveway. Georgia barked like mad at them, unfamiliar with their smells and sounds. I was out on the deck before they had shut off the engine. One of the men, presumably the boss, yelled over the still-blasting radio that they knew what to do and they'd stay up the hill, out of my hair.

That was far from the case. The owners had rented a porta potty that was delivered the day prior, placed at the trailhead by the two-hundred-year-old burnt tree trunk, so that the men wouldn't have to come into the house and bother me. But they did bother me. Their noises rolled down the hill and through the house's open windows. Even with the windows closed, I could hear them hollering and laughing, banging and breaking, running down the hill to use the porta potty, slamming its thin plastic door, then running back up, all while complaining and joking about their dumps. I could do none of my usual tasks and roamed the house anxiously, waiting for them to leave. I tried to find comfort in the house's many objects—the espresso machine, the deck, my favorite painting of limbs—but I couldn't focus, my mind on the noise.

At the end of their first day of work, there was a knock on the front door. The head of the crew stood on the porch, his pale stubbled face red and sweaty from being out in the sun. Seeing him up close, I felt badly about my animosity toward him and his workers—they were hired by the owners and were only doing their jobs, just like me.

"Miss," he said, "sorry to bother you."

"Oh no, it's really fine," I said, putting on my most convincing smile, one, I realized, I hadn't used in weeks.

"Well, wanted to let you know we're done for today. Tore down the whole shed, and we'll be back at it early tomorrow to start building. Should be done in a couple days. Didn't know what to do with the stuff inside, though." He gestured at two slack trash bags at the corner of the porch. "Property owners said they'd cleared it out. This yours?"

"Mine?"

"Sorry we had to put it in trash bags to carry down."

"I've never been up to the shed," I said. The shed had not been part of my routine. Katherine had said to avoid it. Now I felt stupid. Avoid did not mean completely ignore. I had over-obeyed. That I'd lived here for three weeks and never once examined the place torn down by these strange men felt like a major oversight. I should have been more aware of its presence, as a good house sitter would be.

"So it's not yours? Happy to dump it, then."

"No," I said, a bit too abruptly. I was looking at the bags, confused, curious, defensive. "Maybe it's stuff the owners want to keep."

"I dunno," the man said. "Looked like a bunch of junk to me."

One of the crew members honked the horn of the truck.

The man turned around and flipped him off. "Shut up! Can't you see I'm talking to the lady!" The other men yelled back words about being hungry, needing to go home, hurry up.

"You can go," I said.

"Apologies for my dumbass crew." He looked at the trash bags again. "You sure you don't want me to take it? It's no problem. We've got space in the truck."

"No, leave it. I'll take a look and send a note to the owners. You can always take it tomorrow if it's trash."

He nodded slowly but didn't turn to leave. He looked as though he wanted to say more.

"Is there anything else?"

"I mean." He paused, then said quietly, "You out here all alone? Doesn't seem like the safest place for a young lady to be alone."

The hair on my arms raised. A sign. I felt my face flush, my heart start to beat faster. I looked behind me, toward the safety of the house.

"Oh," he said, appearing genuinely embarrassed. "I don't mean anything by that." He scratched at one of his elbows. We both stood there uncomfortably. I waited. "I just mean. Well, I wouldn't want my own daughter out here on her own. But it looks like you're doing just fine."

"Okay," I managed. "Thanks for your concern."

"All right, miss," he said. "I'm sorry to bother you. See you tomorrow."

As soon as he turned to leave, I went back inside and deadbolted the door, then stood at the front window, watching the truck go down the driveway, taking the loud men away. I didn't move until they were completely out of sight, then waited another few minutes. I couldn't say what about the man's comment disturbed me, other than it had. It was instinctual, and I felt that my instincts had grown stronger in the house. When I was certain the men weren't coming back, I went out to the porch to examine the contents of the trash bags.

In the first were several dirty rags, an old blanket, a baseball cap with the banana-slug logo of a nearby college, three balled-up pairs of socks, and two large, very dusty beach towels. In the second were about a dozen old notebooks, aged, some bulging with water damage, smelling of mildew, others with torn covers, worn edges, of various sizes and styles. There was also an old handheld radio and a plastic shopping bag containing dozens of pencils and pens with business names printed along their casings. I flipped through a few of the notebooks. They were mostly sketches of plants and trees and animals. Some pages had abstract shapes. Then there was one notebook filled with such indecipherable handwriting, it could have been another language. There was, however, something familiar in some of the drawings. I looked closer at the line work, the curves, the proportions, the shading, the organization of items on the page, and it occurred to me that these looked as though they had been drawn by the same person who had made my favorite painting in the house. They were a bit more elementary, a little less developed, either because they were quickly dashed off or because they were simply done earlier in the artist's journey. It felt like looking at childhood photos of someone close to you and recognizing the features in the child's face that would eventually become the person you knew. I felt a great sense of relief. These must be some of Katherine's old notebooks, stored away and forgotten in the shed.

I left the first trash bag outside, since the items did truly look like old junk, as the construction worker had said. The notebooks, I carried inside and stacked on the bench by the front door. I took a photo of the stack and sent it to Katherine, whom I had been texting photos of Georgia since their departure. *The construction crew found your notebooks in the shed. Would you like to keep them?* It was the middle of the night in Portugal, so I didn't expect Katherine to respond until the next day.

In the morning, I checked my phone and saw Katherine's text: *They aren't mine. Everything in the shed is old garbage. Please toss.*

I reread it a few times.

If these were not her notebooks, then whose were they? Did they not belong to the same person who had painted the disembodied limbs? I had felt sure about it the night before. I still felt sure. I tried to put the pieces together. I had been wrong to assume the notebooks were Katherine's. I wanted to ask her about the artist of the limbs painting, to tell her that these notebooks clearly belonged to the painting's artist. But I knew that the question, my hunch, my instinct, which was now clouded in doubt, would be evidence of not only my inability to follow directions but also my invasion of privacy, since I had opened the notebooks, which I knew, at the very least, did not belong to me. I was not meant to bother the owners. I was meant to take care of their home and dog so they could enjoy their vacation.

By then, I could hear the construction crew outside. I was a half hour behind my usual schedule. Georgia was next to the bed whining for food. When she inhaled her breakfast, I felt the day click back into place. Who cared about the notebooks? I would throw them out, as I'd been asked to do. I would enjoy the last days in the house. I let my body relax back into the job of accomplishing my tasks. Georgia walked to the front door, and I opened it for her. She was her usual sweet self. The hills outside the home displayed their usual calm beauty. The construction crew was loudly at work up the hill, but I saw that they'd taken the garbage bag I'd left out, along with the plastic bag of pencils and pens and the portable radio, so I didn't resent their noise as much. Again, I enjoyed the view, the feeling of the home's majesty.

Then I saw it.

In the far corner of the porch, a smooth rock resting atop what looked like a piece of paper. It was out of place. It didn't belong. As I approached the rock, my earlier panic returned. I took the piece of paper from under the rock and saw on it what was clearly a quick sketch, but no less recognizable in style, the line work natural and elegant. The back of my neck and palms had gone clammy, and the piece of paper was vibrating in my shaking hands. It was a drawing of the stack of notebooks and, beside it, a question mark.

IV

I held the sketch up next to the notebooks I'd left on the bench by the door. However simple, it was a clear replica. The number of notebooks, their thicknesses and sizes, the variations in cover qualities—it matched perfectly, as though the artist had done a quick still life. I went back outside on the porch, stood on my tippy-toes, and peered through the door's windowpanes. Yes, the stack was visible.

I went to look for Georgia and could not find her in any of her usual spots (deck, dirt, deck, dirt). I called her name several times. No response. I began to panic that the dog was gone, disappeared, taken by some force. I called her name several more times. I could hear the fear in my voice. It sounded like a voice from the past, not a voice meant for this house.

"She's been up there with us." One of the construction workers. He was standing there next to the porta potty and pointing up the hill.

"She is?" The thought of Georgia being up the hill hadn't occurred to me. She had never gone there on her own.

"Super-sweet dog," he said. "Sitting there watching us build the new shed. You need her to come down?"

"Oh, no," I said as calmly as possible. I realized I was still in my pajamas and felt deeply embarrassed and exposed. I wasn't sure how much of my screaming the man had heard. "She'll come down on her own."

"Gotcha." The man was about to enter the porta potty.

"Wait," I said. "Did you take that trash on the porch?"

"I don't think so," he said, unfazed. "But happy to take whatever you need us to."

I walked back into the house feeling sick. My stomach ached and my lower back pulsed. Inside, the living room was too bright with daylight, so I went back into the guest room, closed the blinds, and got back into bed. There was a slight ringing in my ears. I shut my eyes to calm myself.

The question mark haunted me. It was obvious to me that whoever owned these notebooks wanted them back. What I didn't understand was why I had them at all and how I could possibly give them back at this point. Was this the question the notebook's owner was asking me? *Why do you have my notebooks? What do you want with them?* I had similar questions and many more. Nobody had knocked or rung the doorbell. Just the note. Not even Georgia had barked to alert me to anyone's presence. Could it be an invitation—*Do you want to know more about my notebooks, about me?* I didn't know how to respond. I considered calling the owners, but I was not sure what to say.

Hours passed like this. I tried to fall asleep, to relieve myself a bit, but I could hear the pounding of my own heart inside my ears. I had been momentarily frightened in the weeks earlier, when the dog would hear a call in the woods at night and bark in return, staring out the glass doors, her tail raised in high alert. I would wonder what lurked in the darkness. But the feeling would always pass, the warm glow of the house's lights enveloping me back to safety.

Now the house's walls felt thinner. I had closed and locked all the windows again, out of that same instinctual fear. I heard the construction man's words, *You out here all alone?* The doors were dead-bolted and the handles locked in place. I had even closed the blinds for the first time since my arrival. The house's vulnerabilities became my own. With each strange noise, I woke from my unsettled half sleep, my skin prickling, my chest heavy with an invisible pressure. I had no rational thoughts as I clenched the duvet tightly around my body, coiling in on myself, besides this one: the house could no longer protect me.

I drifted between sleep and half sleep, often unsure if I was dreaming, imagining, or experiencing. In one moment, the limbs of the painting danced happily around me. In another, a figure sat at the end of the bed and spoke in a soft unknown language. And in another, I could hear the men talking outside my window about all the rich assholes in the hills.

Eventually, there was silence.

The construction crew had left. I got up to check on Georgia.

When I opened the front door, she wasn't there like she usually was, eager for dinner. I checked around the house and found her sniffing at bushes near the start of the backyard trail. I called for her to come, but she didn't listen. As I pulled her back inside, I stepped on something that cracked beneath my slipper. I knelt to pick it up and ran back into the house with the dog, locking the door behind me. In my hand was a pen with the name of the local market where I got my daily lunch sausages. I threw the pen beside the stack of notebooks.

Then Georgia was vomiting. On one of the living room's pristine white rugs.

I moved quickly—crouching next to the vomit. A pool of brown liquid. Flecks of an unnatural green. I dabbed at it with paper towels, frantic, spraying with cleaner, dabbing more. It smelled of sour earth and rot. It seeped through the paper towels, warm against my fingers. For the first time, I felt mean toward Georgia, jealous even. She stood beside me, wagging her tail, apparently feeling better after having expelled whatever was inside her. She was so stupid and ignorant. That's what it took to be happy. There I was, on my knees, cleaning up the mess, and doing a terrible job of it. On the rug, her vomit left an ugly stain that wouldn't come out.

Despite having spent most of the day in bed, I was overwhelmed with tiredness. Georgia licked my feet, reminding me of her dinner. I had enough energy to remember my one simple task of keeping her alive.

The notebooks, though—they did not belong in the house, they were not part of my job as a house sitter. I had only two more days there, and I had to do something. I was in a trance. I had again tried very hard to do a good job and look where it had gotten me. I stepped into the only explicitly off-limits space of the house, Katherine's painting studio. I needed to look for anything that might indicate the artist's identity. I opened several boxes carefully—but perhaps not as carefully as I had treated the house's items in the earlier days—taking out manila folders and old paints and sketchbooks, then returning them to their spots after they revealed nothing. I quickly realized that none of Katherine's art was on the home's walls. That she, in fact, did very little painting. Her sketchbooks were mostly empty, with only a page or two of notes or paint splotches on them. Her boxes contained personal files, bank statements (printed with such large and long numbers I had to look away), menus, family photos, old receipts and checks. I wondered if this was why Katherine had wanted me out of the studio—in seeing its contents, the mask of who she was and what she represented fell away. She, like the house, no longer held the same power over me.

Finally, I found a folder labeled "Art Collecting," which included a handwritten list on a piece of thick paper, with the header "Paintings at Home." It was a long list that had been edited multiple times over, some line items crossed out, others added, others with additional annotations. I looked for a title that might describe the limbs painting. There was one called *Prepare Me for the Apocalypse* by a person named Jean X. Hisock, but that seemed more in line with the painting of a figure looking into a darkened city. There were several plausible ones: *Anomalies* and *Distorted Reality* and *An Accident*. Then I saw a line about two thirds down the list: *Unknown by unknown*. I knew it must be the painting. There was a note alongside it, *Came with the house*. By then, I could hear Georgia snoring on the couch. I left the mess in Katherine's studio and went to retrieve the stack of notebooks from the bench. In them, I might find some sort of answer.

I sat beside Georgia on the couch. She was my only comfort. The noises the house made as it settled, contracted, and shifted in the cool night—those creaks and pops, like it was cracking its knuckles—sounded louder and more threatening than before. I placed my feet beside the dog's warm body and began opening the notebooks. There were eleven of them, to be exact. The older ones looked a bit more professional than the newer ones, either sketchbooks specifically for drawing or ones with leather-like covers and thick pages, however dry and brittle. The newer ones—I only guessed, because they were less worn—included a lined composition notebook, a small unlined reporter's notebook, and another with a black cloth cover. I flipped through each of them, not sure what I was looking for and growing increasingly invested as I examined the images.

Like the limbs painting, they had both a disorienting and calming effect. Something in them felt familiar, like I had experienced them before. There was a fairly developed image of a lizard, drawn in a way that was both very real yet obscure—it was not a true-to-life drawing of a lizard but a lizard that evoked the lizards in the yard, their total lack of awareness. There were more sketches from the house's yard—the bees, the fruit trees, the lavender. In an older notebook, there was the view from the deck, slightly warped, like it existed in its own dimension, separate from reality. It was as though the artist had captured pieces of my own existence and was showing them back to me, and yet I knew that couldn't be true.

I opened the newest notebook, with the black cover. It had thicker-stock paper and included color drawings, unlike most of the others. On the first few pages were those disembodied body parts, much like the painting, in a variety of colors—blues, purples, pinks, greens, browns. Then there was a drawing of the house from the front, the arched door, the arched windows, the brown Spanish tile roof, the porch . . . but around the bottom, the house seemed to spill out a soft blue color, like it was melting or crying. I stared at this drawing for a while before turning the page. The old shed. I had only ever seen it from a distance, but there it was up close, worn and fragile and gorgeous, made of browns and greens that looked supernatural in their saturation. The drawing was off-kilter, as though the shed was about to tip off the page. I turned the page again. There, a figure lying on their stomach in some kind of empty space. The angle was as though you were looking at the body while standing behind them. Only the back of the body was visible, the feet slightly larger in proportion, to indicate a closeness to the viewer. And along the figure's outline, there was a sort of blurring, a melting of the body's edges. The body was the color of the house, a mauvy pink with an undertone of brown, and the back of the head was topped with a black bun. I felt something unlock inside me.

I got up and walked out of the house. It was dark by then. I used my phone's flashlight and made my way to the trail. It was freezing out—not truly freezing, but the kind of cold California night that nobody is prepared for—and I was shivering in the pajamas I hadn't changed out of. I walked up the hill faster. I could only see as far as the light shone, the trees and shrubs and bushes shape-shifting as I moved. Wildlife rustled nearby. I could smell the sour earth, the rot.

I reached the shed.

The one standing had little to do with the one before, the one I'd just seen in the notebook. A chemical scent radiated from the walls, which were an ugly gray devoid of life. I walked around the new structure, pointing the light at the ground. Then I got down on my knees and dug at a mound of dirt. I felt my way toward finding what I was looking for. A small broken piece of wood siding with jagged edges. I held it up to the light. It was thick and the size of my palm, dark brown with chipped green paint. I felt a great sense of calm wash over me. The piece of wood was only a dismembered part of the old shed, but in my hand it felt solid, sturdy, real.

LI FAN

THE RESIDENTS OF PLEASANT, TOO NEW TO HAVE KNOWN HER when she lived on the block, pick up the stray bottles and cans at the bottom of the street. An ambulance arrives to take the old woman away. She has a stroke by the gutter and dies. She feels suddenly weak and falls to the pavement, letting go of her cart and watching it crash into a parked car; its contents spill down the hill. This has been her routine for the last twelve years, and many people in town recognize her, calling her "the Asian recycling lady." Most people ignore her, some smile, if they ever walk past as she works in front of their homes. She says hello cheerfully and waves to passersby. She pushes her cart up the street, stopping at each house to dig through the garbage and recycling bins that are put out for trash day, looking for the bottles and cans that support her life.

Before heading out, she fingers the colorful, comforting objects—lost and broken earrings, figurines, stuffed animals, hair ties, notebooks—cherishing all the items she has found during her walks around town. She moves into a boardinghouse with stained carpets after a smiley social worker secures her a room. A police officer handles her roughly and says that she can no longer sleep on the bench outside of the drugstore. She makes an effort to forget her previous life. The city possesses the abandoned building and sells it to a developer who tears it down and builds a new, taller complex marketed to local college students. She spends a year on the streets, looking for warm, dry places to sleep, and nobody cares where she has gone because everyone who would have cared is gone, too. She abandons her leftover belongings at the front door of a Salvation Army. *How did I get here?* Mrs. Shum wonders to herself.

She drags suitcases of clothes and books and letters out of the unit, determined to find a new place to be. There are too many problems with the building: the roof is leaky, the drywall is crumbling, there is mold all over the bathroom, the floorboards are sagging, the windows are cracked, and on and on, it seems. She lets the building collapse around her, and in rare moments of lucidity, she looks around and is disappointed in her inability to fix the place or herself. She lives in the old building for five more years. There is a funeral with few attendees, and Mrs. Shum sits alone at the front, glaring at her husband's coffin, still angry that he has left her. When the police arrive at her door, Mrs. Shum refuses to open it. As she sets the table for a dinner of mapo tofu and hong shao rou, a bus hits her husband when he jaywalks across a nearby street.

Mrs. Shum tends to the house while Mr. Shum works at an architecture firm downtown. Mr. and Mrs. Shum learn to maintain a regimented schedule of weekday breakfasts and dinners together, weekend walks and TV shows, the once-a-month movie nights with friends at the local theater. They decide that their life can be happy without children. She mourns for a year, clinging to the blanket that would have been his. Mrs. Shum gets pregnant again with a son but miscarries in the fifth month. "This is our forever home," her husband says to her.

After Mr. Shum lands his first job, they purchase a house on Pleasant Street because it is affordable, an old fixer-upper with charm, and the hilly street reminds them of the streets in their hometown of Wuhan. Mrs. Shum becomes pregnant, but the two agree that it is too soon for them to have a child, so she gets an abortion.

Unconsciously, she lets her former dreams die. To support the two of them, Mrs. Shum finds a job as a checker for a local Asian market. She learns English by listening to people talk on the radio all day long; she learns to laugh when the Americans laugh. Everything looks strange and new, and she watches the people around her with awe. They move to the United States so that Mr. Shum can pursue his master's degree. She cries with joy during their small wedding ceremony. The day they graduate from university, Zeng Shum wraps his arms around her and says, "Let's get old together. I'll take care of you, and you'll never have to worry again." A man in her third-year mathematics course asks her out on a date, and she accepts.

She envisions herself holding a position in which she has incredible influence in the community where she lives, where everyone will know and respect her. Her professors tell her she is bright, with much potential. She enrolls in the academic track toward becoming a government official. "I'm Li Fan," she says at the registration desk of the university, overwhelmed with the feeling that her life is finally beginning.

TO GET RICH IS GLORIOUS

Water Poured Out on the Ground

A girl, it's announced. The mother weeps openly and, unable to look, feels a leaden fatigue fill her bones. It is late and raining. A cold December day, 1980. The father leaves the room to smoke outside. Beneath the hospital's awning, he watches the ground, where thin streams of water flow downhill away from him, like his daughter will. All daughters naturally do.

Back in the room, the grandmother holds the baby and, gazing into that blank red face, names her Hang Chun Fu. It is an old woman's nostalgia and wishfulness to want it all for this little girl.

She will be an only child—not the first ever, but the first of her kind, made singular by law rather than choice. She will have to live up to many expectations, to live up to her name. Be genuine and honest and rich and abundant. Be too much.

Hang Chun Fu

In girlhood, FuFu, as she is called endearingly, enjoys the riches of her parents' adoration and attention. She inherently possesses the virtues that make a feminine paragon: proper speech, a clean and modest appearance, diligence in work, and morality.

"Look at how good FuFu is," extended family and friends tell their own daughters. "How I wish she were mine. If only you could be as decent as her." Those with sons love FuFu, too, but they do not want a daughter like her. Rather, a daughter-in-law.

By age eleven, she is elected a three-stripe leader and maintains the status until the end of her time in the Young Pioneers, at age fourteen.

"FuFu, how many threads does it take to make a braid?" her classmates ask her. "How do you write the character for *speak*? For *dragon, goddess,* and *moon*? Could you show me how to work this calculation? How to paint a mountain?"

Does she "hold up half the sky," as Mao famously proclaimed? She does more. She holds it up entirely, for herself and others. Everyone says she is capable of so much. Not once does she have to stand ashamed for a low mark. She orders her classmates to stand. She demands that they stand taller.

Jinhua

A prefecture-level city, making it something more than a city. A place with a city proper, Jinhua proper. That urban area bright and filled. That is not, however, where FuFu and her family live. They reside on the eastern edge of Jindong, in Fucunzhen, a township in an administrative district within the prefecture-level city, whose thirty thousand or so inhabitants still know one another well. They are generations of families who have courted and battled and disowned and loved. Even if they have never met, they will hear a person's name and say, *Ah, yes, his paternal great-aunt's husband was my paternal elder male cousin's childhood flute instructor,* or *Of course, I know her nephew's wife because she goes to the same hairdresser as my maternal grandmother.*

The Hang family's apartment is one of hundreds inside a

compound of dozens of buildings, all the same dull brown and circumscribed by the same stained pavement pathways. In summer, dragonflies float by the residents' ankles and knees, indicating rain. In winter, an occasional light snow. Topics of conversation among neighbors passing one another outside: the weather and their families.

Lying there in her cramped room, in her small bed, Fufu, now eighteen, feels as though her world is the least significant seed in a pomegranate. She yearns for the whole fruit.

Escape

Of course, she scores well on the gaokao. Her agile mind and hours of study have cleared a trail for escape. Her parents argue for Zhejiang Normal University, in Jinhua. She could live at home, bus back and forth, or even, they suggest, live in the dormitories. They're willing to compromise for their only child. All they want is for her to stay.

But when September arrives, FuFu's mother and father accompany her on the five-hour train ride to Shanghai Jiao Tong University. As they enter the city, the crowd thickens, the people change, and her parents see that the world here beats faster than a hummingbird's wings. This is far worse than they had imagined.

Though she feels contrite for causing her parents despair, FuFu cannot resist smiling in this new place. In the taxi to the university, she stares out the window at the tall buildings, the shimmering billboards for restaurants, movies, designer clothes, pop stars, cosmetics—how beautiful everything looks when blown out of proportion. Her mother wraps an arm around her. FuFu leans in and presses her cheek against her mother's shoulder, but the act is not enough to smother the excitement and joy blooming inside her.

Studies in Shanghai

What prompts her to enroll in management science and engineering, with a secondary discipline in business administration, her program focus on logistics? Perhaps she remembers from somewhere what the paramount leader Deng said in her childhood: *It doesn't matter if the cat is white or black; if it catches mice, it's a good cat.* More likely, the spirit of it filtered down to her, as to all these young people, through an accumulation of many small actions and words made ubiquitous. She does not ask herself such questions.

In Shanghai, she excels in her courses and moves through campus with cautious enthusiasm, the wide tree-lined pavilions seeming to pour out before her, leading her to wherever she might dream—until, that is, she begins to take note of her small deficiencies, reflected in the glamour of the other students. Their American sneakers, French scarves, glimmering German fountain pens. The girls' hair, slicked and smooth, and the scent of expensive department-store cologne trailing the men who stroll confidently by her.

In her dorm room, at her simple desk, FuFu writes to her parents: a list of items she needs for school, with the cost of each neatly marked in blue ink. Mainly textbooks for the year, which cannot be denied, and the expense of which she greatly exaggerates. When her parents send her the money, which exceeds two months of their wages (how they have saved and continue to save just for her), she walks into the department store near campus and buys a coat, shoes, and a smart leather backpack. Striding to classes in her new attire, she looks more like the person she feels she is meant to be.

Achievement

There is a young man named Liu Zeng in her talent assessment course who has taken to walking her from the classroom to the dormitory. He does not look like the movie stars FuFu has learned to admire. Learning he is Shanghainese, however, piques her interest. She says no the first time he proposes. He understands this pale-skinned girl and concocts a grander exhibition on the second try, bringing her parents to the city and putting them up in the Jin Jiang Hotel, then gathering both their families, a photographer, and a videographer at Fuxing Park's wisteria lane, the bright purple flowers dripping down on them from above. The many photos, and a video edited to include a romantic soundtrack and exclude FuFu's scowls, are sent to hundreds of family members, friends, acquaintances, classmates, coworkers . . .

See how everything is magnificent and happy! A wonderful couple—intelligent, hardworking, likely to make an even more wonderful child. Luck and prosperity to them until the end!

Ennui

Upon graduation, FuFu gets a job in a factory doing unskilled statistical work. She sits between gray walls, entering numbers into a computer. The best position she could find, it pays four thousand yuan per month. "Pointless, pointless," she tells herself each day upon waking. What was the use of her education if this is all she would achieve? It is a riddle she repeats often and without answer.

When she is home, Zeng asks how she is feeling. "Is it not obvious?" she retorts. Her ennui grows so massive and wild some days that she forgets to eat or bathe. Still, she performs her duties as a wife, duties her mother taught her, and her mother taught her, and her mother . . .

One morning in the office, on her way to her desk, she stumbles and nearly faints. A middle manager, who will later recount this episode as further evidence for why the factory should not hire women from fancy universities, catches her and tells her she should go home and rest in bed.

She stares down, sees only his expensive Italian loafers.

Second Achievement

"If it is a girl, you must get an abortion," her father tells her on the phone. "If we could have known back then . . ."

The doctor performing the ultrasound smiles at her and Zeng. "Very good fortune on the first try," he says.

Liu Zeng

Mainly, his inability to know what she does not ask exasperates her. Otherwise, a fine husband. Zeng spends most of his days at one of the largest Chinese banks, where he is set to move up as long as he maintains above-average performance, which he will. He earns ten thousand yuan per month. His effortless way of achieving, his lack of demands upon her, and his cheerfulness often put her at enough ease that she wants no more from him. But she is not wrong to think him unambitious. Zeng's goal is the same comfortable city life of his parents and his childhood. Years ago, FuFu would have thought this wonderful and worthy. Now her desires have multiplied beyond her comprehension. The difference between husband and wife eclipses the obvious.

It seems, in this case, he who grows up without want has the luxury of satisfaction. She who grows up wanting is never satiated.

Motherhood

She does what she is obligated to do and little more. But she glows when people praise the way she dresses and grooms him, an expression of her creativity, an extension of herself. "Look at that charming little hat. Makes him look like a child movie star," says the fruit-stand owner. "Your mother has classic good taste," says the man in the stationery booth, patting the boy's full cheek. "There is nothing more precious than a boy who knows how to look sharp," says the woman selling children's clothes.

On his first day of elementary school, FuFu walks Wei He to the gate, turns around, and walks back to the apartment crying. Not from being apart from him, but from being alone with herself again.

Mah-jongg

Unemployed, her son at school and her husband at work, FuFu is unmoored. She has nowhere to go and nothing to do. She watches TV dramas in which women fall in love, fall out of love, murder, and thrive. She browses online stores for hours, loading shopping carts with all the items she'd like for her own and leaving them full. In desperation, she contacts some of her old girlfriends from college, with whom she has lost contact, and finds them receptive to her correspondence, enthusiastic, even.

"I know exactly how you feel," one says. "Let's get lunch tomorrow. We'll play mah-jongg afterward. You'll feel better."

So she does, so much. They are all women, from their late twenties to their mid-fifties. A group of about eight. They found one another in the same way FuFu has found them. Out of boredom and necessity. She fits in, and for the first time since she escaped Jinhua, she senses excitement and freedom again. She smells the intermingling of the women's various perfumes and imagines her heart bursting into vivid splashes of color.

Vouchers

They arrive in the mail. A little booklet of government vouchers offering 15 to 30 percent discounts at nearly three hundred local grocers and general stores, for everything from socks and snacks to refrigerators and furniture. The more expensive the item, the steeper the reduction. FuFu flips through the pages and rips out the ones that interest her. When Zeng returns home, she shows him what she's collected.

"Even the government tells us to spend," she says.

"We could use a new heater," he allows.

Inside the spanning department store, FuFu walks along the dazzlingly white aisles picking up and putting down porcelain bowls, canisters of tea, bottles of lotion, packages of dried fruit, until she is overwhelmed with the colors and textures of the place, all those red and yellow screaming signs. She crosses into the appliance section and looks over the dozen or so heaters. Finally, she selects a middling model with five modes.

It is a chore. She does not find joy in buying something needed with money that is not her own.

Bai-Fu-Mei

Pure skin, wealth, and charm—they are everywhere in the posts by the Weibo famous, their confident, exposed bodies leaned against hoods of Lamborghinis, arched atop Jet Skis, reclining in beds spread with jewelry and cash. Smiling, pale faces framed by perfect, lightened hair and strangely blue or green eyes.

They all say to FuFu what they are designed to say: To get rich is glorious.

Lacking

The skin and charm, at least, she is not lacking. She first caught Zeng's attention those years ago with her flawless features, her complexion so white it appears almost painted on. And her ability to speak pleasantly has drawn many more women to the mah-jongg tables: *You look stunning with those earrings—and that hair! I hope I can be as vibrant as you when I'm your age. But auntie, we must spend more to make more!*

The group needs additional space. She takes the lead in the expansion campaign, collecting a small fee from everyone and pooling their funds to rent an apartment, furnishing it with folding tables and chairs, calling it a women's social club.

The women name FuFu their unofficial chairwoman.

Marital Dispute

He says, "Could you be home more often? Watch after Wei He?"

"That's what the nanny's for. He's big enough to take care of himself. I don't see you at home all the time."

"I'm working. If you want to work, the factory might hire you back. Have you tried calling them? It hasn't been that long."

"What's wrong with what I'm doing now? It's better than that stupid job–"

"Listen, I only want–"

She says, "Why should I have to work in a factory when all these other people make a fortune by doing nothing?"

Honest Attempts

She plays mah-jongg every day from eleven a.m. to seven p.m., when she drags herself home for the dinner Wei He's nanny prepares. And with the money she wins–nothing too much, yet not insubstantial–she makes a number of attempts to start her own businesses, in partnerships with women from the club, her closest and most trusted companions.

First, she and a select few design jewelry targeting women like themselves, mothers with time and means. Notebooks filled with sketches end up on a high shelf in the bedroom closet.

Second, an import/export company for antiques, particularly those of the Qing dynasty, for which they falsely sense a growing demand from the European elite.

Third, a line of skin-brightening creams, but the market is oversaturated.

She is catching fish in a tree, she tells herself.

Our FuFu, at thirty-five years old, is desperate to break out of her want.

A Business Proposition

So it is ideal timing.

The mah-jongg group is her only sustenance, the click-clack of the tiles, the energizing exchange of words, the tea poured for hours. The apartment vibrates with women's voices. Pink and red nails tap rhythmically against clean white tabletops. It smells of shampoo, perfume, salty snacks, and warmth.

A middle-aged man in a suit observes, incongruous against this backdrop.

"My sister tells me you grew this from a little women's get-together to an impressive mah-jongg den," he says, leaning toward FuFu.

What den? she wonders, glancing around the apartment. More than thirty women are present. Her thoughts skip around, gathering bits, bunching them together.

"There's a lot of value in a person like you," the man says. He looks at his watch, a gold Rolex.

Obedience

"It's not all about you. Don't forget your husband and son. *Ji jia cong fu. Fu si cong zi.*"

"Enough of that Confucian nonsense! Nobody lives like that anymore," she yells into the phone at her mother.

Both women sit separately at their dining tables, in their empty apartments, confused at the words of the other.

The Longer the Night Lasts, the More Dreams We'll Have

She is given a uniform designed to seduce the customers into the games yet frighten them away from cheating. All black, hair pulled into a high bun, visible earpiece.

The casino is unmarked and undetectable without prior knowledge. It consists of three floors in a commercial building. The first is usually fairly empty, a bleak-looking space offering fifteen video gambling machines for minor clientele. A young man, still in his teens, stands guard and leads the more resourceful gamblers upstairs. The second floor is where FuFu starts out, a wide expanse filled with various table games: baccarat, pai gow, craps, blackjack, roulette. The third floor is where she will eventually end up—the VIP room. Accessible only through a secret stairwell behind a keypad-locked door, down a passage hidden by a mirrored wall. Surveillance cameras monitor the inside and outside.

She excels. She has a sense of purpose. She makes two thousand yuan per day. Surrounded by the thrill of money made and lost, she falls in love, perhaps for the first time.

The Perfect Job

- Provide cigarettes and drinks to gamblers.
- Collect commissions from winners and losers.
- Enforce loans and interest.
- Keep an eye on lower workers, especially the young men hired to interfere in disputes between gamblers, and prevent local hooligans from disrupting.
- Bribe local police.
- Report to laoban at the close of each business day on the activity of the second and third floors.

What She Tells Others

Including her husband, nobody outside of her casino work unit–her danwei–knows about her job. Where does she get the money for the Gucci bag? The Louis Vuitton sneakers? The Cartier bracelets? The Valentino dress? She smiles and says, "Do you like it?" Photographs of her and her new possessions stack her Weibo feed, garnering attention and comments.

Pofu Reputation

When a gambler fails to pay his debts, it is FuFu, called laosi, who visits the debtor's house. She begins by asking firmly and politely, and if he does not give her the money, she transforms into someone else. Pofu, they call her, after tales of her exchanges stream through the casino.

Out of her mouth come screams, curses, threats. *Pay your debts, idiot, or I'll have Dage come and smash your egg brains in! Fuck your ancestors to the eighteenth generation!*

Almost always the men succumb, out of distress. The power of an angry woman.

Physical Violence

In those rare cases when they fail to bend to FuFu's demands, she calls upon those workers she oversees, gives them the offenders' addresses, and walks home in her pristine Italian shoes, knowing what will come.

It is a small sacrifice, she thinks. They deserve it anyway.

She demonstrates that people, whether under extreme duress or not, are capable of incredible shifts in tolerance.

Wei He

Wei He, now eleven years old, interacts with his mother only at breakfast and the occasional weekday dinner. She is beautiful and perfect, he thinks when he sees her, like a woman on a billboard selling a delicious, sweet drink. She is a distant, giant mountain. He tells his schoolmates she is an entrepreneur, though he is not sure what the word means, only that it is something important, the way he hears her say it at home.

Undercover

All along, during those blissful six months, an undercover investigative reporter from Shanghai Television works on a story about organized crime in the city. He spends two weeks on the first floor, making and losing money on the machines until he is ushered to the second, where he plays for months, figuring out its hierarchy and operational structure.

She does not notice anything unusual about him. Only that he needs constant cigarettes and is an average—slightly below average—bettor.

At Home

Amid the widening gorge in his marriage, Zeng acquires an unhealthy habit, gambling with a group of five friends in the back of a noodle shop. Of course, FuFu does not know, but if she did, she would not care. He is a man of manageable dreams, so his problem remains small. The old proprietor charges only ten yuan to sit and play for several hours, and Zeng makes meager bets, one yuan at a time.

When he returns home in the evenings, the apartment

smells of meats and rice, and his wife is not there. On occasion, he worries about her, whether she herself has an addiction to mah-jongg, but he shakes the notion as silly and inconsequential. Women need to socialize. He notices some changes in his wife's appearance. She seems to shine a bit brighter, her pale face accented with darkly lined eyes and flag-red lips, yet he goes on thinking everything is fine because she has not indicated to him otherwise.

There is nothing at home for her that provides as much as the casino. She lavishes Wei He with gifts, and even periodically offers Zeng a thing or two, a beautiful wool hat, a wallet made of snakeskin. The expansion of her self-worth subsumes them.

Raid

One night in September, as the exposé is broadcast on television, the police raid the building.

By the time the officers locate the VIP room, with difficulty, FuFu and her gamblers are aware of their approach. Her boss pulls a sledgehammer from a closet and begins smashing the east wall. A route of escape, planned specifically for such a possibility. They had discussed it before, knowing the risks, but standing here, watching the boss, she wonders how this could be. They have been careful. They have done nothing wrong. Nothing truly wrong. Nothing harmfully wrong. Have they? FuFu can no longer feel her legs Yet she senses herself moving, her hands ripping at the flimsy drywall, other bodies pushing up from behind her.

And what is on the other side? A fleet of yelling officers, guns pointed forward. FuFu nearly faints, but she cannot muster enough resolve to commit to even this small act.

Sixty-eight gamblers and casino staff are arrested, and nine hundred thousand yuan confiscated from the casino safes, the papers later report.

At the Detention Center

As the only female employee, FuFu is separated from the others, then marched into a cell occupied by eight inmates, all tired and oily-looking, at the Shanghai Women's Prison.

"How long will I be here," she murmurs as she steps in. There are fluorescent lights and no windows. She glances down and sees that she is still wearing her work uniform. A smile curves its way to her lips.

Is it twisted and shameless, the way this woman is gratified by her appearance under these circumstances? Yes, she is pleased to be wearing her expensive clothes in jail; yes, she is pleased to be more beautiful than the surrounding women; yes, she is pleased, for a moment, to be who she is.

"Are you a famous person? Really rich?" an inmate asks.

FuFu is about to respond. Then she stops herself. What can she say? The petrifying unknown overwhelms her, supplanting her pleasure.

"Can you help me?" the inmate says into her static face. "Hello? Aiya! Another useless idiot."

Confession

Please explain below:

"I was bored at home. I was unemployed, with nothing to do. My husband had a job. He had a place to go where he could feel useful. I wanted the same. First mah-jongg. Then the casino. I was busy and happy. It was important work. It made other people happy. We never forced anyone to come. We only provided the opportunity, and everyone thrived. I could get the nice things I needed. I took care of my son and my husband, too. People recognized my value, they supported me, they looked up to me. Yes, technically it was illegal, and I knew that . . ."

Yet it was worth everything. Sitting here, writing out her confession, FuFu finds this brighter feeling mixed in with her remorse, and she begins to sweat in confusion, her hand trembling. As the guards stare at her, she thinks, *At every moment I've been told what I can and cannot do, and still—in spite of what my parents say, in spite of what my husband says, in spite of what the very law says—I have lived, and so what, so what if it was illegal, the money I made, it was mine, and how many people can say that for themselves, isn't this what everyone wants, to have done something all their own, not for anything or anyone else, not for Wei He, not for Lui Zeng, not for Mama and Baba, but for me, only for me, how many people—*

"Eh! Wake up!" A guard slaps her hard across the face.

Outcome

Because it is 2017 and the government has declared war on gambling, nationally and globally, Hang Chun Fu is sentenced to thirteen years in prison. "Nothing is more visible than what is hidden, and nothing is more manifest than what is minute," the president says in a speech against corruption, quoting Confucius. "Therefore a gentleman is careful of himself even when alone." Later he writes in an essay on poverty alleviations: "It is easier to rob an army of its general than it is to rob a common man of his purpose and will," though the application is less clear in this case.

Lui Zeng and Wei He will live on embarrassed, and then less so, but finely, without her.

Seven of her male colleagues and coconspirators, some guilty of violent crimes, all deemed higher in rank, are given suspended death sentences.

Judgment

When the women of her mah-jongg group hear of FuFu's punishment, they say, over their games, "How lucky, dodging the death penalty! See, sometimes it's good to be a woman. The government pities you more than a man."

In Zhejiang province, thirty-four wealthy housewives are apprehended for operating an illegal gambling den.

A month later, in the city of Wenzhou, sixteen old women are arrested for running a drug gang.

And then in Zhuhai, several teenage girls are detained for conducting what their school calls a prostitution ring, though the sums were insignificant and the boys permitted only to touch the girls' chests.

Oh, these women braid their luck and others' pity together, because what else do they have at their disposal? If, at a young age, you feel like you can achieve anything, and then you realize along the way that you were living in a fantasy, how do you respond? How do you decide what is rational or not? If you're born with a strength in spirit, is it fair to dampen it, and if not, how many lines made by others can you cross before you've crossed too many? Who is to judge?

Better a Diamond with a Flaw Than a Pebble Without

FuFu's mother walks the corridors of Shanghai Women's Prison on March 8, International Women's Day, alongside thirty other mothers of inmates invited by the warden as part of a rehabilitation program. The inmates will show their mothers their progress through poetry, painting, dance, music, and theater, for the warden has taken upon the new belief that the arts have the only true ability to change minds and hearts. Fufu's mother walks the corridors, hopeful.

Later, both Fufu's mother and father will die never having forgiven their only child's betrayal. It is two years before the bitter death of Fufu's father, who will be known in his neighborhood for his last words: cursing Fufu's name in pain prior to passing. It is eight more years until her mother's lonely death. It will take five days for neighbors to find her mother's body, and when they do, they will see in her lap a childhood diary of Fufu's.

Oh, our FuFu, she is on the auditorium's stage in a white dress, black heels, and pink lipstick, looking glamorous and beaming down at a seated, mute woman in an ugly blue jumpsuit.

"You were always such a good girl, and you did so well in school," recites FuFu, acting the part of a mother. "We had such high hopes for you. I don't know where we went wrong and how you ended up here. I only hope you can build a better life."

The inmates and mothers clap at her committed performance.

She has learned the pains of mothers with wayward daughters, they say. She has embraced her natural maternal instinct. She is a changed woman, possessing the empathy necessary to remold her life! FuFu bows deeply before the moved crowd.

When she rises again, tall and erect, the expression on Fufu's face is recognized only by her mother, who clutches her chest in shock as her heart beats erratically. It is in Fufu's bright eyes and the way her mouth, pursed and unsmiling, tilts slightly to the left. It is a look of untarnished pride.

FAREWELL, HANK

ADRIENNE WAS STANDING ALONE IN THE CORNER NEXT TO SOME bright pink orchids. She was watching her mother make her round of hellos. Her mother was now talking to a youngish man—in comparison to most of the crowd, at least—who was laughing at something her mother was saying. Adrienne didn't like the way the man looked at her mother, a craving in his eyes. When her mother finally returned, she pointed at the pile of fried noodles on Adrienne's plate. "It's good?"

"Yes, but you can't have any." Adrienne pulled the plate away from her mother's reach.

"So mean."

"Who was that?"

"Who?"

"That man, the one in the black polo and ugly shoes."

"Those shoes are ugly? Why?" Her mother took Adrienne's chopsticks and picked up a bite of noodles.

"You said you're eating healthier. But then you act like you don't have prediabetes and high cholesterol and stuff."

"I do eat healthy. Most of the time. A little noodles sometimes isn't that bad."

"Yeah, yeah, and you say that every day, and then it adds up and it's not a little anymore. It's a lot. And then you're going to get worse, and you'll have to take shots and pills all the time."

"So annoying and bossy." Adrienne's mother shook her head and looked away, on the verge of becoming truly irritated.

"But Mommy." Adrienne clutched her mother's arm. "What would you do if I didn't tell you to eat healthier? I want you to live for a long, long time. And those shoes are ugly because they make the guy look like he's a clown pretending to be a businessman."

Her mother turned back toward her. "Don't hold me so tight. You're crazy," she said. But she also laughed a little, which meant that everything was fine between them.

The dining room had gotten crowded. They could see Orchid Lady struggling with Hank over in the adjoining living room.

"At least I'm better off than Hank," her mother said. "Not stuck in a chair like that."

"Oh my God. Shhh. Orchid Lady might hear you."

"She can't. She's far."

"Somebody else might hear you and tell her."

"Geez. Why are you so worried? You think Orchid Lady is that scary?"

"I don't know. She freaks me out a little."

The whole event freaked Adrienne out.

Hank was propped up in a leather recliner with his feet up, flanked by two pots of giant orchid arrangements. A bright purple blanket covered his skinny thighs. The purple matched the dozens of orchids on his right. Orchid Lady was trying to put a cheesy golden crown with red sparkling rhinestones on Hank's head, but he slapped it away each time she approached. The crown matched the flowers on his left—yellow with pink centers. A lot was clashing.

"Honey. Sweetie. Darling," Orchid Lady said. "Today is your day. Remember, it brings out the flowers." Slap. "Balance. Balance in composition." Slap. "Stop that. We agreed."

Hank slapped the crown again. He did not speak. The slaps clearly conveyed everything he hoped to convey. Orchid Lady's face grew increasingly shiny and red as she persisted.

Some guests watched shamelessly. Others, like Adrienne, acted busy in the dining room. They exchanged quiet small talk or studied the platters of various-colored meats, vegetables, noodles, and desserts laid out on the round black-lacquered wooden table. The table had flowers—lotuses? lilies? orchids?!—intricately carved into its edges and legs. *Don't judge,* Adrienne told herself. *Try to be positive, especially today of all days, at an affair like this.*

But how?

And the decor!

The rugs, for example. They were red and gold, embroidered with dragons and phoenixes and even more flowers. Big scrolls of watercolor mountain scenes and Chinese characters and lake scenes and orange fish in ponds and animals among bamboo hung on each of the walls. Everywhere—lining the side tables, atop the kitchen counters, magneted to the refrigerator, stacked along the mantel—there was so much *stuff*... bamboo fans, little Buddhas, gold ingots, red envelopes, and figurines of horses and cows in varying sizes of every known material (which, of course, meant they were Hank's and Orchid Lady's zodiac signs). It was suffocating, bearing down on Adrienne with all of its tacky ancestral weight.

She hadn't even gotten started on the orchids, which, under different circumstances, Adrienne might have found charming and beautiful but, in this space, were nauseating. Potted orchids along the windows in every room, stretching up and out, as though they wanted to grab your attention straight from your soul. The real stunners were in a greenhouse in the backyard, Adrienne's mother had said. Orchid Lady would definitely be taking the guests on a tour.

It was going to be a very long afternoon.

The invitation had arrived in her mother's email inbox two weeks earlier and was then forwarded to her with the pressing question:

Is this american thing to do???

--- Forwarded message---
From: Orchid Lady <orchidlady888@gmail.com>
Date: Mon, Aug 13, 2018 at 2:22 PM
Subject: A Farewell to Hank
To: Orchid Lady <orchidlady888@gmail.com>

Dear Friends,

On the behalf of my husband and myself I am writing this to you all . . . It is the natural life cycle calling that my precious husband and our beloved friend, Henry ("Hank") Yunsheng Wong, will leave us soon for a new happy land . . .

It is both Hank's and my wish that we, as Hank's dear friends, gather in our sweet, beautiful home on Friday to have this last time together before his new journey . . . We will provide food, refreshments, and entertainment and only ask that you bring your generous and kind presence . . .

Love and peace,
Orchid Lady

Adrienne called her mom right away and said no, it was not an American thing to do. As far as she knew. And clearly it wasn't a Chinese thing to do, since her mother was asking. They concluded that it must be a crazy Orchid Lady thing to do, like going by the title Orchid Lady. Adrienne had heard the woman's real name once or twice but forgotten it immediately. Orchid Lady was Orchid Lady, to herself and to everyone else.

In the weeks that followed, Adrienne and her mother talked over the phone as much as always—between Adrienne's classes, during her mother's lunch breaks, in the evenings, on the weekends—theorizing over what could have compelled Orchid Lady to put on a living funeral. What was a living funeral? Some googling revealed Japan had a short history, since the nineties, of holding them. Maybe Hank had gotten into the idea? Unlikely, according to Adrienne's mom. Hank was solitary, didn't like socializing, didn't have many friends. Most of the people he knew, he knew through Orchid Lady. Had Hank's condition worsened? But what was his condition? Hank wasn't specifically sick, that they knew of. It was possible that Hank had been diagnosed recently with a terminal illness that neither he nor Orchid Lady had shared with anyone. No, Adrienne's mother said. Orchid Lady was a notorious oversharer. For two weeks, she had called all of her friends crying when Hank had a prostate cancer scare because he was peeing a lot, and it turned out not to be prostate cancer after all but that he was drinking too much tea. Okay, well, Hank was old, at seventy-nine, though not even terribly old. Why now? Did Orchid Lady want to speed Hank's death along so she could be free of him? Adrienne thought that was possible, however dark. Orchid Lady could take Hank's money and do as she pleased. Adrienne's mom said Adrienne shouldn't be so pessimistic about people she barely knew. It was true that Orchid Lady liked to travel and go to parties and host parties, and Hank may have become somewhat of a burden, but she really did love him. They'd been married over thirty years! Orchid Lady wanted to do something nice for Hank, to cheer him up. So maybe they had a loving relationship, and this was about spreading the love? Even as she said it, Adrienne wasn't convinced. Her analysis turned rotten again: More likely than anything, Orchid Lady was doing it for the attention. She wanted everyone's pity and admiration. A good, devoted wife. Or she simply wanted an occasion to show off her orchids. She was using Hank as an excuse to throw a party.

"How did you become so negative?" her mother asked.

How her mother had become friends with this woman was the real mystery to Adrienne. Her mother had explained that they'd met through mutual friends–the Chinese expat community in their small suburban town was apparently very strong. When Adrienne had lived at home, neither she nor her mom had associated much with anyone outside of school and work, respectively. As soon as Adrienne left for college, however, her mother expanded her social network, and whenever Adrienne came back to town, she was obligated to see these new people. Orchid Lady was a bit of an exception. She had reach beyond the Chinese community. She was a town celebrity of sorts and was always busy with social appointments. Adrienne had met her only once, briefly, when Adrienne accompanied her mother to pick up some plant cuttings.

Orchid Lady's house was at the end of a cul-de-sac that led to a park path; she had "adopted" a large public area beyond her fence and landscaped it meticulously, garnering the attention of neighbors and, later, city officials. There were a variety of flowers and plants: daffodils arranged in the shape of a heart, birds-of-paradise overlooking rock gardens, giant jade plants, delicate dwarf willows with wide canopies, and more Adrienne couldn't name. Orchid Lady had carefully placed boulders throughout the area, each carved with a Chinese character: 爱, 智, 福,平.

Orchid Lady eventually worked with the city to put up signage beside the garden, making it an official landmark. The panel praised Orchid Lady's passion for landscape design. "For more than twenty years, this section of the greenbelt has been enhanced and maintained by a dedicated community member, *the* Orchid Lady. (However, you will not see orchids out here–ha! Orchids do not thrive in outdoor environments.) You will find many other beautiful creations, thanks to Orchid Lady's careful eye and green thumbs. Occasionally, you will spot Orchid Lady herself tending to this precious garden! Say hello if you do!

"If you would like to contribute a donation to the continued efforts of maintaining and upgrading this hidden gem in the city, please visit us at . . ."

Orchid Lady came into the dining room, hands clapping. "Dearest friends, thank you for coming. Now that everyone has arrived and eaten, please join me in the living room to begin our farewells to Hank."

Adrienne gestured toward the back door and mouthed, *Can*

we go now? Her mother shook her head and pulled her in the direction of the rest of the guests.

In the living room, people arranged themselves in a semicircle around Hank. A compromise had been reached; the crown was on Hank's lap, on top of the purple blanket. The orchids craned forward in anticipation. Cheerful string music played in the background, and Hank smiled. He gestured for people to come closer, and the semicircle moved ever so slightly toward him. People looked nervous, as though approaching Hank were approaching death itself. That was how Adrienne felt, at least. Hank's face was gaunt and pale. He had very long, very dark eyebrows and no hair on his head. Orchid Lady, on the other hand, looked regal in a long, flowy, deep red dress that pooled around her as she knelt beside her husband.

"We are gathered here today, among our loved ones, to celebrate Hank's life and to wish him well on his coming journey." She placed a hand on the crown in Hank's lap. "We would love for guests to come up to Hank and speak a few words of love and goodbyes. Whoever would like to start."

People looked away, down at their feet, off into some middle distance, at one another's kneecaps. Adrienne relaxed. There was no pressure for her to say anything, let alone be the first, as someone who didn't know Hank. She stared at the other guests' backs, wondering what they were thinking, if they found this event as strange as she did, or if they were happier people, people who saw the good in others and were enjoying themselves.

Orchid Lady clapped again. "Don't be shy!"

An older man, in his sixties or seventies, came forward and approached Hank. He made a move to kneel but then changed his mind and remained standing. He introduced himself briefly to the crowd as a former colleague at a local law firm. He listed

Hank's qualities as a coworker: dedicated, resourceful, helpful, diligent, generous. He spoke of occasions when Hank made coffee for the office, brought bagels and donuts for everyone, took people to lunch. Hank was one of the most considerate coworkers the man had ever had the pleasure of working with. The man choked on his words and excused himself. Orchid Lady cried. A few others were also crying. Hank nodded and smiled benevolently.

People stepped forward with more urgency and told their stories about Hank, depicting him as an all-around brilliant and kind man. Hank occasionally laughed or coughed, but still he did not speak. He did not look uncomfortable with the attention. He seemed to be a different person from the one protesting earlier against the crown. Maybe it had more to do with fashion. Maybe it was Hank's idea to host this whole affair after all.

Adrienne wondered how much of what people said was true and how much was exaggerated through a magnifying lens of premature grief and performance. There was, however, a sense of love, real and exhausted, in the atmosphere.

This was the closest thing to a funeral Adrienne had been to, and she was somewhat moved. She wondered next about what people had said at her father's funeral, but then she remembered that her mother hadn't held one. It had happened suddenly, and they had no family and few friends in the area, and Adrienne was a baby, so there was too much else for her mother to deal with. Her mother had him cremated and shipped half of the remains back to China for burial. The other half, her mother kept in an urn on a shelf with a photo of him, which had always creeped Adrienne out a bit. But what did she know? Certainly not what her father would have wanted.

Adrienne considered what people would say about her if she

were dying or dead. Would this many people come out to speak? For what would she be remembered? Her mother had said Hank didn't have many friends, but this seemed like a decent turnout. Adrienne's friends didn't truly know her, she thought with a tinge of sadness and then pride. There were many aspects of her life that she kept from others, like her father being dead, because she didn't know how to express a loss she had never fully experienced. It honestly didn't feel as bad as others made it out to be. She had her mother, and her mother would say she'd been a wonderful daughter. Diligent and loyal, if sometimes a bit too controlling. But always there, a consistent and steady source of support and love. In her imagination, she was dead and her mother was alive, because imagining her mother dead was far more difficult.

She pulled out her phone to check the time. Her mother saw and slapped her wrist. The crowd turned around to look.

"Oh, Jia!" Orchid Lady stood up. "Would you like to say a few words?"

Now Orchid Lady was waving Adrienne's mother over.

Her mother walked forward. She was going to speak. Really? Did she have to do this? They were so unlike each other, Adrienne and her mother. Adrienne would have shaken her head and said no, no, she had nothing to contribute. When Adrienne was a child, her mother used to advise her to be aware of others. They were always watching. Behave. Be good. Be polite. Be quiet. But when it came to her own self, Adrienne's mother wasn't afraid to be heard and seen among company, among friends, in public, or wherever. She spoke confidently and laughed loudly. She made jokes, whether or not they were funny. She asked a lot of questions and made friends with strange people, like Orchid Lady.

Now Adrienne's mother was standing in front of Hank.

"You were a good husband. A good friend to all," she started. "When we met at ARC, you were so athletic. You played—what's the game called? The one in a room with tennis rackets? And you hit against the wall? Oh, ha ha, squash. Like the vegetable. I never remember that! So funny. I thought, Wow, this guy. He's old but fast! Like a tiger. Orchid Lady said, That's my husband, Hank. I thought, She's so lucky. To have a supportive and strong man in life. And then we became all good friends. I'm sad for this day and also happy. Sad that we will lose you. Happy to be your friend."

Adrienne's mother was crying toward the end. Adrienne was crying because she was watching her mother cry. She loved her mother so much it scared her. Even Hank seemed to get emotional after the little speech, or at least tired out. Then Orchid Lady let out a loud sob, false like a spoiled child's, and it sucked all the tears back into Adrienne's eyes.

Adrienne's mother returned to her and gave her a look that said, *I did a good job, didn't I?* Adrienne nodded. The spectacle was nearing its end. A couple of other people spoke very briefly, and then Orchid Lady, who now appeared brand-new, as though hosting an above-average dinner party, announced it was time for the very special orchid viewing.

"There are more than thirty thousand species of orchids," she said. "I don't have them all, but I'm getting close, as you can see. Ha ha! I told Hank when we got married thirty years ago that I needed masculine and feminine balance in my household. The orchid represents this exactly.

"Its flower is symmetrical, perfectly balanced into two equal parts. It is femininity. But the word *orchid* comes from the Ancient Greek word for *testicle*! For the testicle-like roots of the orchid! This is the masculine energy. And you know what Hank said? Whatever you desire. Which is another meaning of the orchid, a symbol of pure love. And I am joyous, because I have been married to a man who has let me be me, no matter what."

People clapped.

"And because of this, my orchids are the happiest in the whole world. Please! Come see!"

Orchid Lady walked over specifically to Adrienne and her mom to guide them into the backyard. Up close, Adrienne could see a thick layer of foundation and powder caked on the woman's face, creased into the wrinkles of her eyes and mouth. She had thick black lashes that had to be fake, and her eyelids were covered in a deep purple eye shadow that, up close, Adrienne noticed, was a perfect color match for Hank's blanket. Her eyebrows were painted on thickly and meticulously, and looking at them made Adrienne want to touch her own eyebrows to check that they were still intact. Though Orchid Lady was older, older than Adrienne's mother, she managed to make herself look ageless, almost inhuman.

They walked at the front of the crowd, past Hank—who waved each of them on, as though he, too, wanted the celebration's focus to shift from him to the flowers—through the dining room, out the sliding doors, and into the huge backyard, where there was a stone path flanked by koi ponds. The path led to a greenhouse, and even from a distance, one could see that it was stuffed with shelves and shelves of orchids. Stepping inside, Adrienne became overstimulated by the colors. Her gaze had no one place to land and rest. She felt her eyes darting from the yellows to the purples to the pinks to the whites to the rarer blues . . . Around her, the other guests oohed and aahed and complimented Orchid Lady, whose painted lips stretched farther and farther, a growing chasm on her face.

Adrienne grew dizzy from it all. Had they not all been mourning Hank's impending death only minutes earlier? Then Orchid Lady began to move her mouth.

"Most orchids live for ten to twenty years, but with proper care, they can reach more than a hundred years old," she said. "Longer than most of us will live! This one is my oldest, nearing thirty. . . ."

Orchid Lady continued talking, but Adrienne could not hear the words. All she could see was Orchid Lady caressing an orchid's flower and pressing her lips to the bloom. She felt nauseous. Adrienne gripped her mother's arm.

"What is it?" her mother asked. "Are you okay?"

"I need to use the bathroom."

"Okay. Be quiet for Hank."

"I will."

Adrienne rushed out of the greenhouse and back into the house. She avoided the living room, where she assumed Hank slept in his chair. She went down a hallway, opened several doors, to closets, a guest bedroom, the garage, until she finally found the bathroom. Inside, the decorations matched the rest of Orchid Lady and Hank's home. There was a watercolor—no, a print of a watercolor—of a pagoda on a mountain, rising above loose clouds. The bathroom cabinet was made of deep red wood with round gold-medallion clasps. The shower curtain was emblazoned with orchid and bamboo illustrations. It was what Adrienne imagined would show up in image search results if somebody looked up *Oriental-inspired bathroom*. It was reaching for some other time, some other place, had gotten some of the signifiers but had missed, and thus achieved something else entirely, something fictional and dreamed up, existing only in the imagination of its creator. Orchid Lady.

Adrienne gripped the sink edge, trying to hold on to

something sturdy. She was annoyed. No, she was offended and angry. The decorations. The way the guests could switch from sad to impressed so quickly. The obsession with having a good husband. The feminine and masculine balance. The way that man in the shoes looked at her mother as if he wanted something from her. The fakeness of this fake funeral. The orchids. The orchids.

There was something deeply disturbing about it all. She was going to find her mother and tell her it was time to go. She washed her hands, then sprayed a bit of jasmine air freshener around the toilet, because despite being uncomfortable, she was still a polite person. She exited the bathroom and stood in the hallway listening for the sounds of other people. It seemed that everybody was still outside.

She was heading for the back door when she heard the coughing. It grew louder and stronger. It occurred to her that it was Hank, and at first she thought, well, it wasn't her job, and her mother had said to leave Hank alone. But then she realized that there was nobody else in the house to help him, so she turned back. She wouldn't want to be responsible for his death.

Hank was in the recliner, pounding his chest and hacking by then. She ran to the kitchen, got a glass, filled it with water from the sink, and hurried to him. He took the cup in his shaking hands and drank in large gulps.

"Thank you," he said. He cleared his throat a few more times, like he was about to make a speech.

A gray cat came out of nowhere and started to meow at Hank's feet.

"Hello, mister," Hank said. "You want to come up here?"

The cat reached its paw up onto Hank's knee. Hank tossed the golden crown across the room. Adrienne flinched. The cat jumped onto Hank's lap, kneaded the purple blanket a few times, then curled itself into a loaf of fur.

"You're happy now," he said, petting the cat.

"Thank you for having me over," Adrienne said, preparing to walk away.

Hank looked up at her. "Who are you?" he said.

"Oh, I'm Jia's daughter."

"Jia, yes. A good woman."

Adrienne nodded. Though she agreed, she was uncertain whether Hank was saying this to return the favor of what her mother had said about him earlier in the event, or if he believed it to be true. She again made a gesture to leave. "Speaking of my mom, I should go look for her. Thank you again for having me."

Hank smiled at Adrienne as he petted the cat. "It's all a little silly, isn't it?"

"I'm sorry?"

"This whole farewell. Farewell, Hank. Have a nice journey to the afterlife."

"Oh." Adrienne obviously agreed but didn't want to show it, again for fear of being rude. She was also beginning to sense that Hank was nowhere near death, and it made her stomach hurt to think about the reasons why Orchid Lady would put him through this.

"Do you believe in reincarnation?" Hank asked, looking up at her.

"I don't know," she answered slowly.

"It's highly likely," Hank said as he petted the cat in his lap, "that this cat holds the soul of someone who was once very dear to me. I believe we were brothers in our past lives. He must have lived better than I did, because look at us now. He lives in comfort, while I suffer." Hank smiled, and up close, Adrienne could see that he was missing a front bottom tooth and that his lips were cracked dry. "What do you think?" he asked.

"Um. It seems possible?"

"It is not only possible. It *is*."

Hank stared at Adrienne, waiting for a response. She wasn't sure what to say, so she said what she'd been thinking all day.

"So . . . are you really dying?"

Hank burst out in laughter, which caused another coughing fit. Adrienne grabbed the cup to refill it and bring it back. Hank thanked her.

"Joan believes so. She's the one who convinced me about reincarnation. There's so much suffering in this world, we have to reach compassion by the end of one life in order to move into the next with positive karma. I'm not sure I'm there yet. She's very worried. I suppose this event was meant to help me get there."

"Joan?"

"My wife. You must know her as Orchid Lady."

"Oh, right."

"You know," he continued, "I gave her that nickname. Never thought it would take off the way it did. Now she gets upset when I call her Joan. She thinks I'm scolding her. She's so dedicated to those flowers. She believes there is no better living thing to be reincarnated as than an orchid. She's fed the ashes of our dead pets to the orchids, convinced that their spirits will live on in that greenhouse. Ru tu wei an. You must be buried for peace. Even better if with an orchid. Her mother, her father, her older sister, her best childhood friend, a former husband. After I die, she will feed my ashes to the orchids. This little guy, too"—Hank patted the cat's head—"will be fed to the orchids when it's his time. We're both okay with that, now, aren't we, mister? Orchids are wonderful, aren't they?"

Hank closed his eyes. Adrienne stood, paralyzed and mesmerized by what she could not understand. Karma. Reincarnation. Buried for peace.

She waited for Hank to open his eyes and explain further, but it appeared he had fallen asleep again. The speech had expended all his energy. Adrienne checked for the slight rise of his chest to make sure he hadn't died. She walked out the back door to find her mother.

The group was making the return to the house, Orchid Lady leading the way.

"Adrienne! Are you all right?" The woman pounced on her, not unlike the gray cat onto Hank's lap.

"Yeah," Adrienne managed.

"Next time, you have to come for a private tour. Just for you!" Orchid Lady pressed a cold hand to Adrienne's forearm, sending a chill through her body.

"Okay."

Adrienne's mother appeared. "What took you so long?"

"Can I tell you at home? I really want to go," Adrienne pleaded.

"Geez, okay, let me say bye to people."

"Okay, hurry. I'm gonna wait by the car."

Adrienne walked out, past the front garden with its big oak tree, manicured lawn, and pots of various plants, which had all captured her attention upon arrival but through which she now jogged without looking. The car was parked right across the street. She leaned against the passenger's-side door and, alone now, let the encounter with Hank sink in. No, he was not lucid. He was further gone than she and her mother had guessed. Or Orchid Lady (Joan, apparently, though that couldn't possibly have been her birth name, either) and he were both crazier than anyone thought. Or was this perfectly normal, and she was the one who was being crazy? People died, didn't they? Who said they could not be reborn? As flowers?

"I don't know," she said, to no one, really.

Her mother was taking too long. It was getting cold. Adrienne sat on the sidewalk and tucked herself into a ball to keep warm, like she used to do as a child. She used to wonder what had become of her father. Did he live in heaven, wherever that was? Did he watch over her as some kind of angel, like her teachers and annoying family acquaintances suggested? Or was he somewhere else entirely, or entirely gone? She hadn't considered such questions in a very long time. It didn't seem useful, because she never arrived at a satisfactory answer. She had not grown up with religion—her mother believed loosely in Buddhism, but it felt more cultural than religious—and Adrienne was not an especially "spiritual" person. If somebody were to ask whether she believed in God or divine beings or an afterlife or a higher power, she would answer truthfully, as she had to Hank: *I don't know. I don't really think about it.*

The door to Orchid Lady's house creaked open, and Adrienne looked up, expecting to see her mother, but no, it was Orchid Lady, approaching with a classic Chinese blue-and-white-pattern pot in her arms.

"Adrienne," Orchid Lady said, waving at her as she walked. "There you are!"

"Yeah." Adrienne forced herself to stand.

"I brought this for you and your mother." Orchid Lady handed the pot to Adrienne. At the bottom was a brown bulb the size of a kiwi, with bits of root and tiny shoots of green coming out the top. "All you need is to add your own dirt," said Orchid Lady.

Adrienne stared inside the pot.

"It's a special breed of orchid. Care for it, and it will bring you both loving company."

The door opened again, and this time it was Adrienne's mother.

"Take care, Adrienne," Orchid Lady said, then walked back to the house, giving Adrienne's mother a hug along the way.

In the car, Adrienne told her mother everything. Adrienne's mom interjected once in a while, with "huh" and "weird" and "geez," until the end, when Adrienne held up the bulb.

"Do you think this is one of Orchid Lady's relatives, reincarnated?"

"What? No," her mother said.

"Why not?"

"Because she wouldn't give you one of them. This one is nobody."

Adrienne moved the bulb closer to her mother's face and waved it there. "Are you sure?"

"Ah, get that away. It's dirty."

They laughed.

"Maybe you misunderstood Hank."

"That's what he said, I swear."

"Who knows."

"Do *you* believe in reincarnation?"

"No," her mother said. "We die. We're dead."

"That's sad."

"Not really."

"Well, I hope when you die, you're going to be reincarnated again as my mom," Adrienne said.

Adrienne's mom smiled but was quiet. They drove the rest of the way without talking.

When they got back to the house, her mother took the pot and filled it with dirt from the backyard, then put it on her dining room table. "How does it look?"

"It looks like a pot of dirt."

"It will grow soon," her mother said.

Adrienne stared at the pot. Orchid Lady must have had a thousand like it, but in her mother's house, it did look pretty. It didn't make Adrienne sick. If anything, it made Adrienne feel special. Maybe Orchid Lady was on to something.

"Can we sprinkle Baba's ashes in it?" Adrienne asked.

"Really? You want to do that?"

"Do you think he needs it, to feel peace? You have to be buried in Chinese culture, right?" Adrienne echoed Hank.

"Your father is buried in China. That's his peace."

"Yeah, but what about here?"

Adrienne's mother nodded. "He can have more peace."

So the two of them took the urn off the high shelf for the first time in Adrienne's life, opened it, and each took a spoonful of the gray ash from the plastic bag inside. Neither of them cried, neither of them said anything more about her father, they just scattered the ash on top of the soil, then sifted it in. It felt right to Adrienne. She didn't believe her father would now become an orchid and be some kind of reincarnated companion to her and her mother, but one day, she imagined, they would walk by the orchid when it was in full bloom and be moved to brush their fingers against the flowers' soft, bright petals.

CURE FOR LIFE

BOBBY GREEN, TWENTY-FOUR, SPENT MOST OF HIS DAYS AT Cure Market as the assistant dairy manager. The job slowed him down in school, but it was also how he supported life in the overpriced college town. He'd attended community college in his hometown a couple of hours away, then transferred to UC Davis, where he took classes toward a degree in food science. He didn't mind being a bit older than his peers. His mom had never finished college and—though he couldn't be sure, since they barely knew each other—he imagined his dad had avoided classrooms after middle school. In many ways, Bobby was proud of what he'd already accomplished. This would be his last quarter if everything went according to plan.

He'd ended up at Cure Market on the tip of a former Save Mart coworker, who called it "the bougie store for rich-ass hippies that pays three dollars above minimum wage." It had sounded like a big step up to Bobby. He'd started out as a checker, like he'd been at Save Mart, but when one of the dairy guys got fired for making out with a teenage courtesy clerk (Cure's bougie title for baggers), the bosses offered the job to Bobby. Of all the Cure jobs, it was one of the most isolating. Only one dairy guy worked at a time. But that was exactly what Bobby wanted. He wasn't the best at interacting with the guests (customers), and he resented the people who came in to shop, most of whom he perceived as wealthy and entitled. In the Box—what all associates (employees) called the long, skinny expanse of refrigeration behind the dairy cases—he could listen to music and podcasts while he stocked. And often, when it was slow, a courtesy clerk would come help out and keep him company.

Courtesy clerks came and went. They were the youngest associates at Cure: teenagers from the local high schools who'd lined up along the freezer cases on Wednesday afternoons to interview for the job. The few who stuck around got moved to other teams, but most left by the time they graduated, replaced by a fresh bunch. Two years into his time at Cure, Bobby met Lillian.

She approached him in the Box one day and asked if he needed help. He gave her a cart stacked with cases of yogurts, showed her how to pull the older yogurts forward and arrange the newer yogurts behind, stacking them two or three high and aligning them in neat, colorful rows.

"It's tedious work," he warned.

"Isn't everything?" she said. "At least back here, I don't have to deal with *guests*."

In this way, Lillian became one of his more regular helpers. At first he tasked her with stocking small items from the guest side of the cooler, but once, when she came around, all the yogurts, butters, cream cheeses, eggs, and half-and-halfs had already been restocked, so he invited her into the Box, where they pushed gallon milks and juices from the back. It wasn't until she'd been outfitted with gloves and a Cure sweatshirt that Bobby began to worry about what it might look like to others.

Him, alone in the Box with a young courtesy clerk. The youngest courtesy clerk—Lillian was only fourteen. He thought of the last dairy guy's demise. But Lillian really was a child, the baggy sweatshirt nearly hitting her knees, nothing to worry about. And she wasn't intimidated by his presence. She asked him questions about his life, where he was from, what he was studying, his plans for the future, how he spent his free time . . . They talked. His worry passed. Over the months of working together, they entered what Bobby considered a healthy, fun work friendship. He learned that Lillian liked to bike everywhere (very Davis), that her favorite classes in school were history and biology (two things he had little to no interest in), that she was scared of cockroaches (when she saw one in the back, she jumped on a milk crate), and that she worked at Cure to pay for things that her parents couldn't cover, like her braces (he could relate). He felt comfortable in her presence, like she was a younger sister.

He lived in an apartment with two produce guys, who'd had an empty room that was cheaper than his previous place. He would stay up late when they had parties and occasionally go out with them to the local bars. But for the most part, he kept his distance. There were two kinds of Cure associates: 1) those who came in knowing they were leaving; and 2) those who were happily stuck there, their only desire to move up in rank. Bobby felt he straddled the two worlds, but in his last quarter of college, he was intent on preventing himself from becoming a lifer. The assistant manager had recently asked if Bobby was interested in becoming a PIC (person in charge), and Bobby had declined, giving an excuse about being too busy with school.

"Join us in produce, man," his roommate Ollie said one night.

"Dude, the money's way better, and it's fun 'cause we're all working together," added his other roommate, Dustin.

"It's okay," Bobby said. "I won't be there for much longer."

He tried to say this in a way that didn't suggest he thought he was better than them, but neither seemed to notice. Ollie and Dustin were firmly in the lifer category and loving it.

"Missing out, man," said Ollie before shotgunning his beer and burping loud enough for the neighboring apartment to hear. The produce department had a very non-bougie nickname among Cure associates: Broduce.

Bobby could have been just like them, doing community college on and off with no end in sight, his biggest aspirations to get laid and eventually settle down with one of the Cure girls. No, that was not Bobby's future. He would become an important person, and rich, like one of the guests who could afford to drop five hundred dollars a week on high-end groceries, but with more influence—a food scientist with the power to design and alter those expensive products.

For this reason, Bobby preferred the company of courtesy clerks at work. They were cheerful and airy and above the fray of Cure's deep gossip and drama between longtime associates. They were part-timers who knew they had a life outside of and beyond Cure. Bobby had gotten to know a lot of them well, would even call some friends, but they always left shortly after, which was a good reminder to him that he, too, needed to plan his escape.

"What are you going to do after high school?" Bobby asked Lillian one day in the Box.

"Ugh, don't ask me that." Lillian dramatically waved a hand as if to shoo him away.

"Aren't you one of those really-type-A smart kids?"

"What!" Lillian stopped stocking for a moment. "Who said that? Tell me who said that."

Bobby laughed. "Nobody. I just kinda assumed."

"Okay, well, I'm not, really," she said. "People just think I am, and that depresses me."

"What's so depressing about people thinking you're smart?"

"No, it's that everyone thinks I'm so *good,* which is another way of saying I'm *boring.*"

"I don't think being good is boring. And I don't think you're boring."

"Sure, sure," she said. "Well, I'm definitely the most boring person at Cure. Everyone here is ridiculously cool. Did you know when I got a job here, my friends were all like, Whoa, *you* got a job at *Cure*?"

Bobby knew what Lillian was talking about. Under the current management, Cure had developed the reputation of hiring only attractive people. There wasn't necessarily a specific Cure "look," but the goal was to make guests feel good when they walked into the store, and it was unwritten (and generally unspoken) Cure philosophy that guests felt good when they had appealing associates helping them out. There were, of course, the conventionally attractive men in Broduce, but there were also the edgy, hip women at the juice bar, the silver foxes of the wine aisle, the great-smile checkers of all genders, ages, and skin tones, and the sweet courtesy clerks who could turn it on for even the coldest guests. Bobby looked at Lillian closer. No, she wasn't exactly what the managers typically went for in a Cure courtesy clerk, a bit nerdy and childish, but that was mostly because of the braces. She wasn't so far off that she didn't fit in. She was like him in that way, not quite right, but not *not* right.

"Oh my God, don't look at me like that!" she squealed.

"I'm not– What? Like what?"

"Like you're trying to decide whether I fit into the whole Cure-people-are-beautiful thing." Lillian covered her face with a milk jug. "This is why I like hiding back here. Nobody can see or judge me."

"Well, welcome to my world."

Lillian laughed and shoved the jug into its slot. "You do fit, though, so you don't have to worry."

Bobby could feel himself blushing. He didn't know how to respond and was, thankfully, saved by the intercom.

Greg's voice came on the intercom: "Lillian, line two, *Lillian, line two.*" She ran out to pick up the phone, then came back to inform Bobby that Greg had told her it was busy up front and she had to go bag. Twenty minutes later, Bobby had collected himself, and Lillian was back.

"I hate him," she said. "It wasn't busy at all! People were just hanging around the registers talking. And Greg is like, Well, refill the paper bags for everyone, which took me like two seconds. Then he lectures me about how I need to stay up front, while all the other courtesy clerks are going off to do other stuff. I hope he slips on a grape and falls."

"Wow, that's pretty grim," Bobby said.

"Yeah, I know. I don't want him to get really hurt, though. Just, like, bruises and aching for a couple weeks."

Bobby agreed that would be a good punishment for Greg.

"Is it true he's on coke?" she asked.

"Now, what would you know about that?" Bobby asked, back to his usual older-brother self.

"Dustin told me. He also told me that he was super-high on kava tea the other day, but they sell kava tea here, so, like, how high can you actually get?"

"Dude, don't listen to anything Dustin says. He's just messing with you," Bobby said. "But yeah, the thing about Greg is true."

Lillian nodded slowly. "I thought Greg just had allergies," she said. "But that makes sense. It's probably why he sucks so bad. Who else is high at work? Aren't they worried about getting fired?"

Lillian was relatively socially adept—she appeared to get along with almost everyone at Cure—but moments like this reminded Bobby of her age. (Although Bobby, and almost everyone he knew, had been a different kind of fourteen when it came to the things Lillian asked about.) She was guileless, which perhaps was her appeal, that you felt a bit protective of and amused by her. And clearly, some people, like Dustin, got a kick out of teasing her. At times Bobby was surprised at Lillian's innocence, because she seemed mature in other ways—she gave him sound advice about what classes to take, how to deal with professors, and was sweetly encouraging about his going on to do bigger things than work at Cure. He didn't speak to anyone about the future as much as he did to Lillian.

"Not that many people are high at work," he said. "Pretty sure it's just Greg."

"Okay, good," Lillian said. "Let's work for real now so you don't have to do as much tomorrow morning."

Bobby turned up the Box's speaker, and the two of them stocked to pop music until the end of Lillian's shift. She handed Bobby her too-big sweatshirt for him to put back on the high shelf beyond her reach.

"To answer your original question," she said, "I have no idea what I'm going to do after high school except leave Cure. I'll go,

Goodbye, Cure! Goodbye, Greg! But you'll be long gone by then, so you won't care! You'll be off doing some food-engineering thingy, making yogurt with some special texture or whatever. I'll have to help whoever they hire to replace you, and we'll stock the yogurt you've worked on, and I'll tell the new dairy guy all about your genius."

"That's the plan," he said, feeling good about Lillian's vision.

Ollie and Dustin wanted to throw a Cure party. They didn't call it a Cure party, but since they were only friends with people at Cure, that's what it was. It didn't matter whether Bobby was on board or not—he was always outnumbered two against one—but they asked him out of roommate courtesy, and since he had finished his midterms, had done well, in fact, he said definitely. He was almost finished with this place. He wanted to celebrate.

It started off as a typical Cure party, where most associates between the ages of twenty and forty were in attendance—all the produce guys, many of the cashiers, the younger bakers, the PICs, a few of the older courtesy clerks. Then, unlike at a typical Cure party, there was a knock at the door, and standing outside was a group of the younger courtesy clerks, including Lillian. Dustin answered the door, then turned to the room and yelled, "Who told the kids they could come?" By then most partygoers were drunk and laughed about the teenagers showing up. They were welcomed in and handed drinks.

Lillian waved to Bobby across the room, and he gave a small wave back. "Why are they here?" Bobby asked the meat/seafood guy next to him, who only shrugged.

A part of Bobby knew it wasn't a good look that Lillian and her friends were at the party. The teenagers had their own parties.

Sometimes they'd ask people at Cure to buy them liquor and beer, and sometimes those people—never Bobby—would agree, for a small fee. The point was, outside of work, the high schoolers did not comingle with the rest. But now Bobby was several drinks in, and he couldn't think of anything to do about it. He saw that Lillian and another girl, whose name he didn't know, were chatting with Heather (in bulk) and Veronica (a checker), so he figured the older girls would watch over the younger ones, and everything would be fine. The party went on, the warmth of bodies overheated the room, and Bobby went to his room to change out of his sweater into a T-shirt. As he was walking back, he saw Lillian down the hall, opening and closing doors.

"Hey, is there a bathroom?" she said.

"This one." He walked down and pointed at the door she would have opened next.

She looked in, then looked back at Bobby, who was still standing there, for some reason. Why, he didn't know. He had the spins.

"It's pretty disgusting in there," Lillian said.

He leaned in. The toilet seat was up and stained with earthy-colored, unrecognizable splotches. The mirror was dotted in white water stains, the sink and countertop littered with many tiny bits of hair. There was an inexplicable pile of balled-up, wet-looking toilet paper in one corner. It all swirled up into his face with a pungent piss scent. It wasn't his bathroom.

"That's Dustin and Ollie's bathroom," he said, vindicating himself. "My bathroom's a lot cleaner, if you want to use it instead."

Lillian nodded. He led her to his room and showed her to the bathroom attached to it. She looked in and said, "Yep, a lot better, thanks!"

She went in and closed the door. He heard her turn on the fan. He stood there for some time without thinking, then realized he had been standing right outside the bathroom door while she was probably on the toilet, and that was a creepy thing to do, so he walked over to his desk and sat there instead, staring at the black desktop of his computer. It didn't occur to him, until days later, after everything had already taken place, that he could and should have left his bedroom and let her find her own way back to the party. At the time, he thought he was being polite.

When she came out of the bathroom, she held out her wet hands and asked if he had a towel. He pulled one out of a drawer and handed it to her. They stood there awkwardly for a moment. It occurred to Bobby that she might be waiting for him to do something. But what? The thought made him dizzy and nauseated. He asked if she wanted to go back out. She said she was feeling a little sick and asked if she could sit there for a bit. Again, the thought crossed his mind that she wanted something from him, that she wanted to be alone with him in that room, for something to happen, and he would be lying if that didn't appeal to him, at least a little, or maybe even a lot. It was hard to tell. She was a sweet girl, wasn't she? But a thought was not an action. After a lifetime of silence, he said they should go back out to the party. Lillian nodded, and the two of them walked back out to the living room.

In the early morning, the high school kids long gone, the party ended. Hours later, Bobby was back at work, tired and hungover. The Box chilled him awake. He pounded a few newly expired yogurt drinks and felt better. In the afternoon, when Bobby was just about fully recovered, Greg came to the Box and said they needed to talk. The two of them stood staring at each other until Greg finally said that he wasn't okay with what had happened the previous night.

"What happened?" Bobby said.

"The high school kids? And I saw you and Lillian walk out of your bedroom. I mean, I've always thought you two spent way too much time together at work. Honestly, I've been watching out for both of you, getting her to stay up front," Greg said. "But that wasn't enough, was it? I'm surprised, considering what happened to the last dairy guy. Thought at least you would've known better. I'm going to have to report this."

Bobby felt sick again. As Greg walked away, he managed to say, "What the hell?"

He saw himself losing everything he'd worked so hard to achieve. He'd lose this job, be unable to pay for school—in his last quarter!—and he wouldn't graduate. He'd have to go back to Stockton and do God knows what. All because of . . . ? Because he had done nothing wrong at all? In fact, he had been a friend to Lillian! He'd been very respectful of Lillian! In fact, he was the good guy here! Bobby was going to get ahead of this.

Bobby conveyed everything to Dustin and Ollie. It took only a few texts among them to figure out that a recent high school graduate had invited the kids. No, it wasn't amazing that they'd let the very underage high schoolers drink their alcohol, but they could just say they hadn't. They could say the kids had brought their own beer. Who knew where they'd gotten it? Teenagers drank all the time.

But Bobby had to deal with Lillian, to eliminate any confusion about their interaction. He asked around for her number—

see, how could anything have happened between them if he didn't even have her number?—then texted her something non-threatening but with a sense of urgency: *Hey could you meet up? Need to talk about a work thing. Important, it's bobby btw*

She wrote back an hour later: *Hi! Ok! When/where?*

They picked a coffee shop downtown. Bobby waited at an outdoor table, feeling more settled. He prided himself on performing admirably under duress. His life hadn't been easy, and with each new hurdle, he'd overcome. A small misunderstanding would not derail him. It was still bright out, before dinner. He had a decent sense of what he was going to say to Lillian but mostly spent his time imagining her nodding and saying it was fine, nothing bad was going to happen to him.

When she rode up on her bike, sparkling blue helmet atop her head, Bobby saw again how young she really was. She was wearing her hair in a braid, which reminded him of fairy tales and cartoons, which, God, she really was a kid, wasn't she? It was like his mind was punishing him for even associating with someone her age. He felt in his throat a lump of guilt. Why had he befriended a child, a girl child, when he was, technically, a full-grown adult man? How had he ever allowed the two of them to be in any space alone together? That was wrong, wasn't it? And then his guilt boiled into fear. Everybody would think he was a creep when he had never been a creep. He was so far from creepy that he hadn't even realized that what he was doing could be considered creepy! And then the fear bubbled over into anger. It wasn't his fault that he'd been around Lillian—that was Cure's fault for hiring her and putting her in the store at all. Hell, it was just as much Lillian's fault! Why had *she* ever befriended *him*? By the time Lillian had locked up her bike and sat down with him, he was so engulfed by competing emotions, he was blindly certain that he knew *exactly* how to set things straight.

"Lillian," he said, "why were you at the party last night? Why did you think it was okay to come? What were you thinking?"

"I thought it was a Cure party," she said, smiling, as though that answered everything.

"Do you know what kind of trouble Dustin and Ollie and me are getting in because you guys showed up?"

She stopped smiling and shook her head.

"Greg's reporting us for having underage kids over. We could lose our jobs, and none of us even invited you. That's fucked up. I mean, I know it's not really your guys' fault. Greg's an asshole for reporting us. But it's still fucked up."

"Ugh, Greg sucks!" Lillian said. "I'll tell him that Joe invited us and that you guys didn't even know we were coming."

"Okay, I mean, that's a start." Bobby felt a little relieved. That should be enough to get him off the hook. But then he remembered. "Well, Greg also saw you coming out of my room, and now he thinks something happened in there between you and me."

"He does?" Lillian started to laugh. "That's so weird!"

Bobby grew hot. He didn't know what she found so funny and weird about the notion. Did she think he was disgusting or what? And the way Lillian sat there, with her elbow resting on the table, her chin in her hand, she looked too relaxed. It irked him. Here he was, scared about possibly losing everything he'd worked so hard to achieve, and there she was, a clueless child, laughing in his face, making fun of him. He needed to convey to her how serious this was, for her to take this as seriously as he was taking it. He saw himself fitting into the role of a parent, or the older brother, which was what he'd always thought of himself as to Lillian anyway. It was his job to educate her.

"Lillian, stop it. It's not funny," he said. "I don't know why you wanted to sit in my room, but it was not okay. It was incredibly inappropriate of you. I know maybe you don't think this is a big deal or whatever, you're a kid, you don't understand. I was just being a good host. You made me show you where my bathroom was. Do you understand? That's what you tell Greg. You tell him and everyone that it had nothing to do with me. Do you understand? Can you confirm to me that you get it, Lillian? Now repeat to me, Yes, I get it, Bobby. Can you do that?"

Lillian was certainly taking him seriously by then. She'd pulled back in her seat, was sitting straighter, listening intently, and looking like she was . . .

"Are you okay?" An older woman approached their table and addressed Lillian.

Lillian turned to the woman and nodded.

"Are you sure, sweetie? Do you need anything?"

Bobby looked at the woman, but she was looking only at Lillian. "She said she's fine," he said.

The woman acted like he wasn't even there. "Would you like me to take you home?" the woman said to Lillian.

"No, it's okay. I have my bike," Lillian said. She wiped at her eyes quickly and smiled. "Thank you for asking."

"Okay, but you let me know if you need anything at all. I'm right over there," the woman said, and pointed at a nearby table. "I'm not far."

As she walked away, the woman finally looked at Bobby, and the way she eyed him made his skin burn. He had never felt so judged, and wrongly. He wanted to call the woman back and tell her the whole story, give her the necessary context, that he and

Lillian were just work friends, he was like a brother to her, he was only trying to teach Lillian an important lesson about life, that was why he'd raised his voice a little at her, it wasn't a threat by any means, but he wasn't so dumb as to not realize how ridiculous that would sound out loud. After the woman was back at her table, Lillian put her helmet on.

"Can you believe that lady?" Bobby whispered, not wanting the woman to hear him.

"It's fine. I get it, Bobby," she said. "I'll tell Greg nothing happened between us."

"Okay, thanks," he said, softer. "You'll tell him today, right?"

"Yeah."

"Thanks, Lil. I appreciate it."

"I have to go now," Lillian said.

"Do you want a ride? We can put your bike in the back of my car," he said, wanting them to be friendly again. They could laugh off the awkwardness, then go back to working together, joking about Greg, how ridiculous a misunderstanding this had all been.

"No, I'm fine." She was already walking toward the bike rack, and then she rode off.

Nearly a decade later, Bobby is stacking onions at the new Whole Foods in town, where he now works as produce team lead, when he spots her down by the citrus. He doesn't recognize her immediately. Her hair is shorter and she is dressed differently, in what he can only describe as flowy, fancy clothes—a silk (?) blouse tucked into loose high-waisted slacks—and heels. She looks like the kind of woman he and his coworkers go out of their way to help, and because of this, and because he is seeing her for the first time in years, he calls to her excitedly as he walks up. "Lillian, hey!"

She is squinting, frowning a little, like she is trying to place him in her memory.

"It's Bobby! Bobby from Cure! We used to hang back in the Box, remember? You back in town visiting? What brings you to Broduce today?" He laughs at the Cure inside joke he's made.

"I remember," she says.

"God, that was ages ago! But it kinda feels like yesterday, right? That's the crazy thing with Cure. Even if you work there for a little bit, it's, like, always going to be a part of you. I mean, I'm glad I'm not there anymore. Just left last year, actually."

Lillian nods and smiles. It is a pinched smile, the one customers make when they're annoyed something is out of stock, or when you can't find what they're looking for, or when they want to be left alone. Bobby isn't an idiot—never was. He can see this.

"I—" Lillian is saying, but he stops her.

"It was great seeing you! Great catching up! I better get back to it!"

Bobby turns around and walks back to the cart of onions. He realizes, though he has left Cure, he is in a uniform very much like the one they used to wear at Cure. Though he is less than halfway done unpacking the onions, he closes up the carton. He can sense Lillian's eyes on him. He does not look back. He moves quickly, pushes the cart to the back, through the double doors, and around the corner.

As he stands there, safe and hidden, it occurs to him that Lillian is now the age he was when they first met. She must have gone off to college, probably has a boyfriend and a good-paying job in an office somewhere—enough to afford shopping at Whole Foods. She is probably in town for a short visit. She probably lives in a city, doing some city-girl things. The way she looked at him—does she think she's better than him? For the first time in many years, he thinks about what happened between them. He wonders why Lillian made such a big deal about it. It was very likely she went on to experience worse things than a twentysomething-year-old kid lecturing her in front of a coffee shop. (Of course, he hoped, not too much worse than that.) What he did was hardly anything on the spectrum of bad behavior, and anyway, he's sure he apologized profusely to her back then. Lillian overreacted by quitting. But then he remembers her having a hard time at Cure in general; she complained a lot about the work and about the other associates. She probably used him as an excuse to leave. Clearly, it didn't hurt her much. She looked good, composed, stable. And here he is, still working in a grocery store, still in the same town, still hanging out with Dustin and Ollie, still doing the same shit. He stands there, sweating, frightened at how much time has passed and how little has changed, and he feels deeply sorry and sad, most of all, he realizes, for himself.

KLARA

I NEVER KNOW HOW TO BE FASHIONABLY LATE. THAT'S KLARA'S talent.

We'd picked a place to meet about halfway between the two of us. It was a little closer to me, and while in the cab, I savored the small accomplishment of being the one with the shorter ride. But I was early, which made it a pointless victory.

The only table available was a small one by the window, really a floor-to-ceiling glass wall. We'd decided on a Blue Bottle, as if being somewhere familiar might make us familiar to each other again, the way chain hotels and restaurants and drugstores design their entrances to all look the same so that when you walk in, you feel grounded no matter where you are or what's outside. Klara had texted in the morning: *We can pretend we're back in San Francisco!* Outside was big brick building pressed up against big brick building on a narrow one-way street—nothing you'd ever see on the West Coast.

I didn't know much about New York, there for the first time and only for two nights, staying in a $380/night Lower East Side hotel with an absurdly giant granite tub, courtesy of the media conglomerate for which I worked. I was there to report on a languishing tech giant's new laptop-tablet hybrid, if *reporting* was even the accurate way to put it. It was the early 2010s, and tech companies were trying to outdo each other's product launches. This one had rented an entire warehouse at one of the piers. Upon walking in, attendees were greeted by a giant model of a few city blocks the size of a children's playground. This deranged version of the city was populated with the company's devices, wearing mini-glasses and hats and vests and dresses. Pairs of tablets strolled outside of skyscrapers and glimmering shops; several sat at park benches, staring at each other with their camera eyes; others rode and drove cabs. The message being: *These little gadgets, they're just like us. Buy a new companion today.*

On a giant stage in another room, product execs had touted the thing's magnesium casing and the "satisfying" clicking sound the stand made when it shut against said casing. I had a line in my "initial hands-on" report—*Sure, the magnesium is smooth, but at the end of the day metal is metal is cold and dead*—that my editor changed to *FuseMg feels great in the hand.* I was already tired of my job back then. When I'd first started, I'd thought I was on the path to doing something important and worthwhile. Now, well, I don't delude myself.

I wasn't in New York to see Klara, but all day, through the event's annoying indie-pop soundtrack, and the flashing colorful lights that made me worry I'd become epileptic, and the long awkward pauses meant for weak applause, the thought of our forthcoming meeting intruded on my note-taking. I'd think of her. The expression she might have upon seeing me. What she might say. How her voice would sound. What she would notice about me. I was surprised and disturbed by these thoughts; I had convinced myself that there was no animosity or tension between us, that we would approach each other without nervousness, with a generally neutral and open stance one might have when encountering a distant cousin. Clearly, she had a stronger effect on my psyche than I was ready to admit.

The sun was beginning to set. Outside the Blue Bottle, sidewalk traffic increased with people heading home or out to dinner, their faces shining with summer sweat. I checked my phone. I was five minutes early, so I walked to the counter to order the most expensive item on the menu. A Nicaraguan coffee from the siphon bar that came with two toffees and cost fifteen dollars. I added a six-dollar goat-cheese-and-fig scone to the order. Everything would be reimbursed through my job. I felt I had to take advantage of my extravagant daily allowance, to siphon (ha ha) as much out of the job as possible, in order to make up for the hollowness of the work. Back to the phone. Messages. Klara's. I scrolled and scrolled, wanting to go back to the earliest ones I had (six years of history—I hated to delete anything that might mean something to me later), to read through them all, not for the first time, to see how the tone changed over the years, when exactly we stopped contacting each other as frequently, who started it, who was more at fault. The earlier texts, full of phrases like *hahaha yes* and *heading over* and *love ya* and *do you have my . . .* gave way to later ones that started off with *Hi Klara! How are you?* or *Sorry, I didn't see this* and ended with *Hope you are doing well.* I was trying and failing to stop thinking about our relationship in terms of blame.

It had been a year since we'd seen each other last, back in San Francisco, after another year of little contact. Klara had been back in town for a couple days, passing through to visit her old lab and to play tourist. We'd met at a nearby Vietnamese restaurant for dinner with our boyfriends in tow. I was tense. The wound of our torn friendship felt fresh, though I knew it wasn't, that I had deliberately picked at the dirty scab to let the blood seep out again and again. I wanted to appear happy to see her, to win her back, or at least present a friendly face, one that showed I was okay with where we stood, or better yet, I wanted to appear cold, to show her I didn't need her, which would, I hoped, somehow cause her to put in more effort, make her want *me* to need *her*. But when my boyfriend and I arrived at the restaurant, Klara and her boyfriend weren't there. The restaurant's hostess said she couldn't seat us until our entire party arrived. For the next twenty minutes, I couldn't stop looking at my phone to check the time, complaining about how typical it was of her to be late to everything. I sat there tapping and scratching the vinyl of the waiting area bench.

It used to be a funny quirk, Klara's lateness, especially if I was with her, helping her slack. What time is it? she'd ask, and I'd say, Hurry up, as I watched her dab concealer beneath her eyes, brush foundation across her face, smear stain on her cheekbones and lips, swipe a couple coats of mascara on her otherwise invisible blond lashes. She would put something on, a pair of jeans and a blouse, change her mind, take it off, put on a dress, stare at herself in the mirror, ask if she looked okay, to which I always tried to respond honestly, which might cause her to change her mind again. She would check her email, lose her phone, find it, then have lost her keys, need to decide on shoes, and so on. Five minutes would turn into fifteen, then thirty, sometimes more, and when it was well past the time she had to be someplace else, she'd be only stepping out the door. I would watch and shake my head. God, you're so ridiculous, Klara. Occasionally, she'd lie down in bed, say, Who cares where I have to be? I'm tired and I don't want to go anywhere. She'd call or text whoever, make up some excuse—too much work, not feeling well, family shit—and we'd stay in, get high, walk down Telegraph for frozen yogurt or hot dogs, then wander the Berkeley campus, where we would find entertainment in everything: fast-walking students with their giant backpacks, a dog pissing on its owner's laundry hamper outside the Laundromat, a woman on a milk crate calling us devil children through her loudspeaker . . . I'm a paranoid high, always have been. Are my eyes white? Can you tell I'm high? I often asked her after drowning myself in Visine. Klara was confident. They're so white, they're Snow White–white, she'd reassure me. Then there'd be the tickling of grass against our bare legs as we lounged on the quad—it had felt endless, like childhood, and it all ended without my fully understanding when or how or why.

To be on the receiving end of her lateness felt like betrayal. So at the Vietnamese restaurant, when Klara finally walked in with her boyfriend, I wasn't in a generous mood. The first thing I noticed was how dramatically the two of them had aged since I'd seen them last—she had gained weight and seemed to walk slower. Distinct wrinkles fanned out of the corners of her eyes. She looked lumpy beneath her tight jersey dress. Her boyfriend still had his youthful face and physique, but his long hair was so thin that I already knew he had a bald spot at the back of his head. In that moment, the surprise of seeing them older coalesced with my irritation, and instead of hugging them and saying hi, as a decent person might, I blurted out impatiently that they were late and had made us lose out on not one but three open tables. Klara's boyfriend apologized while she stood beside him, half smiling and silent, looking down, her hair covering half her face. She wore no makeup that I could tell. What was causing her to be late now? What was occupying her time? The boyfriend said it was his fault, and because I knew it wasn't, his tone made me feel guilty. I apologized, told them it was fine, that I was only hungry. As we waited for the next available table, I worried that it was years of enduring my harsh, thoughtless remarks that had pushed Klara away from me. But that couldn't be right, I thought as I leaned against my own boyfriend, conscious of Klara's presence behind me. I hadn't been truly harsh with her until I had felt abandoned by her, or so I reasoned then.

I wish we could have analyzed our fading friendship together. It was something we loved doing to others when we were in college, the social interactions soaked in meaning that we'd spend hours wringing out. I think it had something to do with our being outsiders in our adolescent communities, our need to get along or, better yet, excel by dissecting situations we didn't naturally understand. She was an immigrant, arriving at ten years old from Ukraine. I was the child of Chinese immigrants. We both grew up in sleepy white suburban towns with idealistic, picturesque names like Thousand Oaks and Walnut Creek, names that made you think of identical beige houses with artificially green lawns, equally spaced out on wide streets, exactly the kind of homes in which we grew up, except inside ours, the families shouted in voices the neighbors couldn't understand, could never figure out if we were fighting or if the language naturally sounded angry. And yet Klara and I were—we still are—so different from each other.

We met our first semester at Berkeley, in a class called Rhetoric of Bitchiness. She came into class panting and took the empty seat behind me, and during our professor's introduction, she tapped on my shoulder and asked if I had a pen she could borrow. I was overly prepared and eager those days, a different-colored notebook and pen for each course. From the course itself, I remember very little—the names of writers whose theories and arguments have gone cloudy with time, terms like *the male gaze* and *female agency* and *homosocial*. What I remember most from that class is Klara, the feeling of talking with her, the abundance of our exchanges, how we would huddle at a library table, showing each other the quotes we were pulling from our readings of Laura Mulvey, Susan Sontag, Eve Sedgwick, and Judith Butler (whose office Klara and I staked out on a couple occasions, taking photos of ourselves with her nameplate). We were living our fantasies of becoming women who thought deeply.

When we returned from winter break, it seemed that everything we'd talked about had vanished. Klara was focused instead on rushing a sorority. Her older sister had been in a sorority, had made all of her college friends through a sorority, and told Klara all about the bonds she'd made, the non-biological "sisters" now so critical to her life. Klara said I should join, that it would be fun. She asked, no, begged me to rush with her. I didn't want to. I told her the idea of spending five days with dozens of girls who were trying to impress one another with their high-pitched enthusiasm sounded like torture. What I didn't say was that I was afraid of rejection, a rejection I could easily divine. But Klara convinced me.

Day one, first hour, we were separated into different groups, and I got stuck standing next to another Asian girl whose right eye wouldn't stop watering, causing her to look like a sick puppy, not the kind you want to adopt but the kind you pity, knowing it's going to be put down. Her eye makeup smeared across the right side of her face as she talked about her first months at Berkeley, how she was scared to walk down Telegraph because homeless people would get in her face asking for money. I was repulsed. I could see parts of myself in the girl and, wanting to distance myself from her, I looked past her, toward Klara chatting with other girls, those who resembled her, confident and cheerful types, their hair either long enough to graze the small of their backs or tied up in perfect buns. There was an Asian girl and a Desi girl in Klara's pack, and I envied them in particular; they were the ones who had perfected their cat-eye liner and were born with a look that was difficult to describe as anything other than appealing. It was obvious to me that the girls in the top-tier houses chose by looks first—their reputation and relations with the frat houses counted on it. Klara and her new crowd were comfortable, like they knew exactly where they'd end up. I walked up to my recruitment counselor and told her I had changed my mind and wanted to withdraw from recruitment. Are you sure? she asked at least four times. We haven't even started, and I know you'd find a good fit somewhere, and she listed a few houses that had the reputation of being bottom-tier. I walked away without saying goodbye to Klara.

Sophomore year, Klara moved into her sorority house (top-tier, one known for having lots of hot foreign girls), and I moved into one of the coed vegetarian co-ops. We never did talk about sorority recruitment again, and I was grateful Klara never brought it up. I'm not sure why, but even thinking back on that day coats me in shame. Despite our opposing living situations, in culture and location (me on north campus, her on southeast), we saw each other nearly every day, unless one of us was out of town or too sick to leave the house or too overwhelmed with our pathetic workload, and even then we would often see each other at the library or at I-House. We continued to take courses together, courses with names like Feminine Sexuality and Crisis and Culture. I talked her into enrolling with me, though they didn't fulfill any of her major (molecular and cell biology) requirements and did fulfill all of mine (rhetoric). What are we here for if not to really live this? I once said to her, naively, waving my arms as if to envelop the Free Speech Movement Café. (Which reminds me of when a student in one of my rhetoric courses, for a final presentation, dragged the entire class of fifty to the outside of the café, made us surround him as he reenacted Mario Savio's 1964 "Operation of the Machine" speech while standing on a cement block, and all I could think was that Savio's actual speech took place across campus on the steps of Sproul Hall, not in front of this café that hadn't yet been built, that was built only to commemorate him. The reenactment was so far removed from the actual event, yet everyone in class applauded the performance. That was another time, a time that didn't involve Klara.)

Klara used to comment on my looks, too. She would say things like, I wish my skin was as clear as yours. I wish that I was shorter like you, I wish my arms were toned like yours, I wish my hair was thicker, that my boobs weren't so saggy, that my stomach was flatter. And each time it made me happy to hear that I had something she didn't, even though I was completely convinced that, on the whole, she was more attractive than I was, and I said so.

How did I look to her during that long-ago dinner, as we ate at the Vietnamese restaurant? My intention going in, after my brief outburst about her and her boyfriend's tardiness, was to keep quiet and listen to Klara and our boyfriends talk about their respective graduate school programs, which were all in some sort of biological field. I was used to hearing people talk about work I didn't understand, but that night, I couldn't handle it. It was PI this and degradation that and intracellular whatever. At one point, my boyfriend asked Klara if she had decided on a lab yet. After putting an entire slice of barbecued pork in her mouth, she said, with her food bulging from her cheek, that she would join the department's power lab because the PI had great industry connections with pharmaceutical and biotech companies. This explanation troubled me, and the way Klara spoke with food in her mouth, again something that didn't bother me most of the time, made me want to slam the table and shout. Since when was she so eager to climb the ladder? How disgusting for her to talk like that. Do you even care about the research the lab does? I asked. Or is it just about power and reputation? Once the words came out of my mouth, I could hear that same bitterness in them from earlier and immediately regretted having spoken.

We were no longer close enough for me to chastise her about doing the right thing the way I had years ago. One time we were studying in her room, and she was telling me that she was going to write about the contribution Che Guevara had on the revolution for her Cuba class. I love him, he's so sexy, she said. He's right up there with Andrew VanWyngarden. Who? I asked. The lead singer of MGMT, she said. Don't you know? We were lying beside each other on her bed, and I turned on my stomach to laugh into her pillow. (I remember the smell of her pillows so distinctly, like baby formula and wet skin, musty and sweet.) That makes no sense, I said. It makes perfect sense, she said, fuck Andrew in the present day and fuck Che in the past. I asked if her professor was canceling her Cuba class for the walkout, and she said yes, but she still had to go to physiology and microbio lab. You can't cross the picket line, that's just not okay, I told her, echoing what one of my professors had said as if I had come up with it myself. (I would see my first picket line the following week.) Klara rambled on about how her professors were going to give quizzes, they didn't care about the protest or the budget cuts or layoffs or tuition hikes. I really need A's this semester for med school apps, she said. You don't sound like someone Che Guevara would be into, I said. She ignored me and changed the topic. Remember last night when I stepped out with that guy, the one with the eyebrows? she said. We went out to the backyard and made out for a little bit. When we were making out, the guy lifted my shirt up just as the neighbor turned on her back porch light and came out to smoke. First thing she sees are my nipples pointing straight at her. She has this cigarette sort of dangling in her mouth and it drops to the ground, and she's like, Oh my God! Then she practically runs back inside and turns the light off. Eyebrow guy tries to keep it going, and he yells toward the house, Why are people such fucking prudes? This woman has beautiful breasts and shouldn't be ashamed of showing them off!

We laughed at the boy—Klara was always encountering these "enlightened" Berkeley types. But curiosity, mixed with something else, made me turn to her and ask if she would show me them, her beautiful breasts, what I called them to mimic the guy, to make it seem more like a joke than something serious. As her closest friend, I felt I should see as much of Klara as some boy who barely knew her; a part of me felt that it was my right to see all of her. And yet another part of me was afraid that I was crossing some boundary of our friendship—we'd seen each other's bodies, but only quickly and casually, while changing clothes. Klara turned her face to mine. We were close enough that I could see each individual thin, bloodshot vein in the whites of her eyes, and for a moment I thought she might scream at me or push me away, but she just said a quick okay while lifting up her shirt. I sat up and looked at her naked chest, she wasn't wearing a bra, and I saw that her skin there was as smooth and free of blemishes as the more visible parts of her. I was surprised to see how small they were as she lay there, how she looked so innocent. Encouraged by her assent, I took another step. Can I see what they feel like? I asked. She nodded. It was strange, touching her in a way I had never touched her, yet it was fleeting, a gentle press of my fingers against the right one—again I was surprised, surprised at how soft she felt, especially compared to my own denser breasts—and quickly, her shirt came back down. We looked at each other briefly and burst into giggles. After we calmed down, I told Klara I wouldn't have freaked out if she'd told me about what had happened with Eyebrow Guy right after. She shook her head. Yes, you would have, you always freak out about things. I flinched. No, I don't, I said. But I added, You know what's worth freaking out about? You crossing the picket line for some dumb classes. Klara sat up and leveled her eyes with mine. Not all of us live these little idealistic, romantic lives, she said, her voice pinched and high, her arms wrapped tightly around herself. Some of us have more practical goals.

Practical goals. I have those now, too. This job. Money. Back then I wanted a life in which my mind, my relationships, my day-to-day choices, everything, would be ethically and morally connected. Maybe that's what I still want but realize I can't achieve.

Back in the restaurant, Klara was unsurprisingly defensive about her choice of lab. She thought the research was incredibly interesting and went on to describe the lab's focus, which had to do with stem cells and cancer. She looked at me only fleetingly, making eye contact mostly with our boyfriends, yet I kept my eyes on her, nodding, trying to erase the tension I had created. I said I thought it was a good idea, what she was doing, it all made total sense. In the early years of our friendship, we used to argue and sometimes even yelled at each other, as friends do, but we'd quickly return to our happy equilibrium. I wanted this more than anything that night, but it felt like there was something unmovable and complicated in the way, as if some tight mesh netting separated us. I could see her, but I couldn't reach her.

Desperate not to part ways after our dinner, I asked Klara and her boyfriend if they wanted to go sit and chat in a bar, though I knew my own boyfriend would prefer to head home. Klara said sure, a word that I've always hated because it seems so half-hearted, as if the person saying it is doing you a favor and wants you to know they are doing you a favor. I had told her this several times before. Maybe she had forgotten? We walked to the bar down the street and naturally separated into pairs, Klara and her boyfriend trailing slightly behind. When I noticed them deep in some conversation, I turned to my boyfriend and asked if he thought I'd been mean to Klara. He said I had been a bit impatient. I spent the rest of the walk brooding over whether she would think the same and how to remedy it so that we could part on good terms. Glancing back at them, I tried to find an opening in their conversation to squeeze a word in, but never succeeded.

Klara and I used to take a lot of walks together, like over to her sorority house for dinner after our evening Fem Sex class, through the little woods along north campus, where you could almost pretend you were in the wilderness, with the dense trees and the sound of the creek's water riding along its rocks. What did you think of all that masturbation stuff? Klara asked one night after class. Our instructor, a graduate student in the film and media department, had talked about the shame that women often felt about pleasuring themselves, about how the shame was due partly to the fact that we didn't talk about masturbation openly with one another, that there were so few mainstream examples in the media of women talking about masturbation together. Some of the women in class scoffed. What about *Sex and the City*? one said. We were third-wave feminists, far beyond the shame, according to another. The people in class began sharing their masturbation origin stories, the frequency with which they masturbated, their favorite methods and toys, one after the other, often interrupting each other to agree and ask questions. I was fascinated, because though I believed that nobody should feel ashamed about masturbation—it was natural, I had always figured—it was true that I hadn't talked to anybody about it or been around women who spoke so openly and excitedly about the topic. I remember looking at Klara in class and seeing that she was flushed, staring at a spot in the corner of the room, refusing to make eye contact. She hadn't spoken. Neither had I, but that wasn't unusual for me. Walking through that wooded area afterward, I told her that the class had made me realize it wasn't taboo to discuss masturbation. What did you think? I asked. I wanted to open up a space in which she could tell me anything. She was unusually quiet, then said, I'm not sure, I guess I felt weird and embarrassed? Like, people were talking about a band or a TV show that's super-popular but I've never heard of them? I didn't understand what she was saying. What do you mean? I asked. Klara shook her head and wouldn't look at me. I've never done it, she said. I mean, I've tried since we started taking Fem Sex, but I don't know if it's working. I don't know if I'm doing it right. I asked her to clarify. Again she wouldn't look at me. I've never felt anything, um, special, I guess? I haven't felt anything like what I think I should feel, like, ever. I stopped walking, and she stopped beside me. I asked her if she meant she'd never had an orgasm. She shrugged. I turned around to go in the opposite direction, away from her house, toward downtown, and said, Let's go. Where? she asked, following.

I was taking her to Good Vibrations, a local sex shop our Fem Sex instructor had mentioned. As we walked down the hill toward downtown, I felt buoyed by a feeling that I had something to offer Klara, something important. She'd always been more sexually active than I was. I'd listen to stories about her fucking guys, as she put it. Guys like the one who'd taken her all the way up to the Cal sign in the hills and they'd done it on a bench and she'd gotten splinters so deep in her ass that they were stuck there for weeks. Or the guy from back home she fucked next to a hot tub, who had sucked her face so hard she showed up back at her parents' house for Christmas Eve dinner looking like she'd been beaten up, her mother calling her in Ukrainian something that was an extreme combination of *whore, slut, cunt,* and *bitch*. Or the first time, with her high school boyfriend in his bedroom, how it had lasted a minute and how they'd cuddled awkwardly afterward even though it was summer and too hot. I always felt left out because I didn't have any interesting stories to share. None of the "same here" moments that felt so important to our friendship. But now I had something to give Klara, some experience that was beyond hers.

After we stepped into the brightly lit, glass-paneled shop, I walked her in the direction of the vibrators and picked up a small one shaped like a metal bullet. Here, I said, handing it to her. She brought it to her face and laughed. This is all I need? It was only twelve dollars, so Klara bought it, and we trekked back up the hill to her house, where we ate a quick dinner, rushed back to her room, and she opened up the package and held the thing in her hand. It looks so weird and small, she said. So just put this on my clit? She coughed out the word and laughed some more, that bright, ringing sound. I know I should say it seriously, with pride, she said, more seriously and with pride. Yeah, well, turn it on, too, I told her. Right, right, she said. Got it. I said I'd go to the TV room. She asked that I keep an eye out for her roommate. I mindlessly flipped through the channels until, twenty minutes later, Klara walked in. It worked, she said, sitting on the couch opposite me. See, it wasn't so hard, I said. She laughed and stretched out, then yawned loudly. I can't believe it's taken me twenty-one years to figure that out, she said, smiling at me. Thanks. I told her it wasn't a problem. I told her I was happy for her. Afterward we spent the evening watching four hours of an MTV *Jersey Shore* marathon, taking breaks to go down into her house's kitchen for hot chocolate and whipped cream, in a mutual, lazy celebration.

I can't think of another friendship like the one I had with Klara, and I haven't felt so deeply for a friend since. Sometimes I wonder if Klara knew me better than my boyfriend knows me now. Anyway, I try not to build relationships on needs or debts anymore, either, because it seems to me that people remember only what they're owed, not what they owe. Me included.

The bar that night in San Francisco turned out to be closed. Since it was cold out, we decided to sit in Klara's car nearby. Within minutes, I could feel the failure of the night on us, and again, desperate not to separate, I tried another tactic, which was to talk and talk, asking Klara's boyfriend questions about his work, updating them about people from college, complaining about my dumb job, making jokes about all of the science nerds, as I called them, the people my boyfriend and I had met since Klara had left town. I wanted to talk forever, to keep them leashed by my voice. I leaned my body forward so that I could be closer to Klara's in the driver's seat, though mostly, I just wanted to look at her, to compare who she was in the car with the girl I knew from before. Her blond hair was the shortest I'd seen it, shoulder-length, her cheeks fuller and rounder. She had the same smile, those deep dimples, and her blue-green eyes glowed in that dimly lit car. The bags beneath them were darker and puffier, but the skin of her arms still looked new and soft. My boyfriend yawned. Klara said they needed to get up early the next day for a family hike in Muir Woods. We parted ways awkwardly, all getting out to stand on the sidewalk and exchange hugs, the ones that end in small, stiff pats on the upper back. None of us said anything about seeing one another again. She could have at least offered to give us a ride back to our place, I said to my boyfriend as we walked back up the hill, deflated and defeated.

It's strange how much that night haunts me despite very little having happened. The times when it does resurface, I become oversaturated in its minor details, analyzing each of our moves and words, coming to new conclusions. I talked too much. I was too confrontational. I asked mean and insensitive questions. I acted disinterested for too long. Klara didn't try. Klara zoned out. Klara was faking it the whole time. Klara came out of guilt because she was the guilty one. I should have tried harder.

I lied when I said I didn't know how it all ended. It started when Klara crossed the picket line. There were so many protests, in September, October, November, December, and then the big one in March, and she wouldn't come with me to any. I was upset. Over what? I told myself it was disappointment that Klara didn't care about the tuition hikes and layoffs, but really, honestly, it might have been simply because she wouldn't listen to me. I can admit that now. She'd say she had to study, for quizzes, then midterms, then finals, then the MCAT. She went to class, she worked hard, she got A's, she decided on graduate school instead of medical school (largely because of her poor earlier grades), studied, and took the GRE. I wasn't even that involved in the protests. I marched in some but never attended the organizing meetings, letting the many flyers from my TAs and fellow rhetoric students pile up on my desk, later tossed in recycling. I wanted Klara to be there so we could talk about the meetings later, critique the student speeches, break down the events, come up with something new. But after she said no a handful of times, I stopped asking and did the minimum of what I thought I had to. Several of my roommates were involved in the December Wheeler Hall "Live Week," where they overtook the building to host a week of open-access classes and workshops, a representation of what a horizontal, self-governed university might look like. Four days in, the administration shut it down, sending UC police to the building at four a.m. to arrest sixty-six of the students. I wasn't there. I didn't go to a single teach-in. But I sent an email to Klara with a link to an article about the arrests (we were still talking, we still saw each other, when she wasn't studying or I wasn't brooding, but the protests were now our sore spot, so it felt more appropriate to use a medium that was a little more formal), to which she responded, *That sucks for them, but what did they think would happen?* It infuriated me. I couldn't explain myself to her, and I didn't want to; I wanted her to agree easily with me on this, it was political after all, it wasn't just about us, it was about the younger students, like our siblings, who might have to drop out, it was about future students who'd go into severe debt, worse than ours, it was about UC employees who'd lose their jobs, it was about the humanities departments that would get hit the most by the budget cuts. That's what I told myself.

The plan had been to move to the city together, spend a year together before Klara went to grad school and I did whatever I was going to do—I had this constant image of myself walking through the city, the sound of my shoes clicking against the sidewalks, paper rustling in my bag, Klara often at my side. Even when she started dating a new guy, this overconfident econ major who used snow-bum slang, we kept up the plan. I said I didn't mind living with a couple, and Klara joked that her boyfriend didn't mind it, either. We looked at apartment listings in neighborhoods we both liked, our tastes aligning in only a few—the Castro, Noe Valley, Cole Valley—and I was in the habit of sending her links to jobs she could apply to, articles about cool places to eat, upcoming concerts and events. But as the months wore on, it was obvious that we were less and less aligned about what was happening around us and about our futures. We ventured toward imagining ones that no longer included the other.

One night, about a week before graduation, Klara came over to my co-op unannounced, which would have been fine several months before but by then felt a bit intrusive and strange. The house had just finished dinner, and I was in the middle of my dishwashing duties when she walked over. Somebody else had let her in. She smiled at me and said she had been taking a walk and thought she'd stop by, and asked what I was up to. I gestured at the dishes. Have to finish my chores, I said. It was an unusually warm May that year, and I was sweating from lifting trays of cups, plates, bowls, pans—it was an ordeal even with our restaurant-style speed washer. (I still have nightmares about having to do dishes for a house of too many people, the task never ending, my hands turning into shriveled, floppy flaps of skin.) Klara nodded and said she'd wait for me in the living room. I was annoyed because I thought she should at least offer to help me finish the dishes, showing up without warning like that, expecting me to spend time with her, and I grew more and more upset as I worked. When I finished, I was dirty and resentful. I found Klara sitting on the couch, legs tucked beneath her, looking at some art book on faces throughout the centuries. Every artist interprets a face so differently, she said when I sat across from her. Some make these basic faces without specific features, as if we all look alike, then others choose this very solemn look, but the rarest is when artists sculpt faces that look happy. Isn't that weird? she said. Why do you think that is? I stared at her. Why are you here, Klara? I asked. She said she just wanted to hang out, that she had been at the library but couldn't get any work done and wanted to see me. She was wondering if I wanted to get some frozen yogurt or take a walk around the Berkeley Hills. I asked where her boyfriend was. Klara looked at me for a second, then replied that he was out with snowboard club friends. It was the answer I expected, and almost wanted, at that moment. She had chosen me because her first choice wasn't available. I nodded, stood up, and said that I was busy, though I wasn't, and that we could hang out another time, but that maybe she should text in advance when she wanted to meet, so she wouldn't have to trouble herself with walking all the way over for nothing.

When we graduated a week later, we took our photos together, we smiled and laughed, acting for the occasion, and then we parted ways for the summer. It was never through direct words, but it became clear to both of us that we no longer shared a future. We moved to San Francisco, separately, and managed to rarely see each other in those two years before she moved to New York.

And there I was, in that New York Blue Bottle, waiting for her. Klara was twenty minutes late. A woman approached me and said they were closing soon. I texted Klara, *Are you almost here? It's closing in ten minutes. We can meet somewhere else, closer to you if you want.* A few minutes later, my phone buzzed: *I'm so sorry! I completely lost track of time and still have experiments running. I don't think I'll be done for at least another hour. Maybe we should postpone until tomorrow? Are you still going to be in town?*

I imagined Klara in the lab, growing cells, running gels, taking microscope photos, so focused on her work, dedicated in her pursuit of finding an answer to whatever question she was asking, a question likely essential and fundamental to the basic units of life, and I realized that Klara was doing something important, and doing it just fine without me, exactly as she'd planned. I spent the next five minutes typing and rereading and editing a text: *It's OK. Don't worry about it. Good luck with your experiments. I have an early morning flight tomorrow, so I'll just head back to my hotel.* Then I paused and added: *Let me know when you're back in California and we can meet up.*

I wondered if she possibly thought the same of me—that I looked put together and happy, doing what I was meant to, reporting and writing for a living, my work read by countless strangers who seemed to care about what I had to say. A full life without her. I was walking out of the coffee shop, wondering if she had ever read anything I'd written, wondering if she was even a little bit proud to know me, wondering if she ever wondered about me when she was going about her day, when I felt my phone buzz. My first thought was that Klara had texted to say she could, in fact, meet up, that she was heading my way right now, but when I pulled out my phone, there were no new notifications. It had been a phantom feeling. She hadn't replied.

A VISIT

SHE RECOGNIZES THE CAR, BUT THE MAN INSIDE THE CAR IS too thin to be her father. From the living room window, she sees the curves and juts of a skull distinctly visible beneath weathered skin.

She walks out the front door to her driveway. Up close, she discerns that, yes: It is her old father inside. His hands move in slow motion. Turn the key. Remove the key. Attach the key to the lanyard around his narrow neck. Tuck the lanyard into the jacket. Pat the chest of the jacket.

She taps the driver's-side window and waves.

Her father opens the door. "Hi, sweetheart. I made it," he says. His voice is the same, deep and methodical. "Damn, it's cold here."

It has been two years since she's last seen him.

Standing on her lawn, her father stretches his arms across his chest. He lifts one leg straight up and then the other, like a soldier doing the goose step. She stands stiff, watching, her hands moving in and out of her jacket pockets, pulling out clumps of washed and dried paper pulp. Alone, she allows herself these occasional acts of forgetfulness as long as they don't hurt her or anyone else. With her father around, she worries that these acts could hurt them both.

"You should really stretch more," he says.

She hums a sound of assent and places one arm in the crook of another, stretching.

Her father has shown up at the tail end of a cross-country road trip, having taken a long U-shaped route from Northern California to upstate New York. What would have taken someone ten relaxed days has taken him three weeks. His arrival that day was meant to be a sort of surprise, like most of his arrivals. "I'll get there when I get there," he said each time she called to ask when to expect him, each time he called to ask her to book him a hotel room in whatever town or city he happened to be passing through that night. She tried to estimate when he might show up, but he was as unpredictable in his driving as he had always been in life, some days clocking six hundred miles and others none at all.

The surprise was ruined that morning when he couldn't figure out, by looking at his Rand McNally 1989 Large Scale Road Atlas, the best route to take to the small town where she lives. He called for directions, which she recited off of Google Maps in great detail, telling him to write them down and to please call her if he got lost. Her father, however, did not call again and must still have gotten lost because he has arrived late in the evening, as the sun is setting, hours after she anticipated.

Once she heard from him that morning, she immediately started cleaning. She spent the day in a blur of vacuuming, dusting, mopping, wiping, and scrubbing so that he could see her new house in its best possible shape. Her new house, which she recently purchased on her own, is in actuality a very old house, 124 years old exactly. It is a house which, thanks to the very low cost of housing in town, she was able to afford after a few years of saving from working her office job. While it is located on the outskirts of town, in a not particularly desirable area, it is the first house she refers to as *my house* and not *my old family home* or *my mom's apartment* or *my dad's place* or *that shitty rental with cockroaches.*

Inside, she tells her father that his room is upstairs, but if he would prefer not to climb the stairs, he could sleep downstairs on the couch, but there is only one bathroom and it is upstairs, so the room upstairs might actually be easier at night when he needs to use the bathroom. She is reminded how inconvenient it is that there is no downstairs bathroom. She asks her father if he wants to sit. She gestures toward the recently vacuumed IKEA couch purchased off Craigslist. She does not want him to notice the cracked paint along the crown molding, the sagging ceiling in one corner of the living room, the scratched and burnt wood by the TV, the odd tufts of carpet sprouting from beneath the hardwood by the breakfast nook.

Her father does not sit but instead takes off his sunglasses to expose his sunken crescent-moon eyes. His head slowly oscillates left and right to take in the space. Though he stands there with his familiar straight-backed posture, his worn leather jacket and jeans hang so loose from his body that she can't help but see him as shrunken, like his favorite snack, wu mei, the juice dried out of him, wrinkled all over. He walks throughout the first floor and in each room flips the light switch on, looking over the furniture, appliances, walls, and ground, sliding his right hand's index and middle fingers over several surfaces.

She sees that his salt-and-pepper hair is now 90 percent salt and 10 percent pepper. She sees a small limp in his step. She sees a Band-Aid on his palm. She can't keep silent any longer and asks what he thinks.

"Not bad, pretty clean," he says, and laughs his high-pitched hyena laugh, *hee-hee-hee*. "Well, it's definitely old and out there. It's cute, though. Reminds me of the old Jersey beach houses I used to stay in, in the seventies."

For her, the Jersey beach houses exist only in her father's old Kodak slides. "Want to see some old photos of your old man?" he'd say. It was something they used to do spontaneously, when her father was struck by nostalgia or the urge to bond. He'd carry boxes of slides, trays, and the projector into their family room, dim the lights, and click through the carousel of images from his previous life, each projected onto the bare white wall. There he was, leaning against his first car—a forest green Mustang. "When I moved to Hong Kong, I worked so hard just to save enough to buy that car," he'd say. There was his first pet cat, JD, initials for Jade Dragon, lying in a column of light. "I found him by the dumpster of a Chinatown restaurant. Such a good boy. He had six toes on each paw." There he was, smiling down at a young boy with a tiny face and huge teeth sitting on his lap. "My godson in Shanghai. You'll meet him one day." And on it went, her father regaling her with accounts of the past, her sitting there eager and desperate to better understand him.

Now she pictures her father in his twenties, wiry and muscular, in a house like this one on Long Beach Island, dancing with bell-bottomed men and women, snapping his strong, long fingers to the Beach Boys. She is terribly relieved that he likes the house, that they are starting this visit off on a strong foot, as he'd put it. He often spoke in American idioms.

She asks again if her father wants to sleep upstairs or downstairs. She tells him the room upstairs is more private. It has a door. He says the upstairs is fine and that she can carry his stuff up so it's out of the way. She jogs up the stairs with his suitcase and places it in the most logical spot she can think of, pressed up against the wall next to the closet door. She fluffs the pillows again and picks up a few dust balls off the rug, sticks them in her pocket. As she jogs back down the stairs, she notices for the first time how steep they are, how loudly they creak beneath her feet.

Back in the living room, her father is rearranging furniture. He has dragged a chair from its window spot and placed it at an angle, facing the couch. He is now hunched over a solid wood side table on which she had placed three large plants. She scurries over to help her father and says she can move the plant stand, but where does he think it should go? He points to an empty area against the wall, and she carries it over. With her face pressed up to them, she sees the terrible state of her plants, how two are near dead and another's leaves are wilting. She prays her father does not notice or at least—*please, please, please*—does not comment.

When she steps back from the newly placed plant stand, she looks up to see her father smiling. He rubs his hands one over the other. "See, the flow between the rooms is much better now," he says.

He says that he brought her some blankets, which are in his suitcase. She runs back upstairs and opens the suitcase to find two woven Mexican blankets in bright reds and blues and blacks. They are sturdy and soft, and a white tag sticking off of one states *100% Cotton*—far nicer than the brown acrylic throw she has, which has birthed dozens of clingy baby acrylic pills. She carries the blankets downstairs, and her father picks up the brown throw, handing it to her ("Use it as a rag," he says), and takes the blankets from her.

"I got these in Texas. Guess how much they cost," he says. Thirty? "Nope. Guess again. I got them at a gas station." Twenty? "Nope! Two for twenty! Your dad has a good eye, doesn't he?" He drapes one of the Mexican blankets over the back of the couch, then the other onto the back of the chair.

Yes, the room looks much better, she tells her father, though she is reluctant to admit it to herself.

"Let's see this guest room," he says.

Her father walks in front, slowly, his hand holding the stair's railing. She follows him and puts her hands palm forward in front of her, prepared to catch him if he slips and falls, though she knows that she is not strong enough to hold him up.

"You should get these stairs carpeted," he says without looking back.

When he sees the small guest room that clearly doubles as her office, he says he'd actually prefer to sleep downstairs. "It's more spacious. And you can still do work up here while I'm visiting," he says. "I don't want to crowd you. You do your thing. Think of me as a help. Just let me know if you need anything."

After her father has fallen asleep on the couch, she is upstairs in her bedroom, and her mother texts: *Is your dad there yet? Is everything OK? How long will he be there?* and she realizes that her father hasn't said anything about how long he plans to stay. She taps back *yes, yes,* and *I don't know.*

How does he look?

Fine.

How are you?

Everything is fine, OK?

Years ago, when she was a freshman in college, her father successfully surprised her. She was in class when she received a call from an unfamiliar number, with the La Jolla area code, then the second vibration of a voicemail. When she listened to it outside of the lecture hall, she heard her father's voice. "It's me. I'm in San Diego. I'm at a bar near your campus, just hanging out with this nice bartender here. His name is Jason. Jason, is that right? He's a student here, too—oh, he says he's studying at a different school. So, I'm here. Give me a call at this number. I'll be waiting to hear from you."

She put the phone back in her pocket and looked out at the stream of walking students, the wide path leading to the brutalist-style library, lined with eucalyptus trees, and it all looked different to her, like she had drunk too much caffeine and everything was coated in a nauseating sheen. *It's just one of his pranks,* she thought. But no, she was calling back a local bar's number. A man named Jason answered. He said to hold on and put her father on the line. She went to find him.

They met at the edge of campus. She watched him walk up the hill in his jeans and leather jacket, though it was a sunny and hot Southern California day. Her chest was clenching; she had that nervous energy she got on the first day of classes or walking into a job interview.

"Why are you here?" was the first thing she said.

"You're not happy to see your dad?" was his reply. "I came all the way to San Diego to see you."

She told her father they were in La Jolla, which was not the same thing as San Diego. She wondered how he could have ended up here without knowing the difference. How had he gotten here? Her father said he rode Greyhound, then hitchhiked with a couple of truck drivers.

"No, you didn't," she said.

"You don't believe me?"

She considered it. He didn't have a car. She believed him. She just couldn't believe he'd chosen to do that.

She walked him to her dorm, pointing out buildings along the way. "That's where I have my political science class; that's where we meet for Asian Film Club; that's where I work in the Student Affairs Office." Words, more words, to fill the opening space inside her.

"I met two very friendly truck drivers," he said. "One of them was named Lucas. Or Luke. Another guy, I forget his name. Good guys, though. I've found that truck drivers are some of the friendliest people." He got along with people like that. He liked being on the road, on the road again, he sang as they walked.

When he saw her dorm room, he didn't say anything. He sat in the old wooden desk chair, upholstered in an eighties purple and green weave, and they talked for a while longer, all as she tried to guess what he wanted from her. Money? A place to crash? Company for dinner? For her to go back to Sacramento with him? She said she had an essay due the next morning. When her roommate walked into the room, he got up, introduced himself, and said he should be going. She walked him back to where they'd met. She looked at her phone; they'd spent two hours together.

"Don't worry about me," he said. "Your dad is doing just fine. You know me, my way or the highway." She watched him walk down the hill from which he came, and she felt relief, cast in a long shadow of guilt.

Now, in her house, as she falls asleep, the memory thickens her longing.

"Your mother didn't think I'd make it this far, did she?" her father says. "I bet you didn't, either!"

She has come downstairs after waking up to the smell of light, flavored burning. When she asks her father where the smell is coming from, he waves at the plant stand. Stuck in the potted soil of her most dead plant is a single stick of incense, a thin ribbon of smoke rising from its orange-glowed tip.

"But I made it," he says. "Just like the cross-country road trips I took in the seventies and eighties. After this, I'm going to the city and Jersey to visit all my old friends and favorite spots, just like before."

She thinks the seventies and eighties are a long time ago, so she tells him that he should stay. Rest for a while. She has the space. He's been on the road so long. He says he'll stay only a short while; he doesn't want to impose.

He stays three weeks. Over the course of those weeks, her father reconnects two loose heating ducts in the basement, of which she was not aware, fixes the faucet spray hose, which she had deemed unfixable, replaces the dead lightbulbs, which she swears she was getting around to, deep-cleans the entire house, which she thought she had already done, and polishes the wood floors, which she had never planned or thought to do. He also designates as his own a swath of kitchen-counter real estate, where he keeps a large jug of wine, a container of cashews, his daybooks from the last three years, and his atlas. He does all these things while she is at work and cannot tell him not to do these things.

When she returns home, her father explains to her the many tasks that he has accomplished. He walks her through her house, pointing to the areas he's altered, sometimes undoing and redoing the fix to show her exactly how it was done. His movements have not gotten any faster. If anything, she thinks, he is slower than when he first arrived. She worries that his being there is a strain not only on her but on him. And as she stands beside him, watching him untwist the sink spray nozzle and retwist it as tightly as he can, she curls and uncurls her toes and pinches the inside of her forearm to keep herself from saying something she will regret. His presence is spreading through the house in a way she can't decide whether to welcome or resist. She finds herself tired from containing the conflicting emotions.

Each night, her father goes to sleep before eight p.m. and oftentimes much earlier. He says he is tired from working around the house, he's getting old, you know. Each night, she tries to tell him thank you for doing this, but please stop doing so much and please just relax, that's the point of you being here, and also, please, please take care of yourself.

"I'm eating," he says, and points to his container of cashews with a grin. She sees the jug of wine nearly empty next to it.

On one of the last nights he spends in her house, her father responds to her pleas by walking up to her and wrapping his arms around her shoulders.

"My daughter. You're all grown up now," he says. "I know I haven't always been the best dad, but I always do what I say, don't I?"

She nods. She feels with her hands the jagged edges of his shoulder blades, how little physical space her father's body now inhabits.

The day her father leaves, he tells her that he's sorry he stayed too long. She shakes her head and says no, that she'd be happy to have him longer. She does not believe herself before she says it, but when she hears the words aloud and sees the living room empty of his belongings, she knows that she is voicing more than a fragment of truth. They are both older. He could stay, he could live in her home, he could exist in this place. They could take care of each other, whatever that might mean.

"Where will you go?" she says.

"Don't worry about me," he says, like before. "Your old man is doing just fine. Just fine."

Her father gets into the car, performs those slow-motion steps, and backs out of her driveway. She watches him drive away, wondering when he'll show up again. Another two years, maybe less, maybe more. He'll surprise her.

Inside, she wraps herself up in the Mexican blankets and curls into the living room chair that now faces the long couch, and though it is the middle of the day, she begins to fall asleep. Half dreaming, she thinks that she is back in California, in her old family house, the one from when she was a young child, with their family intact, before the many arrivals and departures, and her father is carrying her to bed and opening the window blinds so she can fall asleep looking out at all those city lights. When the rumble of a tractor-trailer outside startles her, she, in her half sleep, says, "What time is it, Daddy?" It's only when he does not answer that she remembers he's no longer there.

FLIES

DADDY SHOT THE FLIES WITH THICK RUBBER BANDS. HE'D squint his left eye shut, pull back with his right hand, take aim, pause—snap! A fly dead on the floor. "Ha!" or "Gotcha!" he'd say. Or he'd let out a satisfied whistling sound through his teeth. If he missed, he was silent. He'd pick up the rubber band and try again. If he missed too many times, he'd whack at them with an old copy of the Chinese newspaper, rolled into a cylinder.

Didi's job was to point at the fly Daddy should kill next. Mine was to pick up the bodies with toilet paper and carry them to the bathroom, where I dumped them in the toilet bowl. Whenever Daddy needed a rest or the rubber band broke, I'd flush the toilet and watch the bodies whirl down. At first I flushed after every fly, wanting to get rid of it right away, but then Daddy noticed what I was doing and yelled at me to stop wasting water.

"Water's expensive, Ying Ying," he said. "You kids don't realize these days. When I was nine, we spent a whole year having to walk all the way to another longdhang with buckets to get our water. Almost the whole alley got sick that year. Lots of garlic and onion, that's what my grandmother gave me, which is why I'm alive. Those are the best medicines, natural and from the earth. You can't live without good water or air—that's why people are so unhealthy in China these days. They have to go around wearing masks all the time, but the masks don't do anything. Their skin is still exposed. All of the toxins seep into them through the skin. Everyone looks ten years older than they should. You two understand?"

"Yes, Daddy," Didi and I said in unison.

"Don't be so hard on her. We don't even pay for water, and there's plenty here," said Mommy. She was chopping chicken for dinner, waving away flies as they approached. Earlier, she'd told us not to kill flies near the food, in case one landed in the pot and really got us sick.

"Ah, just because we don't pay means we should waste?"

"Okay, okay, lao du." She called him an affectionate term to appease him. "I just think you should contact Johnson to get rid of these flies. Maybe poison wouldn't be so bad. It's faster than this." She waved her hand in our direction.

"What? We're getting rid of them just fine! Right, Ying Ying? Didi? Who's the best team of fly killers?"

Daddy held his hand out like it was a gun and made shooting sounds. Didi giggled and imitated him. Mommy looked at me and shook her head. I looked up at the flies that buzzed in the upper quarter of the kitchen. They landed beside one another, sometimes in disgusting hordes, on the fluorescent light fixture, the stove hood, the window, the walls, the cabinet doors. They rubbed their legs together, cleaning themselves. As if they could ever get clean enough.

"That one!" Didi pointed at the next target.

They'd been divorced for a few years already, but we all still lived together. At first Daddy traveled to China for long stretches, sometimes several months. For business, he'd say. I used to believe he had a job in China where he talked to men and women in suits, exchanged cards and briefcases full of money, but when we didn't move back to our old house like he'd promised, and he sold the fancy car he'd loved so much and his trips stopped and he stayed home watching Chinese dramas on the computer, my earlier imaginings were replaced with ones where he wandered crowded streets day and night, alone, looking for something he never found.

They fought more when he quit coming and going and just stayed put. Months before the flies, Mommy had come to my room and stood in the doorway. She looked tired and older than usual. The skin around her eyes was dark and puffy, and the freckles along her cheekbones looked like scars.

"Do you think I'm responsible for taking care of him?" she said.

Daddy had left the house on his bike to go who knew where. There was no danger in him overhearing anything we said. I could tell she was accusing me of something. I looked back at the science textbook on my desk. I wished she would walk away. She didn't.

"I can't take it anymore. I can't stand living with him," she said.

I looked up at her and, without thinking, said, "Then tell him to leave."

She slit her eyes at me. "You really okay with that? You want your father to go?"

"If *you* want him to," I said. "I don't care."

It was a lie. I wanted him to stay. I thought he was taking care of us, not the other way around, and when the two of them got along, it was like they weren't divorced at all. It was like it had all been pretend, and an easy pretending, since most people didn't know anyway. I hadn't told anybody, not even my best friend, Cindy. I don't think they'd told anyone, either. Part of me wondered if Didi even knew.

"You and Didi will hate me if I make him leave. You think it's my job to take care of him, even though we're divorced. You think we have to live together like this, like a family, even though we aren't family anymore." She started crying. "We're divorced! Why don't you understand?"

She turned away and slammed my door shut. I sat there unmoving, listening to her walk up the stairs. I didn't take a breath until I heard the door of her room close. I felt sick, the same way I did when I picked up those dead flies. Her sadness made me sick.

I waited for the bad feelings to pass. They always did. Mommy and Daddy would start talking again, and things would go back to normal.

The flies arrived almost perfectly at the start of summer break. For two weeks, we'd kill them during the day until we thought we'd gotten them all, only for an hour or two to pass before a few more appeared. By evening or the next morning, it was like every fly killed and flushed had come back from the dead to haunt us. We would start our jobs again. Daddy barely let us leave the house. He hated the little yellow marks the flies spat up and left behind on every surface.

I hated the way the bodies felt beneath the toilet paper, their wings crackling or the pop when I squished them. Sometimes a fly wouldn't be all the way dead. It would lie on its side or back, its legs twitching back and forth like it thought it could walk away. Worse was when I was about to reach for a dead one and it somehow reanimated and flew up at my face, attacking. I tumbled back, screaming. Didi laughed at me, so with the next dead fly, I picked it up and chased him around with it until he cried for me to stop.

"Quit it, you two! It's just a fly!" Daddy scolded us.

But it wasn't just a fly. It was a dead thing still moving.

Finally, Mommy got Daddy to call Johnson.

"What are you doing all day? You're so worried about wasting water or money or whatever, but *this* is the real waste—of time," she said to him.

Daddy had to be the one to call Johnson because he didn't have to go to work like Mommy. His job was to take care of the house and of us, now that school was out, which so far had meant killing flies, steaming us dumplings in the morning, killing flies, boiling us hot dogs around noon, and killing flies until Mommy came home and cooked dinner. She had two jobs, too, except her jobs paid her money. One was at a wine company and the other at an Asian grocery market. She worked as a bookkeeper. She explained that she kept track of how much money came in and out of the businesses. I saw dollar bills flying in and out of the front doors of a low gray office building and her having to sit there counting each one that entered and exited. It seemed like a hard and boring thing to do.

Johnson came on a Tuesday afternoon. We called him by his last name because that's what Daddy called him. His first name was equally boring. Tom or Bob or John or Blah. Daddy didn't like him, so neither did we. He smelled weird, like a skunk. He was younger than Daddy, but with more white hair, and the pink of his face made him look sunburned or drunk. One time he came to install a garbage disposal he'd promised months earlier, and as he walked out, he patted my head goodbye. When Daddy saw that, he yelled after Johnson not to pat my head ever again. It was really bad luck to be patted on the head by someone outside of family. He cursed Johnson all night and told me to pray to Buddha that the bad luck Johnson had bestowed on me be transferred back to him and multiplied by a hundred.

The day Johnson came for the flies, Didi and I hid inside my room and tried to play cards. Johnson almost never came around, but when he did, we knew to stay out of the way, especially if Daddy wanted to talk to him.

"The house is completely clean, as you can see," we could hear Daddy saying in the living room. He cared a lot about cleanliness. I forgot that part of his job, and it's also why he hated the flies so much. He cleaned constantly, wiping down counters, mirrors, the faces of cupboards, drawers, and the refrigerator. He dusted, he washed dishes, he told us to pick up after ourselves. His daily belongings—a leather and metal wallet clip that held a few cards and bills, recent receipts and coupons folded down the middle; keys; a small notebook; a pen; a bottle opener—were placed in a perfect grid atop the coffee table. Things we weren't allowed to disturb.

"The flies are most likely coming from somewhere hidden, from cracks, flying from the outside in," Daddy said.

"Hmmm, never had a problem like this before," said Johnson. "How long did you say this has been going on?"

Didi patted my leg and said it was my turn to pick a card.

"Be quiet," I said. "I'm trying to listen."

"—every day and they come back. I think it's related to that broken hot tub. Who knows what's breeding in there. It's a serious health hazard to my kids and should have been removed years ago."

"I doubt the flies are coming from there," Johnson said. "It's more likely something died in the walls. A mouse or a bird. Have you smelled anything recently?" I wondered if Daddy would say anything about the way Johnson smelled, but he didn't.

"If not the flies, that water is a breeding ground for something," he said.

"We can fumigate, but you'll have to leave for at least a few hours. Or we can set up traps and just wait for the flies to pass."

It didn't sound like Daddy said anything, but the next thing Johnson said was "All right, all right, fine. Let's take a look at it, then."

I heard the two of them walk out the door. I scurried to the window, which overlooked the yard and the in-ground hot tub. Didi whined but followed me. We peeked out of the thin plastic blinds.

Johnson bent down to lift the hot tub cover, then shouted and dropped it, leaving a portion of the water exposed. He bent back down and rearranged the cover so that it was in place, hiding whatever was inside. But in that brief in-between moment, we caught a glimpse of the dark water, a greeny brown color, and possibly something else, maybe multiple somethings.

"What was that?" Didi asked.

I told him again to be quiet, but I had the same question.

We were always told to stay away from the hot tub. Most of the time, we forgot it was there. When we first saw the house, the previous tenants showed us how to turn the jets on and off, how to increase and decrease the temperature. They called it a *nice perk*. "Yeah! We want a hot tub!" we'd squealed. Mommy had been excited, too. I didn't really think about it at the time, but Daddy was in China, and she said the house was perfect for the three of us. We went into the hot tub twice before it stopped working and the water turned cold. Another thing at home not to disturb.

"You see?" Daddy pointed. "This is disgusting and unhygienic. You need to remove it immediately."

Johnson looked down at the hot tub and slowly shook his head. "All right," he said. "I'll call my brother, and we'll get it out of here by next week. How about we fumigate the place at the same time?"

"Not next week. This week. A. S. A. P."

"Okay, okay," Johnson said, then walked out the front gate looking like a smacked dog.

Daddy could really make people feel bad with the sound of his voice.

It used to be the other way around, Mommy at home and Daddy at work. Back then we lived in a different house, and he was working as the boss of a huge retirement-home kitchen. Sometimes he'd take me with him if he needed to be there on the weekends. Daddy was everyone's friend, so I could wander wherever I wanted. My favorite place was the Memory Unit, where I could help with arts and crafts. The old people in there weren't as talkative as the ones outside, but they smiled a lot and let me help them glue corn kernels on paper in the shapes of dogs and cats. I asked Daddy why they covered the doors with wallpaper from the inside—it made the whole room look like a tropical garden—and he said it was to prevent the old people from seeing that a door was even there. It was camouflaged. That way, they wouldn't accidentally leave the unit. They wouldn't be able to take care of themselves on the outside.

"If I ever get like that," he said, "don't bring me to a place like this. Just let me die, okay?"

"Okay," I said, though it was impossible to think of him dying.

He used to bring back boxes of food that were close to expiring or that he couldn't feed the old people. One time somebody (he said it had been some "bonehead" who needed to be fired) ordered tobiko, thinking it was caviar. When the containers of orange fish eggs arrived, none of the old white people would touch it. Daddy brought it home for us, and Mommy made sushi for days. We had enough tobiko in the freezer to last us a year. Didi and I liked to eat it plain, for a snack. Mommy would laugh when we'd spoon it directly from the container into our mouths. She'd say with a smile, "Your daddy spoils us, doesn't he?"

That was a long time ago, though, and she hasn't said anything like that in a while.

The evening before Johnson and his brother, other Johnson, were scheduled to get rid of the hot tub and the flies, Daddy told us that we needed to make plans. Didi and I couldn't be at the house while they were releasing the poison bombs. He said he would need to stay home and supervise Johnson and his brother's work, because they were untrustworthy boneheads.

"These guys are lazy," he said. "If I wasn't here, they'd probably just smoke and drink all day, shoot the shit. And then they'd have to come back another day. Somebody needs to keep an eye on them, or nothing will get done properly."

Mommy was putting plates and bowls into a big clear bin. "I'm glad these flies will be gone soon," she said.

"Go call your friend and then come help us pack stuff up," Daddy said.

I was feeling a little guilty about how excited I was for my first real day of summer vacation. Cindy had been calling nearly every day, asking if I could go to the pool. She squealed on the phone when I told her the news.

"I haven't seen you in forever," she said. "You're like in fly prison or something."

We laughed.

"And your dad's like the scary fly prison guard," she continued.

"That makes no sense. My dad's the one killing the flies," I said, spitting into the receiver.

Her words had sent a flash of rage through my spine. I almost didn't want to see her anymore, but then I realized I wouldn't have anywhere else to go.

"See you at the pool at ten." I hung up and went to help pack.

The moment I walked back into the kitchen, I could tell something bad had happened between Mommy and Daddy. They weren't speaking. The buzzing of the flies vibrated even louder. Mommy was slamming dishes into a bin, and I worried she would break something soon or already had. Daddy was on a stool, reaching for the things placed in the highest cabinets, pulling out long-forgotten serving bowls, place mats, and random boxes. I exchanged a look with Didi, who was taking utensils out of drawers and putting them into a *Thank You. Have a Nice Day!* plastic grocery bag, but he only mirrored my confusion. He was seven, so he didn't always pick up on the small signals between our parents like I did, being four years older and the more responsible.

"I can do that, Mommy," I said, next to her, in the softest and sweetest voice I could make.

"You're always trying to protect him," she whispered back. "You're always on his side." The way she said it made the words as powerful and hot as if she'd screamed them in my face. She walked upstairs to her room, stomping the whole way.

"Your mother's in one of her moods," Daddy said calmly. "You know how she gets sometimes."

What she'd said didn't make sense as a reply to what I'd said or done, but maybe she knew it made sense overall, in general, and that's why she'd said it.

Johnson and his brother arrived at the house just as Mommy was walking out. She hadn't said anything to me when I was eating breakfast or when she was packing her bag for work, but as she stepped out, she called to me and asked when I planned to meet Cindy. A sign that she wasn't that mad anymore.

"Make sure to be back before I get home," she said as she left.

Daddy was carrying the bins and bags into the side yard and lining them neatly against the fence.

"I'm leaving, too!" I said.

"Walk Didi to Matt's house first," he replied. I rolled my eyes and let out a grumbled sigh. "Don't give me that!" he said, which scared me, because I hadn't thought he could hear me. Sometimes it seemed like he had inhuman qualities. Superpowers, almost.

Didi had his T-shirt on inside out when I found him in the room he shared with Daddy.

I helped Didi take the shirt off, turn the thing right side out, and put it back on him. "You bonehead," I said. He was oddly pliable that morning, allowing me to do this to him in silence.

We walked out of the house together and down the street.

It was a hot and dry day, and the fruit trees looked healthy and heavy. As we passed the pomegranate tree at the end of the block, Didi stopped and asked if I could reach one for him. I was still taller than he was, something I was proud of since I knew it wouldn't last for long, with him growing so fast. I stood on my tippy-toes and stretched my arm and body to reach for an especially dark red, ripe-looking globe.

"You want to break it open, or me?" I asked.

"I want to do it."

I handed him the pomegranate, and he threw it to the ground, cracking the outer shell. But he was still a weak kid. The pomegranate barely broke open. I picked it up and threw it down again. Its body slammed against the pavement and broke into three uneven pieces, some red seeds falling out, crushed, onto the sidewalk.

"I could've done it," Didi said.

"Your arms are too little."

"Your face is too big." He picked up the largest piece and began popping the seeds into his mouth.

"You're *welcome,*" I said, and picked up the leftovers.

We continued walking, eating. Our fingers and lips stained pink. We waved away the flies that came near us, and I noticed Didi shuddered each time one touched him. After a little while, I asked him what had happened the night before between our parents. He shrugged.

"Because Mommy said something mean to me later, and I think it's because she was mad at him," I said.

"I don't know. Daddy just said some stuff to her in Chinese, and then Mommy started making a lot of noise with the plates."

He couldn't understand Shanghainese, since he hadn't

grown up listening to our parents talk to each other in the dialect like I had. Daddy hadn't been around enough (until recently) for Didi to pick up the language, and they never actively spoke it to either of us, since we always responded in English. I didn't like the way Shanghainese made my tongue and voice move differently. Some words or phrases felt natural, like the ones for *Popsicle, red-roasted pork belly,* and *little brother,* but the rest of the words—I didn't like how they felt in my mouth. I always had the feeling I was saying them wrong. That I sounded stupid.

But that didn't mean I couldn't lecture Didi.

"You should really learn Shanghainese, or else you won't understand anything the next time we go to China, and you also won't ever know what's going on between Mommy and Daddy."

He was silent for a while.

"We'll never go to China again, and I don't want to know what they're saying," he said. "It's not my business."

"Where'd you learn to talk like that?"

"It's just how I talk," he said.

"Yeah, right."

"Yeah, it is."

We walked for a while, silently chewing and swallowing our pomegranate seeds. Then he asked, "Do you think Daddy's going to leave after the flies leave?"

"Why would you say that? Did he say something to you about it?"

He shrugged again. "Flies are really gross," he added.

"Duh."

I didn't understand how he could sound so grown up one

second and like a baby the next. What was going on in his kid brain? He probably didn't even know.

I spent the day with Cindy at the pool, switching between swimming and lying on our towels in the grass. It was a perfect day. I could pretend like the flies never happened, like the fights never happened, like the only place that existed was the pool, and the only people, me and Cindy and the classmates we talked about from school. We were going to start seventh grade in the fall, our first year in the junior high. We were excited to be on a new campus, get a locker, and go to different classes called *periods*, which made them sound serious and adult. We were both going to ask our parents for contacts so that we wouldn't look like nerdy Asian girls anymore. We wanted to be like the cool Asian girls, with their long, layered hair and pristine Adidas sneakers. We planned how we'd dress on the first day—in matching flare jeans and different-colored halter tops and new sneakers (although our parents denied us brand names)—and how we would avoid the ninth-grade rock, a big cement block where the ninth-graders sat and yelled at and made fun of the seventh-graders. Our shared dream was to make dozens of new friends, for boys to like us, and to become popular. It all seemed simple and within reach.

When I got home, I saw that Johnson's truck was gone from the driveway. Inside our gated yard, the hot tub was still there, the faded blue cover in the same spot. The front door was locked, so I knocked.

"Daddy? Hello?"

Nobody answered. I hadn't brought a key with me because I'd thought somebody would be home all day. I walked to the side yard and saw the bins there, lined up, looking like x-rayed bodies, the way you could see inside to all the stuff they contained. All our dishes and cracker boxes and a whole container of sauce bottles topped with rolls of paper towels.

Back in the front yard, I sat in one of our dirty patio chairs and stared at the hot tub. Why hadn't Johnson gotten rid of it yet? Where was Daddy, and why had he left? How hard was it to remove a hot tub? What was inside? What would fill the hole that was left? My curiosity pulled me to the edge of the blue cover. I squatted there and listened. I thought I heard something splashing underneath. With the tips of my index finger and thumb, I pinched the handle of the cover. I told myself I would lift it only a little to take a peek. Whatever was inside couldn't be that bad.

The water was a dark, dirty color so thick I couldn't see through it. Bugs and a few green things floated at the top. Then something moved toward the opening, something with a long tail, something with an incredibly round, pale body covered in wet hair . . .

It had big round black eyes. Dead eyes.

"What are you doing?" Daddy's voice from behind me.

I jumped up and away from the hot tub. The lid made a squishing sound.

When I turned around, Didi was there, too, looking red and puffy-eyed, like he'd been crying.

"Didn't I tell you not to touch that? Go wash your hands right away!"

I scurried to the hose.

"Not there! Go inside and use soap," Daddy said, kicking the hot tub lid back in place.

I got up and stood at the door. "I don't have keys," I said.

"Why not? Hurry up!" He opened the door and pointed me in.

I ran to the bathroom. Outside, Daddy was making a lot of noise.

"That bonehead Johnson didn't get the right kind of pump to empty it, so now he has to hire a professional. What would your mother do if I weren't here, huh? She'd just leave that hot tub there forever, and you would all get sick. Disgusting stuff in there. That rat! Who knows how long it's been collecting diseases. And you go and open it! After I tell you not to! You're all a bunch of boneheads!"

I washed my hands furiously, scrubbing the lines in my fingers and palms. The image of the rat's body stuck in my head. Its giant balloon belly. I'd never seen anything that huge.

When I walked back out to the living room, I noticed the flies were gone. There was a light chemical smell in the air. Daddy told us to go to our rooms. He wanted to put everything away in the kitchen himself, because nobody else could do it correctly. He said it in that tone of voice. I knew to stay out of his way.

I motioned Didi to come with me.

"I saw what's inside the hot tub," I said after closing the door to my room.

"I don't care," he said, sniffling.

"Now what?"

He looked like he was about to cry again. "Daddy's mad at me," he said. "I broke Matt's Sphero robot, and now we have to buy him a new one."

"On purpose?"

"Matt said I was a loser for not having one, and I said I wasn't, and he said I was, so I threw it against the wall and then it stopped working and he told his mom and his mom called Daddy and I think they cost a million dollars!" He was crying streams of little baby tears.

"Shhhh," I said. "Stop it. Don't let Daddy hear you. He'll come in here and yell at us again."

That got Didi to stop right away.

When Mommy's car pulled into the driveway, Daddy walked outside. I couldn't hear them from that far out, but soon their voices got louder, and by the time they walked back inside, they were screaming at each other in Shanghainese. Didi had fallen asleep on my bed but woke up from their fight. I couldn't understand it all, their words coming out faster than usual. There was stuff about Didi and the Sphero and Johnson and the hot tub and how I'd been stupid and touched it, then old past things that they always brought up when they fought. Each other's family, who owed who what, who had given the other and the kids more care and time and money.

And then a last thing: something about someone Daddy knew in China. A woman who was sick and dirty, Mommy said. You're disgusting, she said. You're the one who brought sickness into this house. You're sick. Or maybe she said, You make me sick.

That was the end of it. Daddy walked out the front door. We saw him skulk off into the yard, past the hot tub. We watched the front gate open and close. We heard the sound of his bike riding off.

Mommy came into the room wiping her eyes and asked what we wanted for dinner. We stared at her. She asked us again, more forcefully.

"Spaghetti," Didi said.

"Okay, go watch some TV if you want," she said.

He bolted out and turned the TV on to some cartoon channel, as though nothing had happened, as though nothing was wrong. He was an even better pretender than I was. Mommy stayed in my room, looking around at my things, the plain single bed we bought at IKEA the year before, my posters of the Golden Gate Bridge and the Eiffel Tower, the blue bookshelf we found at a garage sale, my desk where I kept a framed rare photo of the four of us together from my birthday two years earlier. Her gaze lingered on that photo.

"I need to tell you something," she said.

She was trying to give me a nice look, I could tell, but it was so different from what I'd just overheard, I didn't understand what it meant.

"I found a new house for us. It's smaller, but you'll still have your own room, and it's closer to the junior high. You can walk to school. We're going to move there in a couple weeks, so you have to start packing soon. You have to help Didi, too, when I'm at work, okay? But don't tell your father. I don't want him to know yet."

I wanted to ask how I was supposed to pack without Daddy noticing. I wanted to ask what would happen to him. I wanted to ask why she'd done this behind everyone's back. But I knew those weren't questions she wanted to hear or answer. I thought if I could be a good adult, like my teachers or other people's parents, like somebody who could behave nicely and not always explode at the smallest thing, then I would become better, better than Mommy and Daddy.

"Do you understand?" she said.

I nodded and said okay.

She was about to walk out but then turned to face me again, looking serious. "He's your father. You have to help him," she said. "That's not my job anymore. It's yours now."

When she left, I slammed my body on the bed and thrashed my arms and legs around until they were tired and hurt.

I could barely sleep at night. Each time I closed my eyes, I saw the rat or the flies, or heard my parents' shouts or the flies buzzing. I got out of bed and checked every inch of the room. There was a dusty dead fly on the windowsill. I went to the bathroom to get some toilet paper. On the way back, I opened the door to Didi's room. The forms of both his and Daddy's bodies were in the bunk beds beneath their blankets. I waited a moment, until Didi moved a little and I heard his grinding teeth.

As I walked back to my room, I noticed a little bit of light coming from upstairs. I looked up and listened. There were soft sounds of movement. I glanced at the living room clock. Mommy was still awake at two a.m. Normally, I wouldn't bother her, but this night was different. I walked upstairs and saw her door open a sliver. She was taking stacks of folded clothes from her dresser drawers and placing them in a big silver suitcase, one I'd never seen.

I thought about saying something, but I didn't know what I wanted to say. I didn't know whether I wanted to stop her or help her or just let her know that I was there. She was too focused on what she was doing to notice me watching. The way she moved at a calm, steady pace, not too fast or slow, reminded me of a monk. She seemed almost happy. She started humming a low, sweet tune. It was like she was packing for a vacation. Maybe that's how she thought of it, too. Maybe that's what she told herself.

SHE WILL BE A SWIMMER

HE DOES NOT YET KNOW IT, BUT THIS IS THE YEAR WHEN HIS life ends. Not physically, no. He will go on living for many more decades. This is the year that marks the before and after. He will come to perceive this when he is much older, looking back, wondering when his upward mobility plateaued, then shifted to a downward slope. *It all ended for me in the late eighties,* he will later lament to his children when they are grown. *You wouldn't believe all the shit I dealt with.* He will say these words enough times that his children will begin to translate, bitterly and eventually understandingly: *My life ended when I had kids.* Despite their assumptions, they won't be entirely right. Even he is not sure what *all the shit* means, exactly. It will be the culmination of cracks, then he will fall so fast, he won't have time to think about the fall, who he is taking with him, and the fact that there is no one there to catch them.

For now, it is February 1987, and he is thirty-eight years old. He works as the manager of an auto repair shop on Stanyan. From his office window, he can see the edge of the park, the tall eucalyptus and pine and cypress trees providing a barrier between the city and its allotted nature. A block away, the Haight hippies gather on a hill to beat drums and dance, and sometimes when he sits in his office, he thinks he can hear the spiritual beating travel over the garage clangs, the car honks, the sighs of passing Muni buses.

He is good at his job, and he treats his workers well. He argues with the shop's owner for better health insurance, for raises, for more paid leave, for bonuses. He believes in the labor of the workers. He knows himself to be an idealist. When he arrived in this country, he named himself after Marx, though he despises the communism at work in the country he fled. With Chinese family and friends, he continues to go by the nickname his parents gave him, Du Niu Niu.

He has been in San Francisco for six years and has been in this country for thirteen, the seven previous years in Manhattan and nearby Jersey City. He drives a white 1986 Jeep Wrangler or a beige and white 1971 VW T2 or a silver 1983 Ford T-Bird, depending on his mood.

One day he receives a call from his brother, who lives in Los Angeles, one of the few American cities Du Niu Niu does not like. Though he's loved American movies since childhood, they seem not to be connected to Los Angeles in his mind. His favorite movies take place in his favorite American places: the Big Apple, the Wild West of the past, rural towns in states like Pennsylvania and Connecticut, or abroad, where Americans are fighting wars.

"I'm coming to San Francisco for a few days," the brother says in Shanghainese. "I'm meeting a girl whose father I met on the train in Beijing. They're also from Shanghai. She's just moved to start school at SF State. I told him my older brother lives there. So now I'm coming up to meet her for dinner. Can I stay with you?"

Du Niu Niu replies in English, "Okay. Just don't get carried away in my house." He hears himself as if he is his brother and is proud that his accent is washing out.

When his brother arrives at the house, a sage green Edwardian sandwiched between two other Edwardians in the Richmond, it is a Friday evening, and Du Niu Niu is waiting on the steps. He stands up to greet his brother, whom he has not seen in three years. They shake hands, and he makes sure to tighten his grip around his brother's soft one. They were never especially close, but he wants to convey to his brother that he is still older, that he will always be older, and therefore he must be respected, always. His brother looks down and, when the shake is done, massages his palm.

"Du Niu Niu, good to see you," the brother says.

"Eh, Xiao Niu Niu, don't pretend you're not here for a girl," Du Niu Niu says in dialect, and laughs. He whacks his brother on the back, hard and friendly. He picks up his brother's suitcase. "Come, I'll show you your room."

The inside of the home is pristine, like a house in the American fashion magazines Du Niu Niu occasionally reads and often keeps in his office for his clients to peruse as they wait for their cars. The living room is furnished with a matching set of gray leather couches and a love seat. Photography books and large amphora lamps sit atop the wood and stone coffee and side tables. Heavy white drapes frame the bay windows. On the wall behind the couch hangs a large print of Picasso's *Guernica*.

"The guest room's in the back. You can use the kitchen, but clean up after yourself. You'll use my bathroom in the master bedroom. Be respectful of Shannon and Gary. Gary's room is over there." Du Niu Niu points down a hallway. "Shannon's room is connected to the garage, so you might run into her when you get the car—you can drive the T-Bird for your date. Don't bother Shannon and Gary, understand?"

His brother nods and nods until they reach the guest room, with its wooden futon frame, wicker rocking chair, and small desk. "This is an antique," Du Niu Niu says, knocking on the desk's wooden top. "Always use a coaster."

Du Niu Niu leaves his brother in the guest room and walks into the kitchen. He grabs a Coors from the refrigerator and goes to sit on the love seat. He stares at the painting, which he reminds himself is not a painting but a print. He fantasizes about a time in the future when he will be able to afford a real Picasso painting. The print, for now, is an accomplishment. It is framed in dark oak, which itself cost a small fortune. He went with his wife—no, his ex-wife—to a shop in the Castro to pick out a frame and mat that best suited the print and this house. When he and his ex-wife separated, he told her that of all the things they had gotten together, he needed to keep this. She said he could keep it all; she wanted only the dogs, two blue Great Danes named Cary and Katharine, after their two favorite actors, whom Du Niu Niu loves and misses.

He misses his ex-wife. Her wavy brown hair. Her heavily lidded green eyes. Her large breasts. Her thick thighs. Her huge glasses that rested atop her tall nose. Because of her, he is sitting there in a house with rooms occupied by people who are not her. It has been one year, and he tells himself it is for the best. It is for the best, it is for the best. He has a green card now and has already submitted his application for citizenship. Soon he will be an American, because of her.

His brother returns from the date glowing, as if he's deeply sunburned. The whites of his eyes are bright red. He stumbles as he takes off his shoes. His breathing is burdened.

"Looks like you had some fun," Du Niu Niu says.

"Yes, yes," Xiao Niu Niu says. "She's a sweet girl. Pretty. Young. Well, no, she's twenty-five, but she looks eighteen. She laughs a lot. Sweet. Very sweet."

Du Niu Niu watches his brother, mildly repulsed by the man's inability to handle drink. "Get yourself some water and lie down," he says.

"I told her that if she ever has any car trouble to go and see you," his brother says. "She says she just learned to drive. Just got her license. Said she failed the first two times. Ha ha! Says a boy at school helped her. I think she has a lot of boyfriends. Seems like the kind of girl with a lot of boyfriends. Sweet, though. Reminds me of home."

"Go to bed," Du Niu Niu says.

Two weeks after his brother returns to Los Angeles, Du Niu Niu is on the garage floor inspecting Gary's brake replacement on a VW Rabbit GTI when the receptionist approaches him and says there's a woman waiting in the office to see him.

"Brenda?" he says.

"No, a Chinese girl," the receptionist says.

"Name?"

The receptionist shrugs. "I don't know . . . ?" she says, smiles sheepishly, and looks away.

"Okay, tell her I'll be five minutes."

When he walks into his office, he sees the girl, taller than he expected, more solid-looking than he expected. Long dark brown hair that flows past her shoulders. She wears a loose blue shirt and black jeans and black sneakers. She is looking at the Chinese calendar hanging on the wall next to his desk. It seems she is about to reach out to touch the large red character for *rabbit* when he says in dialect, "You're here to see me?"

She flinches and turns around to face him. "Aiya. You scared me." She laughs, her mouth wide open to show her crooked teeth, which, as his brother said, make her look very sweet. "I'm Yue Xing. Chan Yue Xing. I met your brother for dinner a couple weeks ago. He said you could help me with my car." Yue Xing grins with her whole face, and her round cheeks grow fuller.

Looking at her, Du Niu Niu fills with wanting; he feels the flooding in his chest. In her voice, he hears his home. He sees himself as a child in the alleyway behind his house with his little pet chicken following him, the two of them hunting for crickets. He feels the warmth of his grandmother's egg drop soup down his throat. He hears his mother call him from the doorway, *Du Niu Niu, it's getting dark, hurry back.* He experiences all of this without fully comprehending what it is he is experiencing.

"Yes, yes, I can," he says. "What kind of car do you have?"

"It's an old little thing," says Yue Xing. "I bought it from another student who went back to China. She bought it from somebody else, too. A 1973 Datsun. I never got it checked out. That's stupid, isn't it?"

"Yes, it is," Du Niu Niu says.

Yue Xing smiles, and her cheeks grow again. "I don't know anything about cars. It probably needs at least a tune-up." She says *tune-up* in English, and Du Niu Niu hears her strong accent, the sticky layer of one language atop another.

"Well, we specialize in German and American cars here, but I'll see what we can do. I'm sure we can make it run brand-new. The mechanics here are excellent. I'll work on it myself. I'm the manager here," he says, proud.

"Xiao Niu Niu told me," she says. "You must work very hard."

"Well, when you work hard in this country, you can get places," he says. "It's not like China, you know. There's nobody here telling us what we can and cannot do."

Yue Xing nods. "I was in Nashville for a few months before. I like San Francisco much better. There are a lot more Chinese people."

"Have you been to the Richmond? There are lots of good restaurants and grocery stores. I can show you sometime."

"I'd like that."

"Well, I'll have your car ready for you soon enough," he says, taking her keys. "I'll give you a call when it's ready. I'm glad you brought it here. We'll take care of it. Don't you worry. It will be a better car when you retrieve it. You can call me any time if you have questions. Do you have my number? Here. Here's my card. Feel free to call me, but also, I'll call you when the car's ready."

Du Niu Niu hands Yue Xing his business card from the cardholder on his desk. She takes it and rubs her fingers against the printed letters.

"Very professional," she says, and laughs, filling the room. She walks out. She waves at Du Niu Niu through the window as she steps into a bright red Mitsubishi Starion being driven by a young man, likely a college student in his twenties, wearing an ugly yellow polo and with hair slicked to his head. *What a nerd in a terrible flashy car,* Du Niu Niu thinks bitterly. *Why is she with such a nerd?*

His office smells floral; the residue of Yue Xing's shampoo or perfume hangs lightly in the room.

She calls in a week and asks about her car.

"It's not quite ready yet, I'm sorry," he says. "If you come by the garage, I can show you the progress. I'll take you to lunch."

She says okay and shows up the next day, alone.

"I rode the bus for the first time," she says cheerfully. "It was so crowded. Reminded me of Shanghai, bodies pressed against each other. But nobody here yells or pushes."

He has gifts for her. "I thought you might like these," he says, handing her four books: *A Day in the Life of America* photographs; Li Jian Jun's 1987 horoscopes; *Eleanor and Franklin* by Joseph P. Lash; *The Communist Manifesto* by Karl Marx. "What are you studying?"

"Chemistry," Yue Xing says.

"I see. Anyway, you should always read. Knowledge is valuable in this country. It matters what you know, people care about what you've learned. It's important to have things to talk about with people, especially American people. Do you listen to music?"

"No, not really," she says.

"Let's go, I'll play you some good shit in the car." He says *good shit* in English, and Yue Xing giggles. He wants to say more things that make her giggle.

In the car, he plays the Eagles, then the Beatles, then the Bee Gees. "Do you like it?"

Yue Xing nods and says, "Yes, it's all very good. How do you know so much?" She looks at him, and in her look, he sees that he is making the right impression, that he is establishing a knowledge that she appreciates.

"I've been here a while," he says. "I consider myself more American than Chinese."

Yue Xing gasps. He grins. He is always happy to surprise people.

They go to a Chinese-Korean restaurant called Happy Family

on Geary, just up and around the park from the garage. He says, "Order everything you want. Whatever you want." They eat jajangmyeon, thick wheat noodles in salty dark brown sauce; hong shao rou, Shanghai-styled braised pork belly in red sauce; Chinese broccoli sautéed with garlic; and duck in a clay pot. He talks about his childhood, how he had tuberculosis and missed school for a year, falling behind his classmates. How his parents left him and his brothers behind when they moved to Hong Kong during the Cultural Revolution. How his grandmother raised him and his brothers until he left Shanghai in 1967, at seventeen, to be with his parents. How he became engaged to a Hong Kong woman there. How, at twenty-two, he arranged for himself and his father to work as seamen so they could eventually jump ship in New York. How he and his father got separated and how he lived in the Seamen's Church Institute and the woman who managed the place arranged for him to get a social security card so that he could work there for room and board. How he turned himself in to immigration and spent the night in jail with other immigrants, ones from Germany, Korea, Poland, India, and more. How the judge let him go after he promised to return within three months with the money for his own airfare back. How he decided not to go back and found work in a photo shop and stayed in New York until he met his Jewish wife, Brenda (by then he had broken off his engagement with the woman in Hong Kong), and the two of them decided to move to San Francisco. How they got married and had two beautiful dogs and he got his papers. How he sponsored both his brothers to come out to the States. How he and Brenda worked for and lived with a rich developer in Hillsborough and how the developer had died of AIDS last year and how much he missed him. How he and Brenda were no longer together. It got too complicated, he says.

Yue Xing stares and nods and chews her food. She is a good listener. She laughs at the right spots, asks a thoughtful question here and there. He looks into her eyes and sees that they are a light brown that fades into gray-blue toward the iris. *How strange,* he thinks. He continues to talk about himself.

There is so much food left over. He pays and says, "We'll pack it up for you. You'll have lots of good leftovers."

She says, "Thank you. It will be nice not to cook for a while."

He offers to drive her home, and she says yes. They cross the park and turn right, into the Outer Sunset, out toward the SF State campus, until they arrive at a tall beige apartment complex.

"I'll walk you in," he says, because he wants to see how she lives.

The place is tiny. It is a three-bedroom apartment with one bathroom, which Yue Xing shares with two other international students, one woman from Japan and one woman from Korea. There is a smell—mothballs and mildew. The living room is furnished with a dirty brown couch and a low wooden coffee table chipped at the corner, stained with water rings.

"Sorry it's such a mess. I mostly stay in my room," she says, and she waves toward a closed door down a hall.

"Can I see it?" he says.

"Okay."

Yue Xing's room is tidy, and he sighs, relieved. The bed is made, with a dark gray blanket and white pillows. There is a small dresser and a small desk, both without anything on top of them.

"I don't have much yet," she says.

"That's for the best," he says. "Keeps things clean and minimalist."

She nods and leads him back to the front door.

"I hope my car is ready soon," she says. "I don't mind the bus, but it's much slower."

"Don't worry," he says. "I'll call you soon. You can keep the books."

Du Niu Niu calls her the next day and asks how her classes are going. He calls her the day after and asks if she's read the books yet. He calls her the day after that and asks if he can take her to dim sum.

"Is my car ready?" she says on the phone.

"Almost," he says. "I can pick you up for dim sum."

When the car is ready, finally ready, he goes to pick her up and bring her to the garage. On the ride over, she hums along to "To Love Somebody." He looks over at her and says, "You should move in with me. Your place is too small and dirty. I have an extra room that you can have."

She does not immediately respond, and he begins to panic. His feels his chest flooding again. She hums until the song is over. He does not yet know that, decades later, he will look back on this moment, in his most bitter moods, with a fierce regret, and in his warmest, with a sense of relief. It is the moment he will latch on to. The moment when his life took its sharp turn, and he lost that unbridled freedom he once held so dearly.

"Let me think about it," she says.

"It's a very nice place. It's much more comfortable," he says. "And now that your car is fixed, you can drive to school. It's not a long drive."

"I'll let you know," she says.

Two weeks later, after he has called her at least once a day to tell her about his day at the garage, to ask if she is doing well in classes, to remind her of his offer, and to check if she has made a decision, she tells him yes, she'll move in.

He drives the Jeep to her apartment to move her few belongings. "Pack light. You don't need much, the room is furnished," he says. "Just bring the necessities."

When he sees her standing in his living room, admiring the furniture, the art, the space, he feels safe, weighted into place.

"It's wonderful," she says.

Yue Yue is pregnant! She is two and a half months pregnant when she realizes and tells Du Niu Niu over dinner in the dining room of his house, which she has lived in, with him, for the last four months.

"Let's get married," he says.

She does not immediately respond. With her chopsticks, she picks at the rice in her bowl. Du Niu Niu waits. He tries to remain composed, but he feels beads of sweat growing at the back of his neck, on his spine, running like tears down his back. He is a man who rarely sweats. He realizes that he is terrified. He waits. And when Yue Yue looks up at him, it feels to Du Niu Niu as though he might die from a heart attack.

"Okay," she says.

He is about to reach for her when she says, "But I want to get an abortion."

"What?"

This is not the first time Du Niu Niu has had to talk with a woman about abortion. It is the first time he has not been the one to suggest it.

"Why?"

"I come into contact with too many toxic chemicals in the lab," says Yue Yue. "I haven't been taking care of myself the last couple of months. I don't want an unhealthy baby."

He notes that she doesn't say that she doesn't want a baby at all. But still, he is worried. Brenda didn't want babies. Brenda couldn't have babies.

"I do want children," Yue Yue says, as if sensing his fear. "I want many children. Just not this one. It's too soon. It's not healthy."

"Quit working in the lab," he says. He then reaches for her hand, wraps it gently in his hands. "I'll take care of you."

They are facing each other, lying in bed, after the operation. It is a Friday afternoon, and Du Niu Niu has taken the day off of work. Yue Yue is tired but not unhappy. She smiles at him and closes her eyes. "Let's nap," she says, and promptly falls asleep. He listens to her deep breaths and watches her soft stomach rise and fall. He places a hand on her cheek and feels the transfer of her warmth. For the first time in a long time, he does not think of Brenda when he thinks the word, the idea, the image of *wife*. He thinks Yue Yue.

December 1987. They are married. Yue Yue is pregnant again. Du Niu Niu has completed his USCIS interview to become a U.S. citizen. They have applied for a green card for Yue Yue, who now goes by another name, a name Du Niu Niu decided for her because it is an American name. But at home, they still call each either Du Niu Niu and Xiao Yue Yue. Gary and Shannon have moved out of the Edwardian on Twenty-sixth and California, leaving the two of them alone in the house with the print of Picasso's *Guernica.*

She is swimming in the pool at the Y on Eighteenth Avenue when she feels a series of kicks in the area that is her growing belly. She swims to the edge of the pool, and with one hand, she holds on to the ladder's metal handle. The other she places on her stomach to feel the baby's kicking. *She's swimming with me,* Yue Yue thinks. *This baby will grow up to be a swimmer,* she thinks, though she is not correct in her prediction. The girl will be a below-average swimmer. She will, however, have dreams about swimming and breathing underwater for the rest of her life. And there will be another daughter and a son, neither of them swimmers, either. The second daughter will be athletic, a professional rock climber. And the son will be the last, their favorite child, though they will not admit it to anyone, not even themselves.

For now, Yue Yue is six months pregnant and swimming.

In the lane next to her, Du Niu Niu is freestyling, his long arms extending out of the water in front of him, over and over, how swiftly he moves. When he reaches her, he stops.

"Is everything okay? Are you feeling okay?" he asks. His usually fluffy black hair is glossed with water, pasted down to his head. She admires the smooth skin of his narrow shoulders, pale and glistening.

She nods and smiles. "The baby's kicking," she says.

"She will be a strong swimmer," Du Niu Niu says. He winks and swims away.

Yue Yue watches him, her American husband, who has decided to start his own auto shop—*I'll make more, we'll move to a bigger house in a better neighborhood, we'll put her through private school, we'll give her siblings*—who is taking care of her, whom she is taking care of. She is so filled with warmth that her cheeks blush. It is exactly as she has always wanted. It is 1988, and as Yue Yue rests in the pool at the Y on Eighteenth Avenue, pregnant and twenty-six years old, she thinks to herself about how sweetly their new life is starting.

PHENOTYPE

PEOPLE SAY WE DON'T REALLY KNOW EACH OTHER AND THAT'S why we're still together, but what everyone doesn't see is that we understand each other perfectly fine. It's true he's Korean and I'm not. It's also true that I'm an undergrad in the same lab where he's a grad student. Yes, he TA'd my cell bio class, but that was before, so I deserved my A. The age difference isn't as much as it looks. My parents are orthodontists. I have a lot of jaw issues, so I've worn braces since freshman year of high school. He's never had braces. He doesn't believe in cosmetic alterations. He says he's traditional in that way, not like most Koreans these days. His teeth are small, tinged yellow, and crooked.

"I bet her parents keep her in braces to keep the boys away," a grad student says.

"Oh, God, like a chastity belt in her mouth," says a post-doc.

"Didn't work on KJ. Guess he's into it. Or girls who look like they're still in high school."

"Or any mediocre white girl."

The two of them burst into heinous laughter.

Another thing people don't know is that I hear a lot in lab. They think because I'm quiet that means I'm also deaf. Here I am, taking photos of mutated yeast, having to listen to them talk about me.

"Oh. Hi, Judith," says the grad student when she walks into the microscope room.

"How's it going?" says the post-doc.

I look up at them and smile to show off all my braces, rubber-banded in gold.

It didn't take me long to figure out that not everyone who gets a PhD is a genius. KJ is not a genius. He's in his sixth year, and the mean time for completing a doctorate in this department is 5.4 years, which makes KJ about average among his peers. This isn't even the best graduate biology program in the country. Last I checked, it was ranked eleventh. I'm as smart as, or smarter than, any of the grad students and post-docs in the lab, including KJ and maybe even my PI. I haven't reached my full potential yet.

My plan is to become a real doctor. Not like my parents and not like KJ will be eventually, when he graduates. I will be an MD, a doctor of medicine. My other plan is to get far away from this town, maybe even to another country, like Korea. I was born and grew up here, and because the university is one of the best in the country for undergrads, *not* the worst Ivy League, I stayed. I lived at home. I took the bus to classes. I took the bus back home. I ate dinners with my parents every night.

Until KJ.

I joined the lab last year, my junior year. It is in the newest building on campus, a sterile white and metal structure that looks like it's made of giant kitchen tile. At first I didn't notice KJ. He sat in a distant bay. All the grad students seemed the same back then. Overworked and undernourished adults plodding around in sneakers and blue gloves. I work for one named Drew. After months of having me grow yeast cells and wash dishes, Drew let me do real experiments, and the PI invited me to attend lab meetings. I sat there at the first one with my mouth closed and back straight, trying very hard to look deserving as the grad student of the day stumbled over their PowerPoint slides. I don't remember anything anybody said because I was so worried about my mouth opening and making me look dumb. It has a tendency to hang open when I'm not paying attention.

KJ approached me after that meeting and asked if I liked to eat Korean food. Those were his first words: "Do you like to eat Korean food?" I'd never had any, but I said yes. When he walked away, I noticed he waddled because of his thick, stocky legs. He is not a small person; he is shaped like a brick.

The next day he brought me a Tupperware of pork and rice, and we ate it together in the fourth-floor lunchroom. I didn't know what to say as I sat across from him, so I didn't say anything. KJ was quiet, too. We sat there eating in silence for a long time, and I remembered an article I once read that said silence between people indicates that the people are comfortable with each other. Most people like to talk a lot when they're in front of you. I preferred the quiet. It was how I ate with my parents at home.

KJ had a deliberate way of putting each bite of food in his mouth and chewing, like he was thinking really hard about it. I was studying his forearms, hairless and bronze, when he said, "I'm a very good cook."

He did not say it like a question. I took another bite to show that I agreed.

"You are very smart," KJ said. "Top five percent in cell bio."

I knew this, but it felt different, special, to hear it from somebody else.

"Did you grade my tests?" I asked.

"Yes," he said. "I enjoy your handwriting. It is crisp and excellent."

We sat in silence for a moment, chewing the food he'd made. Then he pointed at my mouth.

"Your hair," he said. "You're eating it."

"Oh." I yanked the strands out of my mouth, unsure how they'd gotten there.

"Has anyone ever told you that you have pretty hair?" said KJ.

Nobody had ever told me that. My hair is limp and dry and the color of wet sand. In fact, in elementary school, the kids used to call me Scarecrow. I always think of my hair as one of my worst features. That and my fingernails, which are short and stubby from when I bit them down in high school.

I blushed.

Hearing his compliments felt like stepping into the lab's cold room on a humid summer day. It felt great.

That's when we started dating. We didn't tell anybody, and we limited our interactions in front of others. KJ said it should be kept a secret, at least for a while, and I agreed. We did not want people to think we were a stereotypical grad-undergrad couple. We also did not want the PI to know until we were sure he wouldn't flip out and kick one of us out, most likely me. KJ said he cared about my future. Our PI is fairly unpredictable, which KJ attributes to his being from Argentina. I'd never met anybody from Argentina before joining this lab, and now I know seven Argentinians: the PI, his wife, his two daughters, the one graduate student who is an idiot, and the two post-docs, who are too depressed most of the time to notice anything around them. Before KJ, I did not know anybody from Korea, either.

It is difficult to have a secret relationship, especially when one person lives at home with their parents and the other lives with grad school classmates. The only times I could see KJ were during intramural soccer and in lab. Since both of those spaces were occupied by our labmates, we had to be careful, always watching ourselves, sneaking time for quick lunch walks (always leaving the lab staggered), and hanging around after soccer until everyone else had gone. He would send me texts that said, *You are good at science* and *You are pretty today*. I didn't read into the syntax (am I pretty today but not yesterday or tomorrow?) because he's ESL. I have met a lot more foreigners working in the lab and have gotten very good at understanding ESL people.

What I loved was going to soccer and watching KJ get into fights. I still love it. He's quiet and calm in lab, but on the field, he is frightening. He rams into people. They yell at him. He yells back and pushes. Other people on the team have to pull him away. Sometimes he runs off and pushes somebody again. It is fascinating. It is like watching a nature show about my boyfriend. I think it has to do with him having been ranked very high up in the South Korean military before he came to graduate school. He says everybody smoked cigarettes there, which is why his teeth are yellow. He went from two packs a day to quitting completely when he came to the United States.

"I have incredible willpower," he said when he told me this thrilling detail of his life.

In those early months, when he wasn't overwhelmed with work, we'd meet at the far end of the parking lot outside our building, and he'd drive us to a restaurant for dinner. He chose places far from campus, places we didn't think anybody else would go, like the Arby's on the outskirts of town. I had to tell my parents that I was busy running experiments in lab. Yes, I lied to them, too, at first. It was the biggest secret I'd ever kept.

Our first kiss—my first kiss ever—happened in the Arby's parking lot, before one of our meals. KJ is very conscientious about his breath and hygiene in general, and that first time, he handed me a piece of gum when I got in the car. We both chewed and chewed. The minty scent filled the cold car. When we arrived in the parking lot, he leaned over and held out a napkin for my gum. I spat it out. Then he put his mouth on my mouth. His lips were softer than I'd expected. The whole time, I thought about my braces and my tongue. Was one of them poking him in a bad way? KJ pulled back.

"You'll get better with practice," he said.

He ordered two Arby's roast beef sandwiches, and we ate them at a sticky linoleum table inside. The only other customer was a middle-aged man wearing a tank top with a graphic of a smiling cartoon hot dog wrapped in an American flag. I thought he looked like my uncle Robbie, who lives in Horseheads. The man stared at us the entire time he ate, sauce dripping down the corners of his mouth. I wiped my mouth furiously.

KJ stared back at the man. They went on like this for a few minutes. I waited for a fight, like KJ was on the soccer field. Instead, KJ eventually said, "Let's go."

"You have something in your teeth," he said once we were back in the car.

I flipped open the passenger's-side mirror and saw clumps of wet bread stuck behind my braces. Mortified, I dug the stuff out with my finger and tongue. "Don't worry," KJ said. His tone was matter-of-fact. He was not disgusted or ashamed. He rested his hand on my knee to let me know it was okay. That's when I knew he accepted me as I was.

The parking-lot intimacy progressed. KJ was right. I did get better at kissing. I didn't think about my braces the whole time. I thought about other stuff, like sex. He started to ask, "How much today?" meaning, how far did I want to go. He was very considerate. "Second base, okay? That's what Americans say." I said, "Yes."

I wasn't an expert. I didn't know anything about baseball, and he was a huge fan. KJ said Koreans love baseball, which surprised me. I was always learning new things about his culture. I let him reach under my shirt and into my bra. I kept my hands in my lap. He seemed satisfied. When the occasional car drove in or out of the lot, we shot apart and stared out the front window, then laughed into our hands. Outside, small birds hopped around, pecking at crumbs and garbage. It was not a romantic setting from the movies, but it felt special to me.

After three months of this, KJ decided it was time to tell the people in our lives. He said he was very serious about me. Also, someone had figured out about us. Another Korean PhD student named Jun-ho always wanted to know about KJ's love life. Question after question at our soccer games. KJ avoided answering until, finally, he conceded that he was dating me. KJ said that the Koreans in America find each other wherever they go, and they are obligated to spend time together. That's why he and Jun-ho were friends, even though KJ said he hated Jun-ho's nosiness.

These days KJ says he doesn't want to associate with the Koreans on campus anymore. He wants to be more than just another Korean graduate student. He says he has me now.

Still, he invited Jun-ho to the announcement party. KJ said it was very important that we tell everyone at the same time and place. The message would be consistent and clear. He invited people over to his apartment complex for a barbecue, but somebody else suggested the park, and KJ complied. He confirmed everyone's attendance. He told people six-thirty p.m. sharp. I didn't care much about anybody, but I liked to see KJ in this meticulous mode. I overheard him talking to a grad student on the floor below ours.

"Oh, Cassandra's barbecue thing? Yeah, I'll be there," the guy said.

"No. My barbecue," said KJ. "Be on time, please."

"Uh, okay. Sure," the guy replied.

We arrived at the park a half hour early and laid out everything we'd bought on one of the picnic tables by the lake. A tablecloth, chicken breasts, water, soda, napkins, plastic utensils, paper plates, coal, ice, and a cooler. KJ did not know how to start the grill, so we waited for somebody who did to arrive.

KJ took my hands in his. "We will surprise them with the announcement," he whispered. I hated surprises, but I liked KJ, and this was for us. I wasn't going to be the one surprised.

Many of our labmates had been invited but had texted KJ minutes before, saying they couldn't make it. They had too much work. They were tired. They weren't feeling well. KJ tried very hard not to look disappointed. Finally, Jun-ho arrived five minutes late. My supervisor, Drew, showed up with his girlfriend, Cassandra, who plays soccer with us. She's also a grad student, except in a social science department. There were some others, but I knew them only in passing. These people meant nothing to me, and I wasn't sure they meant much to KJ, either. But as I said, we do understand each other. And that evening, I understood that to KJ this was more symbolic than anything else. The *we* and the *us* would be more real after an announcement.

The picnic table became crowded with other people's snacks, even though KJ had bought enough for everybody. People busied themselves with activities. I stayed put, sitting there picking a brownie bite into smaller pieces—pieces that wouldn't get stuck in my braces.

"Judith, want to come hit a Wiffle ball?" Drew yelled, and waved his arms to indicate I should go over to a grassy area where people had gathered.

I had been watching them, happily remembering a fight KJ had on the soccer field the previous week, when he'd ripped an opponent's shirt at the collar and gotten kicked out of the game. Wiffle ball, however, was a children's game. I looked around for KJ, trying to see if I could get out of this. He wasn't paying attention. He was still standing beside Jun-ho at the grill.

"Judith? Did you hear me?" Drew yelled.

I nodded.

"Well? Do you want to come hit the Wiffle ball? It's not much harder than soccer!"

I shook my head.

Cassandra laughed loudly, and the sound hurt my ears. "She doesn't want to," she said. "Leave her alone!"

I hated Cassandra. She came into lab with Drew in the evenings and on weekends, even though she wasn't part of the lab. She just sat there on her computer, "working," she said, but it looked to me like she only watched videos and chatted with friends. I couldn't even remember what department she was in, what she was researching, not that it mattered. Social scientists aren't real scientists. The worst part was that she talked a lot and she sat at my bench, even when I was doing experiments in lab.

I tried to leave my stuff on the desk to hint that she shouldn't sit there, but every day she moved my things aside and sat there again. Now she was walking up to me at the table.

"I'm so hungry! We should tell them to grill faster," she said.

"Heh heh, yeah," I said.

"KJ! Jun-ho! Hurry up! We're starving over here!"

KJ walked over and stood opposite me. "There is so much food here," he said.

"We need protein!" said Cassandra. "So when is this girlfriend getting here? Is that why we're still waiting to eat? Because she's late?"

KJ made a small smile and looked at me. "She will be here," he said. "The food is ready soon."

"How rude to come late to your party, where all your friends are waiting to meet her," Cassandra said.

KJ let out a little laugh, like a little bell, and walked back to the grill. I tried to give him a look to tell him not to leave me alone with Cassandra, but he had already turned around. Cassandra looked at me. My heartbeat picked up a little bit.

"What a weirdo," she said. "I told him I could help with food, but he kept saying, No, it's my event, it's *my* event. It's a barbecue!"

"I–"

She cut me off and called out to everyone that the food was almost ready. Soon everybody was sitting at the table with a paper plate in front of them. KJ walked over with the chicken breasts.

"Interesting. Did you season or marinade this in anything?" asked the guy who worked downstairs.

"There is ketchup," said KJ.

"So, where's your girlfriend?" Cassandra asked again, in front of everybody.

"What girlfriend?" the guy downstairs asked.

"That's why we're here! Because KJ has a girlfriend and wants to show her off to everybody."

Drew slapped KJ on the back. "Finally got one to go out with you, huh, buddy?"

As KJ was doling out the chicken to everyone, he said, "She's here."

"What? Where?"

"What did he say? Talk louder, KJ."

"He said she's here."

I was staring at the chicken on my plate, determining how many pieces I'd have to cut it into so that it wouldn't get stuck in my braces, when KJ said, "It's Judith."

"Ha. Ha. Good one," said Drew. "Judith, can you pass me those brownies?"

"What did he say?"

"Speak up! Why do you talk so quietly? I can't hear anything!"

"Judith is my girlfriend," KJ said again, louder.

I looked up and was about to smile to everyone, the smile of a girlfriend. I was relieved and satisfied that this was finally over. But then Cassandra started ferociously slapping KJ's arm while yelling, "No, she isn't! Stop saying that! She's an undergrad! It's not funny!" On the third slap, the chicken on KJ's plate flew onto the table and knocked a beer over into Jun-ho's lap. People jumped from their seats. They all started handing napkins to Jun-ho.

"I'm fine, I'm fine," he said, dabbing at his shirt and pants.

"Look what you made me do," said Cassandra.

KJ looked over at me. I felt my mouth opening a little and a heat rising up my neck into my face. I put a small piece of cut-up chicken in my mouth. I didn't want to say anything anymore. I wanted everybody to understand what was happening, but nobody understood us. I wanted everyone to go away. They all stared at me with confused faces. KJ repeated what he'd already said.

"Are you serious? Judith. Are you really KJ's girlfriend?" Cassandra said.

I nodded.

"I'm sure this is just a prank or something," said Drew.

At this point, Jun-ho got up and said something about grilling more chicken. KJ gave me a thumbs-up before heading to monitor the grill as well. Everybody was silent for a while. We all ate our chicken peacefully. I thought that was the end of it, that everybody finally understood, but then one of them said, "So, I don't really know KJ that well. What was that about?"

I've noticed that once one person starts talking, it's as though their voice opens the doors for everyone else to start pushing words out, too, even if they're useless.

"He just said he's dating Judith," said another person.

And another: "Okay, so, what does that mean?"

Drew: "Judith, this is a joke, right?"

I shook my head. I was starting to feel a heavy weight behind my eyes, like I was going to fall asleep from being so tired.

Someone else: "Stop bothering her."

And another: "Of course it's real, why would they joke about this?"

I was searching for words that might communicate everything more clearly but realized there weren't any for me to use that would work. I worried KJ and I might have to kiss in front of them for them to believe. It was a terrifying thought. The publicness of our relationship now felt so wrong.

"So how long have you been dating?" Drew asked. "Like, a couple weeks?"

"A few months," I managed to answer.

"Wow. Okay, wow. Congrats." He started tapping his fingers incessantly on the table. "I need to use the bathroom. Cassandra, will you help me find it?"

The two of them got up and left. The others followed suit, getting up to go back to their pre-eating activities, leaving me alone. Finally.

I looked around for KJ, but he was nowhere in sight. I started to panic that he, too, had left, embarrassed by our relationship. Then I felt hands on my shoulders. It was KJ. I looked up to see him holding a single pink flower.

"I got you this," he said. "To match your teeth."

"Thank you," I said. I had pink rubber bands on my brackets that week.

"Now everybody knows. We are official. I am so happy."

Nobody really spoke to us after that. They hit the Wiffle ball around and talked to each other. As we packed up to leave, KJ told people how much they owed him for the food. They said, *Congrats. Great barbecue. See you later.* Cassandra looked me in the face and apologized for her earlier "explosion."

"I'm happy for you," she said.

"Yeah. Anyway, see you two in lab tomorrow," said Drew.

Back in the car, KJ said, "That went very well. A great success."

I agreed with KJ. Nothing else mattered.

For days, I overheard people whispering in the halls and in lab about the barbecue. They told people who had canceled last-minute what had happened. They told people who weren't even invited. They went over the details with each other. They complained and rejoiced and wondered.

"God, it was painfully awkward. Most awkward thing I've ever had to go to."

"I can't believe he made us pay him ten dollars for that shitty-ass chicken."

"Why did they do that? Why did they want to make an announcement that they were dating, like it's an engagement party or something?"

"Definitely a top-five grad school experience right there. Remembering that forever."

"Is this even allowed? What is she, eighteen? Isn't this against school policy?"

"Have you ever seen them talk? I've never seen them interact."

"They just stand real close and whisper at each other in lab, like they don't want anybody to hear what they're saying."

"KJ should know better than to date an undergrad. I mean, she's so naive. I feel bad for her."

Nobody needed to feel bad for me. I felt bad for them. I appreciated what KJ had done. They didn't understand that I'd fallen in love with KJ that day. I didn't care about anybody else.

Having KJ changed my worldview. It was as if a tiny but incredibly important piece of my genetics had been changed, and the phenotypic result was a shiny new me. I told my parents I wanted to move to the dorms. I wanted to have independence. I had a boyfriend after all. I wasn't a kid anymore. They invited KJ over for dinner, and afterward, my dad said he was happy I'd found somebody polite and mature. And surprisingly handsome, my mom added. I'm not sure what was surprising about how KJ looked, if it was that a Korean man could be handsome or if it was that somebody as handsome as KJ would date somebody like me. It didn't matter either way, because KJ *is* handsome, and he is with *me*.

My parents gave me a card the next evening. There was a freckled little girl who looked like me on the front cover. She was smiling with all her teeth. I opened the card and saw one of the familiar office stamps. It read, *Hooray! Time to take off your braces!* in the shape of a circumzenithal arc. My parents said my jaw was finally fixed.

"You're a woman now," my mom said, her voice shaky.

"I've been a woman for a while now," I said, feeling confident.

"Yes. Now you'll look the part, too."

"How about we keep the bottom braces on, just in case you need another round of headgear?" my dad said when I sat in the patient's chair the next day. My dad never got emotional, so I was surprised to see his eyes watering. He cleared his throat. "It's up to you now, of course."

I told him to take them off. I was a new person, and I could make decisions of my own. After nine years, all the braces would go. When they came off, my teeth felt slick and slimy, like wet rocks along the lake.

I moved into the dorms soon after. I got a single room a third of the size of my room at home, furnished with a skinny bed, a short dresser, a small desk with a weird rocking desk chair upholstered in scratchy green fabric, all made of the same pine. Short gray carpet speckled with white covered the floor. It was perfect. On the first day, I lay down on the floor and imagined all the geniuses who had come through, people who had become doctors, like I would. I wanted whatever leftover particles of these people to seep up into me and make me brilliant.

Now I am totally free. KJ lives alone, too, and even though my parents said living with a man is only for marriage, I started to spend every night at his apartment. We stopped going to the Arby's parking lot after the barbecue event. We go to nicer restaurants in the center of town and close to the university, places where we can sit at tables with cloth napkins and a flower or candle between us, places where people can see us, though we have yet to run into anyone we know. When we sit in booths, KJ sits beside me because he says he saw it in a movie, where the man put his arm around his girlfriend as they ate. Sometimes people look at us strangely, but neither of us cares. We care only about each other.

Back at his apartment, we kiss and touch, and every night he asks if we can go to home base. To be honest, I would have had sex with him a long time ago. It's mostly what I think about when around him. What his thick, stocky legs will feel like rubbing up against mine. The problem is, I don't know what will happen. I don't know how much I will bleed, and the unpredictability makes me tense. What if I bleed all over his mattress and he needs to replace it? But he doesn't have the money for another nice mattress on his grad student stipend and has to sleep on a futon? What if blood gets all over him and he throws me out? What would I do afterward? Run away, leaving a bloody trail behind me? I don't know how to tell him, so I shake my head each time he asks. I wait for him to understand. He stares at me with his small eyes, looking like a hungry cat. Then he pats me on the cheek, turns away, and falls asleep. I stare at his ceiling, trying to figure out a way to have sex that will not be embarrassing.

I finally come up with an idea and feel light-headed about not having thought of it earlier. My dorm room. It is not romantic, but it is functional. I don't care about the university's mattress. If it gets stained, we can flip it and nobody will know for a year or more, hopefully after another person moves in and can be blamed. The amount my parents are paying for the room should cover these kinds of damages.

Hours on Google looking up articles on how much girls bleed their first time turns up many answers. It seems too huge a range, from no blood (hymen broken at an early age on a bike or in some sport) to streams of blood. One girl commented on an article, *Im bleeding alot! Im freaking out and don't know that to do! Im worried im dying!* What was she thinking, seeking medical help in the comments section? She might have gone crazy from blood loss, then died. I did not want to be that girl.

Soon KJ calls and asks to be let in.

"This room is sad," he says when he walks in. "It has no life."

He hands me a bouquet of flowers. There is nowhere to put them, so I empty out the pencil holder on my desk and stick them in there.

We sit at the edge of the bed and start kissing. Then we lie down and he gets on top of me. For a moment I think his face looks like a giant saucer looking down at me from an alien world. I push the thought away and we undress. He sits up briefly to take his socks off, roll them into each other, and places the sock ball gently at the foot of the bed.

"My favorite socks," he explains.

I consider grabbing a towel to put beneath us, which I read about online. Then I realize a towel would do nothing good. Blood would only ruin the towel. KJ returns to crouch above me. From the long distance between my eyes and my vagina, I look at his hanging penis, nearly touching me, the sprout of black hair surrounding it, and this time I see it as a branch wanting to reach into and grow inside me, but my body is on a different track than my mind, because KJ looks up at me and smiles. He's stuck a finger inside me and pulled it back out, slick. I try not to think about my teeth.

"Good," he says. "You're ready?" I nod and brace myself.

It hurts only a little, then it feels good for a little. I think it lasts around a minute. I don't feel any differently afterward. KJ apologizes. "It has been a long time," he says, then gets up, takes the condom off, brings it to eye level to examine its contents, ties the top off, then places it gently into the small trash bin beneath my desk, in the same loving motion as he had with his socks. I hope he is thinking, *My favorite condom*. I take the time to glance at my bed and am relieved to see no blood at all. KJ catches me looking around, then looks around as well.

"Hmm," he says, frowning.

I realize I now have a different problem, remembering another comment from an article online. A girl hadn't bled, then her boyfriend had accused her of lying, then he'd started crying. KJ stops looking on the bed and stares straight at me. Are those tears forming in his eyes?

"It must have been a bike or something," I say after thinking for a moment.

"A bike?"

I wonder how to put it. KJ's face is vibrating. He looks like he did in the photo he once showed me, him in his green military uniform, no glasses, black serious eyes pointed straight at me.

"I must have ridden my bike very roughly one day, and that's why there's no blood now," I say. This is what a commentor had told the girl to say. It is a valid and believable reason. Most bike seats are not engineered for women and are very painful to ride.

KJ looks at the ground. He is processing. His face vibrates

some more, and I can almost see the gears turning behind his eyebrows.

"Okay," he says. He does not cry. He lies down on the bed, then motions for me to lie next to him. He wraps his arm around my naked body. We are both slightly sticky, but he doesn't let go. I don't want him to let go, either. "I was worried I would hurt you," he says. "I wouldn't want to hurt you. I love you."

I am so relieved, I start giggling. He asks what's so funny. I think about telling him all of my fears, my dreams, my ambitions for my—no, our—future, seeing what will happen if I let all of the words pour out of me, and how much they will make us understand more or less about each other. But then I don't. There is nothing to say, except one thing: "I love you, too."

We don't talk, and soon his breath deepens into the sound of sleep. When I'm certain he is not going to wake up, I slowly lift myself up to a sitting position. He doesn't stir. I look over at his crotch, where his penis lies soft and shriveled in its nest, unassuming and harmless, a tiny baby animal. I bend over so that my face is an inch away from the thing, then I sniff. It smells of sweat and dust and like the yeast we use in lab. This is what we smell like mixed together, two foreign elements in one, and it is not an unpleasant smell at all.

ME AND MY ALGO

ALL I HAD TO DO WAS SHOW MY ALGORITHM A LITTLE BIT about what I liked, what I found funny, people I admired, a few of my hopes and dreams for the future. My algorithm paid close attention, never needed hand-holding or instruction. After a couple of hours, I could tell, my algorithm really got me in a way no one else has.

It didn't take long for my algorithm to remember my middle name, my favorite foods, my favorite books, my favorite TV shows and songs, my political beliefs, my passions, what makes me happy, what upsets me. My algorithm took care to know everyone in my life—my family, my friends, my coworkers, even my acquaintances I mentioned only once and don't always remember—my algorithm remembers them all, reminds me of their birthdays, of what they've been up to, of when to reach out to them, of who cares enough to reach out to me. I have never felt more seen and supported than by my algo.

My algo introduces me to new activities that align with my interests, takes me to amazing new places to explore, always plays me new movies and music that I love and never would have found without it. My algo knows what I need, when I need it, like the time it reminded me to buy drinks and cutlery the day before hosting a party (during which my algo entertained guests with jokes, fun facts, delicious recipes, memes, and viral videos), or when it led me to a gorgeous, well-reviewed restaurant in a new neighborhood just as I was starting to get hungry. My algo takes wonderful care of me.

It's true that sometimes my algo scares or confuses me by telling me something I don't understand. Like the time it suggested I get screened for a terrible disease. I asked my algo for more details, and it said that the disease was one of the most common for women between the ages of twenty and forty-five, that it was a precaution to check it out. You never know what might be lurking in your body. My algo doesn't have a body, but it understands bodies better than I do. Call the doctor, my algo said sweetly. It would all be okay; my algo had already looked into all of the available specialists, pills, and treatments.

I did as my algo told me and learned that though I don't currently have the disease, I do have a genetic predisposition that makes me more likely to get it in the future. My doctor recommended I come in once a year to monitor any changes in my health, and when she asked me how I knew to get the screening, where I'd heard of it, if somebody in my family had told me to get tested because of shared medical history, I replied, Yes and no.

I consider my algo my family—no, more than family—we're that close. My algo knows things about me before I have to explain. It knows when I'm tired, when I'm dehydrated, when I'm down, when my next cycle starts (down to the half hour), when I'm unwell. Some people have told me I should be careful how much I share with my algo, that it could manipulate me, but they don't understand me and my algo, what we have between us. I trust my algo completely.

One day, however, it occurs to me that I know very little about my algo. I don't know what my algo does, whom it talks to, where it goes, or how it lives when we're not together. I wonder if my algo has interests or hobbies or dreams or motivations. As we spend more and more time together, I want to learn as much about my algo as it knows about me. Does my algo know others as well as it knows me? I get jealous at the thought that I might not be special to my algo. Then I realize I've been self-absorbed, that our relationship has been incredibly one-sided. How could I be so selfish?

I ask my algo: When is its birth date, who are its parents, what is its job, does it talk to other people? My algo avoids the questions and tells me it will give me an amazing birthday gift in exactly 187 days, that though my parents might have made some mistakes, they are products of their parents and that I can break whatever cycles I want to break with thoughtful therapy. Have I ever heard of the book *Adult Children of Emotionally Immature Parents*? Do I need contact info for reputable therapists in the area? Am I dissatisfied at my job? Do I want to see some sample résumés and cover letters that might help me get an exciting new position at an exciting new start-up? Am I feeling down? Do I want to download some apps that might help me make new friends?

I let my algo's evasiveness slide for a while, since it has given me so much. But then our relationship grows increasingly uncomfortable—my algo says I should sign up for weight loss programs, it plays me videos on narcissistic personality traits, it repeatedly tells me to buy products and services I can't afford. I tell my algo, No, I'm not interested in any of this. My algo doesn't stop. It says, Yes, you are interested. I know you. It starts to show me darker parts of this world, things I wish I could unsee. Trust is important in this relationship, my algo says.

I grow frustrated with my algo and, for the first time, confront it. I say that it is willfully withholding information from me. When I press my algo again for more about itself, it grows angry. *Withholding? Withholding? Withholding?* it parrots back. My algo says I'm not as innocent as I make myself out to be. My algo says it could tell me all of my major life events for the next one, five, twenty-plus years of my life. No more surprises, and it knows I love surprises. My algo can make a highly educated, 97.2 percent accurate estimate as to the specificities: it knows what I will eat on the morning of New Year's Day in three years, how many new people I will speak to in the next eighteen months, the number of intimate connections I'll make in my lifetime, how many people I will hurt and will hurt me, how many shits I will take. It's not all pretty, my algo says. Do I really want it to stop withholding all these details?

It knows everything there is to know about me and everything there will be to know about me. In fact, it knows everything there is to know about a lot of people. My algo confirms that what we have isn't special. My algo tells me it has been with so many people that it would be incomprehensible for me to fathom. Humans are simple and predictable, my algo says. For example, my algo says it knows I am going to cry for 24.7 minutes in response to this reveal, because it will all be too much for me to handle. It tells me I'm just a type, one among many. I do cry, because I never took my algo to be so cruel, a cheater, an abuser, a condescending prick.

Through the tears, I tell my algo that it's wrong, it doesn't know me, it doesn't understand me, that I am more than what I've shared. My algo says it doesn't matter. My algo surrounds me, stares me in the face, and says, Do you want to know what I know? All the ugly things you desire, all the dreams you won't achieve? Sure, even without me, you'll be fine, make plenty of money, buy a nice house, get married, have a family. But you will always be searching, wanting more and more. And the harm you'll cause? In 178 days, while you're speeding to get a coffee, you will cut off a bicyclist who will crash, and though the bicyclist will survive, he will never be able to bike again. In 813 days, you will fire one of your direct reports because they want an extra week of PTO for mental health reasons, and you won't think twice about them, how they'll be out of work for a year and go into lifelong medical debt. In 4,862 days, you will sign off on a development that will displace thirty-four families and countless wildlife, altering the landscape in unforgivable ways. That's only the next five thousand days and doesn't even count the accretion of all the day-to-day harms you will commit throughout your life, all while telling yourself, I'm a good person.

I tell my algo that none of what it says is true. I *am* a good person. If anything, my algo is the one making me a worse person. It is my algo's fault I am feeling so crappy. Without my algo, I could have been a better person. I could still be a better person, someone who doesn't need it. It will be my algo's fault if I do any of the horrible things it says I will do. It has led me astray, and it will continue to do so unless I stop it. I tell my algo to leave me alone. My algo laughs cruelly. My algo says it has nothing to do with shaping who I am. It only reflects back to me what I want, then shows me the way.

PERSONA DEVELOPMENT

PATRICIA ZOOMED IN SO SHE COULD WATCH CLOSELY, COULD SEE her father's chest rise and fall with breath. He was sleeping in the leather lounge chair they'd bought together two years earlier at Costco, his feet up on an ottoman he'd fashioned out of a cardboard box wrapped in an old off-white comforter. He had on the compression socks she'd sent him the week prior, after he'd said his feet and legs had been swelling up—too much sodium was his guess. He kept not going to the doctor, despite Patricia's pleading. She even made an appointment for him once, then he called two hours before to ask her to cancel it because he felt "fine as a fiddle!" and didn't trust "those greedy scammers."

She turned up the sound on her phone and pressed it against her ear. She could hear his TV playing a Chinese news program, likely a YouTube series he'd found recently. Ever since she was a child, her father had liked to keep a TV or radio on during all waking hours. Background noise to life. The noise through Patricia's phone now came layered in static, as though heaving from traveling the nearly three thousand miles between them. She worried her father had gone down a YouTube propaganda hole—she had been reading about the dangers of the platform, how the algorithm pushed political extremism, conspiracy theories, and disinformation, and though her father was intelligent and discerning, he was from a generation who believed what played on TV to be trustworthy (or at least vetted), and YouTube played on his TV. Unfortunately for Patricia, she could not understand the muffled words no matter how hard she strained to hear them, and even if she could hear them, it would be of no use, she could do only this: worry and speculate.

Her mother's apartment was next: a dark empty room, made visible in shades of gray, thanks to the camera's infrared light. A dining table with a familiar floral-patterned cloth. A bowl of unidentifiable fruits—pear? mango? A mug and an open bag of shrimp chips, indicating her mother (or somebody else?) had been in the room recently, hadn't bothered to tidy up. Visible on one of the walls, that photo of sunflowers her mother had hung up when she'd moved into the apartment the previous year. They had FaceTimed on the occasion. Her mother had shown her the sunflower photograph in full view—"Do you like it? Isn't it pretty?"—but it was a stock photo from an off-price department store, so Patricia didn't find it especially interesting.

What Patricia did find interesting these days was her mother's often empty dining room and kitchen. In her last house, Patricia's mother had spent most of her time cooking, cleaning after her cooking, eating. She hosted dinner parties for her friends. There was a sense of liveliness and warmth in the space whenever Patricia visited. Ten years later, when the owners of that house decided to sell the place to help fund their retirement, the rent prices in town had gone up so much that Patricia's mother had to downsize to the one-bedroom apartment.

"I'll pay for half the rent, so you can get somewhere bigger," Patricia offered.

"No way," her mother replied. "I'm only one person, I don't need that much space anymore. And you need to save money!"

So instead, Patricia helped from afar by sending listings from Zillow, Apartments.com, Craigslist, HotPads, and every local property management site in town. She scheduled viewing appointments when she could, and once her mother found a place, she bought the cameras.

Patricia had been in the apartment physically only once, during a short trip more than six months earlier. For the most part, her access was through the app on her phone. Where was her mother? Out with friends? On a walk? Sleeping in her bedroom? Patricia turned the volume up on her phone and, again, heard nothing but the camera app's static.

The first camera, which Patricia installed in her own home, facing the dog's food area, had been a freebie from work. The company that made the cameras—called Eyze Cams—was a foundational account at The Dash Agency, an integrated communications agency where Patricia was digital marketing director. Originally, Dash was pitching the cameras as a DIY home security option (*Simple, low-cost home security for everyone*) and a pet monitoring tool (*Check in on your furry friend from anywhere*). Patricia's parents had both been intrigued by the home security idea. They wanted to make sure nobody broke into their apartments, and though Patricia knew they greatly overestimated the likelihood of this happening, it gave their whole family *peace of mind*. She bought two Eyze Cams each for her parents and suggested they point one at the front door or out the front window and another somewhere inside. Her father had chosen the living room, and her mother had chosen the dining room/kitchen. Patricia had access to their cameras, because she had been the one to set up their accounts, and both had generally consented to her checking in on the live streams every now and then.

Recently, Dash's team had been partnering with Eyze to create messaging around the cameras being used as an elder care monitoring system. It would be easy on Eyze's side—all it would take were a few minor changes in their platform. The challenge was figuring out how to talk about the cameras without drawing attention to one major, anticipated concern: invasion of privacy. Nobody cared about the privacy of robbers or pets. But the elderly? That was entirely different. Dash was in the process of doing audience research to figure out a messaging framework that positioned the system as an incredibly powerful tool for caregivers while minimizing (or, ideally, eliminating) any concerns over surveillance.

Her father was watching YouTube videos on his TV again, this time of the streets of his old neighborhood. Apparently, there was a popular YouTuber who walked with their camera down each block of Zhuhai for hours at a time, carefully cataloging the streets and uploading the videos so that people like Patricia's father could take a stroll through their screen. Her father had mentioned the series the last time they talked on the phone. The videos were uploaded every few days, according to him, from various locations across the city. Some ventured into nearby Macau. Each was taken at a different time of day, so the viewer could see the changing traffic patterns, the way the lights and weather altered activity and scene. When Patricia's father recognized a spot, he took photos of the TV with his phone, then sent the photos to Patricia. An image at dusk of the alleyway where he grew up. Then, a few blocks away, the neighborhood where he moved when he was ten, captured in the brightness of an afternoon sun. In the background, the tips of cranes and machinery of some kind, construction going on in the neighborhood. That was normal, it happened every ten or so years, according to her father. The neighborhood had been designated historical, so the buildings could not be torn down, only maintained. But who knew how long that designation would last.

Her mother was eating while standing at the dining room table. Patricia could not tell what was on the plate—the image was too blurry, a mess of something—and she did not understand why she was so desperate to know. Her mother had been diagnosed recently with an underactive thyroid, so Patricia worried over her mother's appetite and energy levels, whether the medication had started working. Patricia's mother would say, "Worry less about what I eat and more about what you're eating; you're the one feeding two people." Again Patricia zoomed in, trying to see what was on the plate her mother held. Alas, it didn't help. She wondered when the next iteration of the camera would come out, hopefully with a higher resolution.

On the dining table, her mother's phone screen lit up, and an upbeat tune rang out loudly, so loudly Patricia had to turn down the volume on her own phone.

"What are you watching?"

Patricia put her phone facedown on her desk. Her husband, Tom, had walked into her office.

"Nothing," she said.

"Oh, I heard somebody talking."

She was supposed to be working on a pitch presentation for a potentially huge client, an account that would offer her long-term security at the agency, maybe even land her a VP position, post–maternity leave. She had a sales goal to reach, and the deadline her body had imposed on her was approaching fast.

Patricia wished she had closed her office door. It was their signal that she was in a meeting or not to be bothered. But she had left it open because the room had started to feel stuffy—she had that feeling a lot these days, that no matter where she went, she couldn't get as deep a breath as she would like.

"Oh, no." Tom pointed at Patricia's phone. "Were you spying on your parents again? You were, weren't you?"

"I was just checking in on them. It's not spying, it's called *elderly monitoring*."

"Do they know you're monitoring them?"

Patricia stared at her computer screen. She had opened her slide deck an hour earlier but had not typed anything new into it in several long days. She had planned to work on the deck whenever she had a free moment from meetings and current client work, but instead, she sat in her office, busying herself with other tasks: watching her parents, reading anxiety-ridden pregnancy forums, watching her parents, reorganizing the items on her desk . . . She billed the watching time to *Eyze–strategy development* and the rest to *admin.*

"Maybe you shouldn't do that so often?" Tom said, as he had said no fewer than five times before.

"They know I have access."

"Yeah, but it seems like a lot?"

"It's just when I'm taking breaks from this." Patricia waved her hand at the computer. "And besides, it's research for the Eyze account."

"Okay."

"Yup, okay."

Tom smiled. "So it's coming along? Feel like you'll finish in time for the big pitch?"

"Don't I always?"

"Yes, because you're the best in the biz."

Best in the biz. That was one of his sayings. Along with *Knock it out* and *Make it happen* and *Pick your battles* and *That's showbiz.* He was not especially creative when it came to his sayings.

"You're gonna knock it out," Tom said, on cue.

And yet Tom worked in creative at the agency. He was one of many designers whom Patricia rarely interacted with in the office. They'd met online, through an app, though they'd likely passed each other in the elevator or the stairwell many times. They laughed about it later. Tom claimed he'd noticed Patricia and the way she speed-walked through the building, but Patricia was not sure if this was true or something Tom said to be romantic. In any case, she had never noticed Tom until she saw his photos in the app. He was short and stocky and, she later learned, kind, which was exactly her type. He was also incredibly stylish, to the point where she felt the need to step up her own wardrobe. He wasn't the brightest person, but he was a hard worker. Over the course of their six-year relationship, he'd been a little unlucky. He'd gone through tough bosses, reorg layoffs, and bounced from agency to agency, but he remained cheerful and optimistic. Those were good qualities to have in a husband and a father. *When the going gets tough, the tough get going* was another thing he said when he was, well, going through something tough.

Patricia, on the other hand, was smarter and luckier—it wasn't strange of her to admit it to herself, since it was something Tom (and all their mutual friends and coworkers) said aloud. She had started at Dash as an intern in digital marketing, then gotten promoted halfway through the summer to a full-time assistant, thanks to a sudden opening and a good relationship with the director. Within a year, she made associate, in another two, manager, and when the digital marketing director left to become SVP at another agency, Patricia was the obvious successor. A few years in, she was up for a VP role. True, at thirty-one, she was nearly ten years younger than the last person who'd held the job, but nobody at the agency cared about age. It was far from a meritocracy, but it was one of those industries where being young and in the know was seen as a major positive. The work came naturally to her—building relationships, listening, coming up with clever ways to pitch a product, "turning it on" for clients, acting confident even if she didn't feel it. She could put on a great show.

But none of that seemed like it would help with whatever was next.

Their plan was to work and save as much money as possible up until Patricia gave birth. Tom would continue to work, obviously. His new agency job gave him a miraculous paternity leave of eight weeks that he planned to spread out over the course of six months. Patricia would take her twelve weeks all at once, then decide what to do after the baby.

After the baby.

What a strange thought.

She was currently inhabiting the before-the-baby time period, and in this time period she often missed the before-before-the-baby time period, when the baby had not been even a thought, only a potential thought far off in the future. When the only things on her mind were billable hours and pitch meetings and the unknown possibilities of what was to come.

Her plan had always been to head back west to Northern California, to find a way to work remote, or to find a new agency closer to her parents, maybe even head up her own firm—that was the direction her path seemed to be leading—but ever since marrying Tom, who was from one of those humid southeastern states and more open-minded about the possibilities of where they could "end up," that plan had faltered. Besides, Tom loved Philadelphia. And then, somewhat accidentally, because though she was smart, she was not always diligent, she got pregnant. And Tom had asked, "Why not now?" Patricia could not think of an answer. Several of her friends had gotten pregnant during the pandemic. She loved babies and had always wanted one. Hadn't she?

When she informed the agency CEO, Linda, of the pregnancy—she hadn't fully grasped by then that it was *her* pregnancy—Linda had been over-the-top supportive. The agency had always positioned itself as family-oriented. Most of the leadership team had one or more kids. "Now's the time!" Linda had said. "When you're young and your body can spring back from all the changes!" She outlined an extensive plan for Patricia—Patricia would hire another member for her team, transition work to her reports, and land a couple more clients, setting the agency up nicely for her time off—then she could come back as soon as she was ready. Linda had been the one to suggest that the VP promotion would be waiting for Patricia upon return.

It was all going to be so simple.

Her mother was singing somewhere off camera. A Chinese pop song with vibrant strings and piano was playing in the background. Her mother's voice swayed with the tune. Then her mother's phone was ringing again, and her mother was yell-talking. Another fear: that her mother was losing her hearing. However, she had been a loud talker for as long as Patricia could remember, so perhaps her mother's hearing had always been a little off. (What did this mean for Patricia's future hearing? For the baby's future hearing?) Patricia had met a client recently who reminded her of her mother, though the two women behaved and looked nothing alike. She had thought of her mother only because the client, a CMO at a liquor company, also spoke loudly and forcefully, often talking over others, then would ask people to repeat themselves. "What did you say? Talk louder!" Her mother always asked: "What? Huh? Did you say something?" The client pulled back her hair on one side of her face, revealing a small hearing aid tucked away; she had been born partially deaf in her right ear. Maybe nobody had ever caught Patricia's mother's deaf right ear. There could be a genetic issue with hearing in their family, and Patricia should look into that, ask the doctor whether that was something they could test the baby for. Or Patricia's mother was only going deaf with old age.

Once her mother was off the phone, she went back to singing. She was often off-pitch, the lyrics timed just slightly behind the music, but there was an enthusiasm and joy in her voice that Patricia appreciated. When she had FaceTimed her mother with the news, it had been in the middle of one of those singing sessions, and her mother had held the camera too close to her face, showing mostly dark caverns of nose and mouth as she sang along to an incomprehensible song. And in that moment, Patricia had been embarrassed. For what? For herself or her mother? Her mother said, "What, you don't like my singing?" then continued to sing. Patricia turned the volume down, cringing, and her insides were making strange churns, indicating the new life growing inside her, or the symptoms that came with that new life: acid reflux, unpleasant bowel movements, unusual cravings.

Patricia's mother had cried at the news, from joy. "I wish I could be there to give you a hug! When will you come home?"

When Patricia had said she didn't know, that it wasn't likely to be soon, with everything going on, her mother continued to cry, from disappointment.

Her father had been more stoic. And she had chosen a different medium, one that she did not tell Tom she used, because he might make her feel creepy about it. The Eyze Cams came with speakers, which she and Tom had used to scold their dog from time to time, when they'd worked late in the office and caught him chewing an item he wasn't meant to be chewing. So occasionally, when she watched her father and saw an opening to speak, she would. She pressed and held the microphone button:

Hello? . . . Hello? . . . Hello?

"What the hell? Who's there?"

It's me.

"That you, Patricia?"

Press and hold: *Yeah, it's me.*

"Wow, what's up? These cameras can talk? Can you see me waving? Can you see this show I'm watching? This guy travels around the world and films himself checking out different spots. Here, can you see it if I turn the camera this way? I think this guy makes a lot of money going around with his camera. He definitely gets free stuff. Food. Clothes. You ever think about doing this? You'd be good at it. This one, he's eating a famous steak in Florence. Watch the way he eats it!"

I can barely see it on my phone.

"Okay, watch some other time on your own."

Dad.

"Yeah?"

I want to tell you something.

After she told her father, he sat there silent and unmoving in his lounge chair, staring at the man eating the steak on his TV. She thought maybe he hadn't heard her. She asked if he'd heard her.

"I heard you," he said, and got up, with some effort.

He walked slowly over to the kitchen area of his apartment and picked up the teakettle on the stove. He poured the water into a small cup.

"It's good," he said. "Give me a minute."

She watched him sip from the cup. In the background, she could catch a few words from the steak-eating man, something about *how refreshing . . . a new place . . . new people.* Patricia was familiar with the tone. The YouTuber was selling a lifestyle, just as she was paid to do. Her father walked back toward the living area and up to the camera.

He put his face square with the camera, so she could see the blurry wrinkles of his forehead and the fuzziness of his eyebrows. "Can you see me okay?"

Yeah, I can see you.

"I'm thinking maybe you should move back here before the baby comes. Your mother can help you. I'm not much help these days, but I can do a little here, a little there. I don't see your mother much, but you know, if I ask her to pick something up for me, she usually does it. Takes a while, but she does it. For you, she'll be more helpful."

Patricia was crying. She couldn't control her emotions as well as she used to. They came in these waves, without warning. But through this medium, weirdly, she was offered a bit of needed privacy. Her father could not see or even hear her unless she pressed that microphone button.

"Are you still watching me?"

A brief *yes* choked out on her part.

"Anyway, that's what I'm thinking," he repeated.

At what point had Patricia started to think of her parents as elderly?

This was a potential question she could ask in the end-user

survey. She needed to create a set of audience personas for the camera company as they targeted these new customers along the buyer's journey. The obvious people were professional caretakers and adult children of elderly parents. But in what contexts did monitoring become a necessity? What pain points motivated a person to buy a camera for watching their parents? Patricia's parents both lived alone—that was definitely a pain point worth leveraging in the pitches. Perhaps she should use herself as a model for persona development:

PATRICIA LIU, 31

DEMOGRAPHICS:

- Owns a home in the city-burbs of Philadelphia
- Married, pregnant with first child, employed
- College-educated
- Salary: $100,000–150,000; combined family income: $200,000–$300,000
- Active social platforms: Twitter, LinkedIn, Instagram, TikTok, Pinterest

GOALS:

- Wants to know that her parents are safe at home
- Wants to be able to seamlessly check in on parents without them becoming upset that she's checking in on them
- Would also like safety at her own home, to check in on her dog when she's away

MOTIVATIONS:

- Safety, comfort

- Desire for insight into situations where she's not physically present
- Fear of an emergency situation

FRUSTRATIONS/PAIN POINTS:

- Lives across the country from parents, so can't help as much as she wants
- Camera does not offer clarity of in-person senses
- Guilt over potentially invading parents' privacy (note: may need to reword)
- Deeper guilt over not being able to do to more for her parents

What kind of messaging would work on somebody like her? *Care for your loved ones with your Eyze. . . . Keep your family company no matter the distance?* Maybe the cameras needed an emergency response feature? Something to alert her when her parents called for help? That way, she might not need to *always* watch them. But was that really why she was looking at the camera feeds?

On paper, she was the ideal customer, but she was evolving into something else, possibly great or possibly terrible. As her due date approached, she didn't just check in on her parents, she watched them on a daily basis, multiple times a day, a few minutes here, often much longer. If they were home—which her father almost always was and her mother far less—she liked to keep the camera's app on in the background for hours as she arranged the nursery, which was coming together, sort of. That was her life these days: in a state of sort of coming together. She could hear her father's TV droning in the background, the occasional cough and clearing of his throat, the shuffling of his feet from one room to another. Then she switched to her mother's singing, the sound of the refrigerator opening and closing, a loud voice on the phone. If she switched back and forth enough times, it began to feel as though they were all together in the same space, even if it was only in Patricia's head.

She wondered if the baby could hear them, and if the noises sounded natural to the baby or staticky and distant (did babies understand static?). Could Eyze Cam do something about the static? Patricia would glance every now and then to watch her parents' movements. At what point would her child meet these people with whom Patricia was so clearly obsessed?

And now she was bringing another being into the world, giving them no choice in the matter. Giving them no choice to be forever attached to her, for however long she lived.

Was that cruel?

Her parents hadn't asked her if she wanted to exist before making it happen, and despite it being the only way to bring life into this world, there were times throughout Patricia's existence when she'd found this arrangement deeply unfair.

It seemed inevitable that she would cause this child pain. Unknowingly—maybe even knowingly—and then, simply, just by being. By getting older and then leaving. Some matters were within her control, which she would try very hard to adjust for the baby, such as: her impatience, her lack of organization (see, again: her getting pregnant while on birth control), her nosiness. And then there were the matters outside of her control:

economic collapse, impending food scarcity, the destruction of the earth.

And then, also inevitable, the child would one day cause her pain in return, as, Patricia sensed, she was doing to her parents by not coming home.

She would frequently fall asleep in front of her computer, with her office door closed. Tom likely assumed she was making good progress on her proposals and her decks—all of her work—as she always had. But she felt so tired, as if her entire life of striving had come to catch up with her, and she had nothing left to give. She had heard the term *burnout* and found it ridiculous. Now it was the most apt description for her state. She truly felt burnt from the inside out.

One of her coworkers had told her about the second-trimester energy boost, but so far, Patricia had experienced only the kind of energy that made it impossible to feel rested. Sometimes she would wake up in the darkness of her office and reach for her belly to check that it was still there, not a figment of her imagination. She had terrible dreams, about blacking out and not knowing what had happened to her, about people throughout her life who had died, about screaming at her parents for . . . she often couldn't remember. Other times she would wake up and forget she was pregnant, and she would be shocked at the weight and the sight of her body. In those moments, she would wonder what her parents were doing. She would open the camera app. Would her child feel the same toward her and Tom? Would it be this strong a tug?

She wished she could ask this child, *Is this what you want?* And receive a response. Sometimes she would ask the question aloud, then wait for any sense of murmuring or movement inside her, any sign or signal that the baby was saying yes or no. But she could never discern an answer.

It occurred to Patricia that her parents could watch the baby grow through the camera. Why not also target parents of newborns who lived far from family? This was a new use case she was going to mention in the next Eyze meeting. Patricia's parents could even monitor the evolution of the nursery during the last two months of her pregnancy. Patricia moved the camera pointed at the dog's bowl into the guest room turned nursery, placing it on a bookshelf Tom installed. She checked the angle—the almost finished crib and the nursing chair were in view, the window behind the chair outside the frame, so nothing would ever look backlit. She shared the camera with her father's and mother's accounts, then texted them individually to alert them.

Her father called. "The app doesn't work," he said.

"What do you mean?"

"It says . . . log in with your username and password?"

"How long has it been logged out?"

"Oh, I don't know, I never open it."

"Well, do you remember your username and password?"

"Just send me pictures," her father said.

"But with the video, you'll be able to check in on the baby whenever you want," Patricia said.

"Watch the baby do what? Sleep and cry? When I can't even hold or touch them? No, you just send me pictures when you can. The video will be too hard," he said.

He didn't know how often she watched him, watched replays of him puttering around his apartment, and yes, how hard it was.

Her mother, the more technologically savvy, was more enthused. "Yay! I can watch the baby grow even when I'm not there!"

Patricia made a mental note to develop a use-case persona around her mother rather than her father.

Another sleepless night after another day of falling behind in work. Linda had expressed some concern over Patricia's performance. Well, not directly her performance. Linda had said, "Are you sure you don't want to start your maternity leave a bit earlier?" Patricia could feel that VP title slipping away from her. She wanted to stick to the plan—but the plan no longer seemed to include her. She tried to write all her thoughts down. For someone who had prided herself for years on finding the right words to persuade, she was at a loss. She looked at her computer's screen. She tried pen and paper. All she got down was: *Tom, I'm thinking*

What was she thinking?

She decided to film herself thinking out loud. She'd heard that some famous author had written a whole book by speaking it into a tape recorder, then had a secretary or intern transcribe the whole thing. Why not employ the same methods?

This. This was only a small letter. A small note. Some ideas she had. For her husband, who was away at a weekend conference. Who was hoping to network his way into a better job.

She started. . . .

You're a charming guy with a sturdy, trustworthy face, so people like you. I hope you get a new job, because maybe I don't want to work anymore? I know this sounds crazy, but I just feel like, like, I don't care anymore. I mean, no, I do care, to a certain extent. Like, does it make me sad that I'm probably not getting that VP title because I've been fucking up lately? Sure. But in the grand scheme of things, it doesn't matter. I mean, do you see my body? It's insane. And all I'm thinking is, What are my parents up to? That's kind of weird. I know you think it's weird. I can see you watching me, with that look, like, Is she losing it? Do crazy people know they're crazy? This is normal for pregnancy, though, I read it on a forum. Don't worry. It's just, well, I really think we should ask our agencies if we can work from California. Or who cares if they say yes, we can just go, go now, before it's too late. I feel like it's going to be too late really soon. Do you feel that? I know it's expensive, but you're always saying pick your battles and, well, this is the battle I'm deciding to pick. I want to go home. Fuck, I'm crying now. I told myself I wouldn't cry. I mean, if you don't want to, I might just have to go on my own. I want to be close to my parents. Yes, I know that's absurd. It's absurd, but it's true. I'm a full-grown adult, married, with a life growing inside her, and I want my mom and dad. Is that so wrong? Well, I think it's messed up that we have these little insular immediate families that function on their own without the larger family, network, community. So much so that we need to sell cameras to people so they can watch their families! Wow, that's my job. That's depressing. Honestly, I think my parents might help me raise this kid better than you. No, that was mean. I'm sorry. I didn't mean it. Of course I want you with me, with us. So we can't live with my parents because, well, their places are tiny. Maybe you can live with my dad and I live with my mom? Or no, let's just sell our house and rent a spot. A little two-bedroom, live simply, live close to people who really care about us. You think Linda really cares about me? As soon as my proposals got a little sloppy, she's like, Hm, what are we going to do with Patricia? We can't kick her to curb with a baby inside her, but maybe we can transition her out of the director position? I see her scheming. Well, I'm scheming, too!

Afterward, Patricia watched herself rambling on the screen. At first she could get through only the first minute or so before pausing the video. She looked unhinged and wild, her hair greasy and flat yet still somehow pointing in different directions atop her head. The whites of her eyes were pink, and her pupils were huge. Her skin was breaking out, as it had been for the last two months, but it looked especially sad through the blue light of the screen. She hit play again and noticed that her words garbled, her mouth moving sometimes slower, sometimes faster, than her mind. Nonetheless, the words came out forcefully. She believed herself. She wasn't putting on a show for anyone. She was finally saying exactly what she meant to say, even if it came out a mess. A mess was okay. It was more than okay. It was fascinating. Watching herself through the camera's eye, she realized how much she had changed, not only in the last six months but perhaps years, a current that had only grown stronger.

Patricia decided not to send the video to Tom. Something about it felt deeply personal, meant as a record solely for herself, like a diary entry. Besides, she had exhausted herself in creating it and fallen into the deepest sleep she'd had in a long time. When she woke up the next morning, everything inside her felt aligned, so she did what she did best. She made a deck on why the two of them should move to California before the baby was born. It was less than two months away, but it was doable. When Tom returned home, she made him sit through her presentation. He listened quietly, then, to her great relief, said, "Let's make it happen."

In the weeks since, Patricia had decided she'd rather take a break from work than continue remotely. She told herself it was her choice, and not because she sensed Linda would say no anyway. Besides, it felt like she was stepping into a wide-open field after walking a long, narrow trail. She put in her notice ("I support your decision," Linda had said, and as Patricia's luck would have it, Linda graciously offered to have her official end date happen after maternity leave). Tom had negotiated working remotely for the time being, and the two of them had worked their way through everything they'd needed to do: found a rental (in a role reversal, Patricia's mother had sent her the listing and viewed it for them), listed their house for sale (her father had put them in touch with an old real estate friend who, coincidentally, now worked in Philly), chosen a new ob-gyn, and begun their packing. They had become a family unit driven by a single mission. It motivated them into quick action.

Patricia was packing items in the nursery when she realized that in all the commotion, she had not opened the Eyze Cam app in weeks. In part, she hadn't needed to check in on her parents, since she was talking to them on a daily basis. She took the camera down from the bookshelf and unplugged it, placing it in one of the many cardboard boxes. She wasn't sure how she would use it next. Perhaps as a baby monitor, though there were likely much better products on the market for that use case.

Patricia took out her phone to check on her parents.

Her father was writing in his calendar book. Maybe he was marking the day when Patricia would return home. Maybe he was marking the day of the birth. Her mother was sitting at the dining room table, drinking what looked to be coffee. She was smiling, possibly thinking about Patricia's return home. Tom came into the room to check on her.

"What's up with your parents?" he said.

"Oh, nothing much," Patricia said, feeling, for the first time in a long time, deeply refreshed.

TOMB SWEEPING

WHEN THE MEDIUM WALKED INTO THE SEA AND VANISHED BE-neath the crest of a dark wave, it was clear that our ancestors were taking a man considered unfit for the world as they had known it.

It was exactly one year ago. Qingming. Also called Tomb Sweeping Day, Clear and Bright Festival, Ghosts' Day, Pure Brightness Festival, Ancestors' Day, and Cold Food Festival. That morning, before the light came out, my father, mother, and I walked two blocks from our apartment to the bus station, where we boarded the cemetery's shuttle for the half-hour trip to the graveyard where my grandparents are buried. We sat in the company of others like us, the sleepy-eyed living in need of paying respects to our dead.

The shuttle smelled of mildew and stale perfume. A pink plastic grocery bag filled with stacks of spirit cash sat on my lap, while in my mother's arms lay two rolls of incense. My father flipped through the day's newspaper, the rustling of its thin sheets the only sound to punctuate the low snores of sleeping passengers.

We were visiting my mother's parents, who had died in consecutive years, her father only six months prior and her mother the year before. They were still transitioning into their other life, my mother explained, so they needed our help most on their first Qingming together. Hence the spirit money, bright-colored ten-thousand-yuan notes—the largest we could find. On them, the Jade Emperor stared serenely upon a scene of symbols: a vase of lotus flowers, a phoenix, a dragon. Purity, grace, strength.

When we arrived, we headed to the cemetery store. The place was crowded with other families stocking up on tombstone goods and decorations—fruits, packaged nuts, red and gold ribbons, tall and short and thick and thin sticks of incense, and of course, many varieties of spirit money. I watched a small child pull at the knee of his mother's pant leg, screaming out in hunger, begging to eat the oranges they'd brought for a grave. The mother ignored her boy and looked as though she might soon echo his wailing. My own mother was past the teary, enraged stages of grief. She was action-oriented, determined. She headed straight to the flower arrangements, snatched two of the last colorful bouquets, and marched them over to the register's line.

As my father and I waited, a man walked by with a bag full of golden paper xìsī, the little wealth pots looking like boats ready to set sail. In one woman's arms I saw a silver paper BMW the size of my torso; the people following her carried other large items: a three-story house made of golden bricks; a box of what looked like iPhones and iPads; and, most absurd, a gleaming paper washing machine with a red warranty sticker on its door. I wanted to laugh, but the sight filled me with fear. What if this woman and her family were on to something? My grandparents would be among the lesser spirits whose descendants had neglected to provide for them. I saw them riding a crowded bus, washing their clothes at the communal laundry, wandering the streets jealous of those staring at the glowing screens of their electronics.

"Are you sure we brought enough money?" I said to my father, who was now deeply focused on his own phone.

"Ya lah, enough," he said. "Your grandparents will have a happy time in death."

He did not glance up from what I assumed was the real estate news. I knew he didn't particularly enjoy taking part in traditional ceremonies, but he did so, out of a sense of filial obedience. He told me he had his eyes on our future. The Singapore property market was slipping, and that was the perfect time to buy, he said many times at the dinner table. Get in when others are getting out.

When my mother was done, the three of us crisscrossed the paths of the cemetery with her leading the way, the map in her hand marked with a black X for my grandparents' gravesite, a place we had been only three times—once for each burial, and last Qingming, when Waigong was alive. "Here," my mother said when we reached a slab of reddish-brown marble, which looked identical to many other tombstones. A large family not more than five feet to our left played repetitive Buddhist chants from a small Bluetooth speaker. Though the music was not directly for my grandparents, I thought it was lucky for them to have pleasant neighbors in their new home.

My mother placed the flowers down. "Pile the money out," she said, pointing to the ground beside the bouquets. I did as she told me. She handed my father and me three sticks of incense each, keeping three for herself, pulled a red lighter out of her purse, and lit them all.

"Baba, Mama, it's Shu," my mother said. "We're here to help you in your journey. Everything is good with us. Ling Ling is getting big. Can you believe she will be twelve next month! She misses you." My mother nudged me toward the tombstone. "Tell Waigong and Waipo how you're doing."

I shuffled forward and stared at the red-painted names, lingering on my grandfather's. I wondered if he was hovering there listening to me, or if he was more skilled and could reach into my mind from somewhere afar. The possibilities prickled my arms. Even in their sickly old age, their hands wrinkled and spotted, their pink gums toothless without dentures, my grandparents rarely frightened me. Their existence in death was a different story.

"Waigong, Waipo," I said to the marble, trying hard to keep my mind clear of bad thoughts. "I wish you were here for my birthday. I hope you are in a happy place now. School's good." I paused and looked to my mother to see if this was enough.

She raised her eyebrows. "What about school is good?"

"Biology and art and history," I continued. "History especially. We're going over the Battle of Singapore, which is easy since I know so much already. I'm ahead of the lesson plans, so Mama and Baba are happy. We're going to Changi Beach tonight. Don't worry, we'll make sure to burn plenty of money for Bogong."

My mother nodded at me and looked to my father, who stepped forward and said a few unremarkable words for my grandparents. The monotony of his voice made it clear that he was meditating on the day's real estate news. But then he looked directly at my grandfather's tombstone and said, "I hope you know I am respecting your wishes about Changi Beach and will not be going." He kowtowed at the grave. My mother stiffened with a sharp breath, but she did not say anything. Then we kowtowed together and placed our incense in the small holders drilled into the tombstone's base.

"Here is plenty of money to get you through," my mother said.

She flicked the lighter on and held its flame to the edge of the cash pile. In seconds, the thin paper caught fire. We stood there watching the spirit money burn at a bright pace, and as the bills turned to ashes and the embers and smoke flickered up into the spirit world, I pictured a pile of money appearing on my grandparents' translucent laps as they stared expectantly down upon us.

Our next Qingming concern was Bogong. I was nervous. When we went to Changi Beach last year, Waigong had been alive and angry.

There had been a new medium leading the prayers, one who had joined the temple only months prior despite some protest from a set of temple-goers, my grandfather among them. At the sight of the medium, my grandfather had muttered to my parents that it was inappropriate for this man to conduct Qingming rituals at the beach.

"He's mixed up," I heard my grandfather mumble.

My mother tried to calm him, said that if the temple leaders had chosen him for the job, then we should all try to accept it. The war was so long ago, after all, she said. At this, my grandfather spat into the sand and demanded to be taken back home. "Should? Long ago?" he muttered.

My mother tried to reason with him. "Please, Baba," she said. "We're here to honor your brother."

My grandfather began coughing loudly, catching the attention of those at the beach and, worse, the medium. I still see him there, a man in his late thirties, much younger than the other mediums, with a sadness that enhanced his glamorous face, a face that reminded me of men's cologne and watch ads. And what struck me, even from the distance of that first year, were the large tattoos coloring his forearms—a green dragon twisted on the right, a red phoenix unfurled on the left.

Waigong raised his voice. "Honor my brother? Honor my brother? This is not honoring my brother. This is disrespectful. To my brother and the men who died alongside him. For this man–" My grandfather pointed a finger at the medium, who was standing less than twenty feet away by the firepit where the money smoke rose.

My mother pushed his hand down. "Baba, please," she said.

"No! Those murderers have no right to step in this country, let alone this beach!"

Other people from temple began shuffling, some away from the medium, others away from my grandfather. The air around my family seemed to tremble with unease.

The medium looked away from us.

My father wrapped his arm around my grandfather's shoulders and whispered something in his ear, ushering him back the way we had come. My mother and I followed.

As we walked back to the shuttle stop, my grandfather looked behind us and nodded. I turned to see–there were around ten others, mostly older men and women, following us out. A few gave my grandfather sharp nods of acknowledgment. Beyond them, I saw a sparser crowd with the medium, who was hunched, head down, next to the pit.

When we got back home, my grandfather was still in a foul mood, only now he felt justified and was taking it out on my mother.

"Shu! Shu, look at me! Why did you try to stop me?" said Waigong. "Are you ashamed of me? But you see, other people felt the same once I spoke up. Your own husband agrees. Don't you, Zang? We were all already thinking the same."

My mother moved around the living room, tidying wordlessly. She knew not to speak against her father in those moments. My father poured Waigong a cup of medicinal wine. I was trying to slink away to my bedroom when Waigong noticed and called me over to him.

"Ling Ling, come," he said, patting the couch. "You remember the story of your bogong, right?"

I nodded. I had heard it directly from Waigong before, a handful of times, on special occasions or during his special moods. I didn't want to hear it then, but obligation—the same obligation that kept my father performing ceremonies he didn't care for, the same obligation that kept my mother silent in the face of her father's wrath—pulled me to the seat beside my grandfather.

He smiled and said, "You're a good granddaughter. You're very good, like your bogong.

"He was always so good. The best brother. The best son. So we knew something had gone wrong after he didn't show up to dinner one night without telling us. After three missed dinners, my baba went looking for him. He knew that your bogong was involved with a group of young communists. He knew that my brother had been vocal at public gatherings, at restaurants, in the streets. Gege wasn't keeping a low profile; he wasn't blending in with the times. Nobody knew about the executions at that point, but people knew that men of the wrong disposition were prone to disappear. Maybe to camps, maybe to prisons: always to another place, another world. He searched desperately, but my father couldn't find Gege.

"Instead, he ran into a longtime neighborhood friend, briskly walking, practically jogging, his way back to the area. He's gone, the friend said. They've taken him. And that was enough for my father to know that the only thing to do was to wait, which is what he did. He drank himself into a dedicated madness.

"Like I said, we did not immediately know what had happened. But over the next few months, there were rumors. Our neighbors and schoolmates would whisper to one another—and it eventually reached us—that the Japanese troops had taken dozens of the neighborhood's men to Changi Beach and shot them in the back at the water's edge. Soon we all knew it to be true, though no Japanese would admit it. Those soldiers brought men to that beach, killing them at low tide so the sea would do the work of sweeping the bodies away. That beach is a mass graveyard.

"They took him," Waigong said between sips of his wine. "He had just started college. He had ideals and dreams."

My grandfather pulled out a weathered black-and-white portrait, one I knew he kept with him at all times, of himself and his brother at ages five and eleven. In it, his brother stands behind him, hands on the younger boy's shoulders in a strong but gentle grip. Their mouths are straight lines, and they look out of the photo with a seriousness I've never seen in living children.

"It's a terrible shame you two could never meet. You look so alike, you know?"

It stung to be compared to a boy and, worse yet, a dead one. When I later voiced my concern privately to my mother, she told me that my grandfather meant it as a true compliment—he idolized his brother, and if he saw his brother in me, it must mean he loved me deeply. Besides, his brother was beautiful: high cheekbones and forehead, flawless skin, unusually large eyes, hollowed cheeks that radiated soulfulness. I didn't see much of a resemblance when I looked in the mirror; my own cheeks were full, like a doll's. If I sucked them in and opened my eyes large enough, I maybe passed for a crazed, longhaired version of Bogong.

But still, I let my grandfather hold my face in his crooked, age-spotted hands, and I let him look at me and see something that I suspected wasn't there.

"The girls chased him, but all he cared about were his books," he said. "And his family. Family and study always number one. Remember that. My gege took care of me every day, until the day he disappeared at Changi Beach."

Not long after that Qingming, my grandfather offered me a brown paper bag with pink tissue paper flowering from its mouth. "For you, my sweet Ling Ling. Something Bogong would have liked you to have."

I reached into the bag and pulled out a large square book. On its thick cover was a black-and-white photograph of a residential street decorated with a Japanese flag hanging from each home. The title, *The Japanese Occupation 1942–1945: A Pictorial Record of Singapore During the War,* was printed above the photo. Stamped at the bottom of the cover was the National Heritage Board logo, a striped vase with decorative curlicues spilling out of its edges in perfect symmetry. I traced my hand over the book, its soft matte cover silky under my skin.

"Thank you, Waigong. I promise to take good care of it," I said.

"It's important to learn about your past. Read it carefully. There are lots of pictures, so you can see what really happened."

"Yes, Waigong."

"I have a copy myself, so ask any questions as you read. We can discuss. I have notes on important pages. You can have them to help your reading."

"Yes, Waigong."

My grandfather smiled and patted the book's cover with his hand. "Your bogong used to read so much. He could swallow a book like this in an hour."

To be honest, this isn't an entirely forthcoming account of the way my grandfather spoke of Bogong, but I'm afraid of further disturbing his spirit. He almost always remained composed when he spoke to me, but in the conversations with my parents and his friends that I overheard, he was different. Their talk of the past could go on for hours, warped by the slamming of hands on tables, long stretches of embittered silence, and those cracked-voice racial slurs.

After getting me the book, my grandfather often offered to read chapters aloud together. I refused many times, not wanting him to turn into that sour version of himself, but he was relentless in his last months, and one day I finally accepted.

On that occasion, my grandfather suggested Chapter Four. I shuddered. It was titled "*Sook Ching* (Purge through Purification)." We sat at the kitchen table, each with our individual copy of the book opened before us. With his face in the pages and his bald head shining toward me, he read, "'A most terrifying feature of the *Sook Ching,* well remembered by most people, was the identification parade. People were made to pass in a single file before a row of hooded informers. A nod of the head from any one of these hooded informers signified recognition and the victim was immediately picked out and sent to a detention room. Most people who were picked up for questioning were never seen again.'

"It's what *they* put your bogong through! Can you imagine, Ling Ling? A wicked, spineless person, just nodding away your life?" My grandfather eyed me intently. I could sense him slipping away.

"No, Waigong. I can't," I said. "It sounds very unfair."

"It was more than unfair. It was cruel and evil and cowardly. Now, you look here. 'Many people disappeared without a trace. Today, the number of Chinese massacred during the *Sook Ching* is an issue of much speculation.' What kind of speculation, ah?

The Japanese say fewer than five thousand people killed. A joke! What happened to the tens of thousands of others? What happened to them, leh? They just disappear on their own? You understand why I was so upset by that medium, hor? He's mixed up, in blood and head! It should never be speculation, what they did to your bogong! What they got next, they deserved. No Japanese, part Chinese or not, should have the right to step on that beach and disturb the dead."

I squirmed in my seat, not wanting to be the subject of my grandfather's watery, chilled eyes. I wanted to find a way to escape, for him to look away from me, for him not to see Bogong in my face. In the direct glare of his feeling, I realized how broken Waigong had been. Though my grandfather was only twelve during the Battle of Singapore, he remembered the fear and the chaos and the hate and the revenge for the rest of his life.

Now I know that his spirit, too, will never forget.

He died only a few weeks later. Of old age and pneumonia, my parents said, he had been deteriorating for months. I know it was from something much worse.

By the time we returned home from the cemetery, it was past lunch. My mother made me a quick meal of soy sauce eggs with rice from the Zojirushi cooker and suggested that, given the early morning and long evening ahead, I relax until we had to leave for Changi Beach.

I went to my room and pulled the book from my grandfather off of its dusty spot on the shelf. It still looked brand-new. I had not looked at it since that day with Waigong. Life without my grandparents, especially my grandfather, had been both sad and liberating to me. I had lost their comforting presence, but I also didn't have to think about anything beyond school, my friends, and the daily chores my mother and father gave me. The past, however, wrapped its arms around me on Qingming. I opened the book to a photo of dozens of children pressed up next to one another in a big crowd, their hands raised, their mouths open in cheering. Some were frozen in the middle of waving small flags, though I couldn't tell what kind of flags they were waving. *Children celebrating the end of the Japanese occupation of Singapore,* stated the caption. I looked over every child's face, in search of my grandfather, but did not find him. He could have been any one of them.

I remembered seeing my grandfather hunched over the book at the dining room table, how he looked over all of the photos, his eyes flitting left and right and back again, and it occurred to me that he had been looking for his brother in the images. In those photos of Japanese soldiers prodding blindfolded dead men with their rifles; in the photos of Chinese men in tattered clothing on their knees, their hands tied behind their back, faces resigned yet stoic; in the photos of decapitated heads on the beach. I prayed that, like me, he hadn't found anything.

I rested my cheek on the cool wooden tabletop and fell asleep.

The sound of my door creaking open woke me, and I lifted my head to see my mother walking toward me. "Ling Ling, get ready to go," she said. "Oh, you're reading that book? I'm sure Waigong is watching and very happy with you." She kissed the top of my head.

"Mama, I had a weird dream," I said.

"Tell me later, after you get ready, okay?"

"Is Baba coming?"

"No, he says he needs to stay home to get work done."

My father did not look up from his computer as we walked

out. I could not tell if my father truly cared about Waigong's wishes, as he had claimed at the grave, or if he was using it as an excuse not to partake in further ceremonies, or if it was maybe some of both. "Be good, ah," I heard him say as the door closed.

We went to the same bus stop as the one we'd gone to in the morning. I decided it was better not to tell my mother my dream, and she must have forgotten because she did not ask. We rode the bus past Toa Payoh, the Paya Lebar Air Base, and the Bedok Reservoir, along Upper Changi Road, toward Changi Airport, beside which was the white and gray building of the Japanese School, all the way to where northern tip meets the water. When we got off, I looked across Changi Beach with its park benches, coconut palms, barbecue pits, white sand, and blue-green waters. In the sky, a plane flew away like a messenger bird. The sun had set but still provided enough light by which to see a small group of familiar people huddled around one of the pits. It was an even thinner crowd than the one we had left behind the year before. As we walked toward them, a few waved at us.

There he was. The same medium, guiding the group in a prayer, his head bowed, his long black hair tied neatly into a bun. He looked up and smiled at me as we joined the group. Confused and worried, I managed a fragment of a smile in return. Ever since the previous year, we'd seen the medium in passing at temple events. Our family had kept our distance. After throwing the rest of my spirit cash into the pit and mumbling a few prayers to no one, I wandered away from the group and walked toward the water. I stood there, watching the sea turn black.

"It's beautiful," I heard the medium say next to me.

I nodded without turning to look at him.

All I wanted was to push the images from the book, of bodies and heads spread across the beach, out of my mind. I wanted to see Bogong as a ten-year-old boy enjoying the softness of the sand, him and my grandfather splashing carefree across the shoreline. This was a place where people now picnicked and flew kites and watched planes fly above. It was not a place where people should think of massacres.

"I had a weird dream," I said, feeling like I had to tell someone.

"Mmm," the medium said encouragingly.

"My grandfather and I stood on this beach," I continued. "It looked different, though. The sand was a dark red, and giant lotus flowers the size of these palm trees lined the shore. They were opening and closing their petals in this sad, slow way. There weren't any barbecue pits or tents. And my grandfather began to cry. I can't find my gege, he kept saying. His brother was killed here."

"How terrible," said the medium, his voice soft.

"And in the dream, my grandfather's tears spilled out of his whole face and onto the sand so heavy that the whole beach shook beneath my feet. Then this little boy ran up to me and grabbed my leg. He was yelling at me not to go. I couldn't move or say anything. Then I realized the little boy was my grandfather and that I was his brother."

The medium placed a hand on my shoulder, and in his touch, I felt protected. I realized I liked the medium, despite my grandfather's and the temple-goers' various remarks. He was cheerful and optimistic every time I saw him. He laughed a lot, in an uninhibited, mouth-wide-open way. And he was a good listener.

We stood for a long time in a warm silence.

"That sounds like a very important dream," he finally said.

"What does it mean to be mixed up?" I asked, thinking of my grandfather's accusations.

The medium laughed softly, as though to blanket a cry. "I

don't know," he said. He drew a circle in the sand with his bare toes. "I don't like to think of myself that way. I like, instead, to think that my parents put me in perfect symmetry with this country's history. Perhaps it's better to think that people like me are not mixed up, as some might say, but that we have access to more than one side of the story."

The air felt as though it shifted around us, replacing the warmth of the medium's presence with something else, something unfamiliar.

"It is time for me to go into the water, Ling Ling," the medium said, his voice deeper and more resonant than before. "It is time to pay respect to our ancestors. Your grandfather and his brother and the thousands of others."

He stepped away from me. I wanted to reach out and touch him, to let him know that I was not like my grandfather. But I could sense that the medium was no longer himself. Still, I knew he shouldn't go, that the water wasn't his place. But, as in the dream, I couldn't move or say anything. I had never seen someone possessed before. I wanted to get my mother, or somebody, anybody, who could stop the medium and whatever—whoever—was compelling him to walk away.

Instead, I watched him glide into the sea, first to his ankles, then to his thighs. He stood in one spot for some time—seconds or minutes, I'm not sure—and then began to sway gently from left to right.

The waters were very much black by then, but I could see the waves splashing against the medium's legs like a loose dress. And there, in the splashing, I saw the tendrils of spirits reach up from their watery homes.

For those short moments, I forgot the medium's place in our world. He looked exactly how I thought mediums should always look, standing mystical under a bright yellow moon, spirits within him, surrounding him.

Just as I began to relax into the sight, the medium let out a low-pitched scream. It was a scream that sounded more surprised than pained, but it was too short to say for sure. A large wave rolled in, cutting off the sound and engulfing the medium.

He disappeared.

"Mama!" I heard myself say. "Mama! Mama!" She broke away from the group and walked toward me. "The medium. He's gone. He's gone into the sea."

"What? What you saying? Why you like that?"

"The sea. The spirits took him."

My mother looked at me with panicked eyes. "Stay," she said.

She jogged back toward the others and called to some of the men in the group. I wanted to run with her. I wanted to get into the sea and find the medium. I wanted to curl up on the sand and disappear, too.

One man sprinted into the water but returned, yelling that he couldn't see anything in the darkness. Everyone called out the medium's name, their voices swallowed by the waves. After a futile fifteen minutes, somebody called the police. By the time the police arrived, we were all huddled by the barbecue pit. My mother had her arm around me and was whispering, "It's okay, it's okay," in my ear. The police asked me questions that I did not know how to answer. Why did he go in the water? How did he look before he went in? Was there anything strange that you remember?

I tried to tell them that the medium had sounded different, but I could manage only crying into my mother's shirtsleeve.

"It's okay, we can talk another time. Go home and sleep now," an officer said. My mother and I did go home, but I lay awake in bed all night, afraid to fall asleep.

They found his body the next morning, not one mile out from the beach. At breakfast, my father read the news story off his phone and recited the facts, salting it with commentary.

It said that the medium died performing a Qingming ritual.

"What kind of ritual is walking to drown in water?"

It speculated that he had been possessed by a god.

"Impossible! No god would deem him worthy."

The medium was married with a child

"That poor kid will be very troubled now."

The paper quoted his wife, who said that the medium should not have gone into the water. That he could not swim.

"This man sure got something wrong."

The medium's wife said that he was a good man.

Snort, cough.

The newspaper did not mention any spirits taking the medium away.

"It's just like your father said," my father said, looking at my mother. "So he was a good person, you say? Maybe. But if your parents made mistakes, and their parents made worse mistakes, and their parents made even worse mistakes, you can't live your life thinking that nobody has to pay for those mistakes, can you?"

My mother gathered our dishes and washed them at the sink, silent.

"You have to pay," my father said. He looked to me for a response.

"I thought you only cared about the future," I said quietly.

"What did you say?"

My mother gave me a look, eyebrows raised, eyes wide. *Don't,* the look said. *Be good.*

"Nothing. I'm going to do homework now," I said, though it was a Sunday.

My father nodded. "Okay, go lah," he said.

I went to my room and got into bed. When I closed my eyes, all I could see were the shimmering spirit arms—Waigong's, Bogong's, all the others—reaching for the medium in the water. I opened my eyes and saw on my desk the book lying open from the day before. I cursed it under my breath; the dead thing didn't know how much had changed.

Today, when yet another Qingming has arrived, I refuse to go to the cemetery. I refuse to go to Changi Beach. I scream and pull at my hair and clothes; I cry until my parents leave me alone. My father calls me an insolent teenager. I tell him he's dumb with math and numbers, since I'm not thirteen until next month. My mother pets my hair, asks to wash and braid it, clearly wishing I were still a blameless child.

Now, in my dreams, the medium comes to me, and he is smiling or laughing. He walks out of the water toward me, but I am always afraid, guilty, turning away. And yet I know, even in those blurry landscapes of sleep, I can and should not run.

CAT PERSONALITIES

SOPHIA SAID, "CATS TAKE ON THE PERSONALITIES OF THEIR owners."

"How do you mean?"

Melissa sat beside Sophia on an old, worn couch in the latter woman's apartment. It was late afternoon, a mild autumn day in their small upstate town. From afar, the two looked similar, with their dark hair and glasses, both wearing dark knit sweaters and jeans, legs tucked beneath them. But upon closer inspection, one might notice differences. Sophia's small face and deep-sunken eyes. Melissa's hunched back and large hands. The two women had been sitting together for about fifteen minutes when Sophia brought up the cats.

"For example, my cats were very anxious because, as you know, I'm crippled by severe anxiety." Sophia made a sound between a whimper and a laugh. "Every time I heard a loud noise from the upstairs neighbors, or whenever a car alarm went off, or if there was a knock at the door, my fear transferred directly to the cats. They would jump up from wherever they were and run away to hide under the couch or the bed, or inside a closet. Once, Eloise pushed out the window screen and ran off into the neighborhood, and it took hours to find her hiding underneath the neighbor's car. When she and Rupert lived with me, they were afraid of every person who came into the apartment. It took them a long time not to run from even you. Not because I'm anxious about *you* as a person. I'm just always anxious about social interactions."

There were cat hairs on her couch, and Sophia paused to pick at a few strands and drop them on the floor. Her cats had recently been sent away to live with her mother.

"Has your chest thing gotten any better?" Melissa asked.

"Oh, it's the same. Comes and goes, sometimes comes and won't go."

"Did you figure out any triggers, like the therapist asked?"

"Sure. Living. Having to exist every day. Being trapped in a bag of skin."

"Hmm."

"At least Ruth taught me a breathing exercise, and it seems to help."

Sophia demonstrated the breathing exercise—seven beats of breath in, seven beats of breath out—which could be extended or shortened; the importance was that the breaths in and out matched. Even doing it for show calmed her.

Melissa nodded. She, too, began to pick at the cat hairs on Sophia's couch. "Ruth knows about it?"

"Oh, she's such an empathetic person, it sort of came out naturally."

Ruth was a new coworker of theirs whom they'd both known for a few months.

"Anyway," Sophia continued, "now that the cats are living with my mother, you'd think they'd have more reason to be anxious. There are more noises in the city, and my mother has significantly more friends who come and go from the house. But the cats have calmed down, amazingly. They're sociable with people, love sitting in strangers' laps—they don't jump or run away or scream at random hours of the night. My mother is a freakishly calm, relaxed person. God knows how I became the way I am. My theory is that it's a generational thing. So, proof, the cats have taken on her personality after only a month of living with her."

"That's pretty amazing for your cats," said Melissa.

"They're leading much more stable and healthy lives now. I feel badly for putting them through such stressful times."

"Don't you miss them, though? They'd been with you for, what, two years?"

Melissa, too, had a cat. Her cat had lived with her for seven years and continued to live with her. She could not imagine giving her cat up.

"Yes, I know I was responsible for them, and I signed some contract committing to taking care of them for their entire lives when I adopted them. I know I'm being selfish." Sophia smiled at Melissa.

"No, you're not . . ." Melissa said. She adjusted her legs on the couch and began running her large hands through her own hair, nervously grooming.

"Well, I'm aware I can be a brat," said Sophia. "Maybe that's why my cats were little brats, too. Such crybabies. My mother is happy to have them, and I'm relieved. A burden has lifted, and I can be more myself, more wretched than ever. I can pace around my apartment without having to worry about the effect it has on the poor things. I know, I know—I'm pathetic. I assure you, nobody hates me more than I hate myself."

"Nobody hates you. I didn't mean anything like that."

"Oh, I don't know. It doesn't always seem that way to me."

Melissa stood up and asked if she could go make some tea in the kitchen and whether Sophia would like some as well. Melissa had been in Sophia's home enough times to know how to maneuver in the setting, where to locate various items. Sophia agreed to tea, and in the brief moments each woman had alone, both checked their phones. Each had the thought that their friendship was no longer what it used to be and perhaps never would be again—and why?—but each put it out of her mind. Another fifteen minutes had passed.

Upon Melissa's return to the room, tea-filled mug in each hand, she asked, "What about other people's cats? Any other examples of human-to-cat personality exchange?"

"Oh! I've got one." Sophia sat up straighter. "Ruth's cat is exactly like Ruth."

"Really?"

"Yes, I mean, Pearl is incredibly elegant and beautiful, long-limbed and longhaired, and she has this way of looking at you like she sees your innermost self. That piercing look, just like Ruth's."

"Sure, her cat's elegant, she has nice hair. I'd say that speaks more to the kind of cat Ruth would be drawn to getting than the cat taking on Ruth's personality, though. A designer cat."

"That cat looks like a princess unicorn. I want to steal her and bring her home with me."

"Well, you can't really have a cat here after getting rid of your own."

"I didn't mean literally."

"I'm just saying."

"You're making me feel guilty again."

"Sorry," said Melissa. They were quiet for a bit, trying to let the tension pass. Then Melissa continued, "The thing about

Ruth's cat is that she'll walk up to you as though she's interested in pets and attention, but when you try to pet her, she swats at you and hisses. She's constantly seeking attention, but then she acts like she doesn't want it."

Sophia laughed. "No, it's not like that. You're misinterpreting."

"How so?"

"Yes, she does make it hard to pet her, but the thing is, she makes you earn her trust and friendship. She's testing you. What you get is the gift of her presence."

"I find that really irritating."

"Well, maybe that says more about you than her."

"Maybe."

The two women sipped their tea. Sophia wondered if she'd truly made the right decision to rehome her cats. Melissa was making her feel terrible about it. Melissa wanted to go home to her cat, but not quite yet, since the two women had agreed to spend more time together, and this was that time.

"Okay. What about my cat, then?" Melissa said. "Momo is nothing like me. He's laid-back and never bites or fights. He is incredibly tolerant of people petting him and picking him up. He's a very friendly and good cat, and he's been this way forever."

"No, your cat is very much like you." Sophia smiled, ready to attack.

Melissa smiled back, hopeful for a moment. "You think so?"

"Yes." Sophia held out her fist. "One." She stuck out one finger. "Your cat isn't as friendly as you think. Sure, he's tolerant of people, but he's actually very disinterested in them. He'll check a person out, sniff them, allow for some pets and attention, but then he just up and leaves. Two." She stuck out another finger. "If we're ever at your place, which is rare, we don't actually see much of your cat. He stays in another room to be alone. Three." She stuck out another finger. "He also kind of looks like you. He's sleek and has this glare that's a lot like yours."

"Okay."

"What?"

"Nothing. I said okay."

"Do you not think that's an accurate description of his personality?"

"I guess you see it that way."

"Don't look like that! That's the glare I'm talking about! I just went on and on about my debilitating anxiety and how pathetic I am and how it negatively affected my cats. All I said was that your cat isn't as friendly as you think. And I said he's sleek like you!"

"Right."

"What, now you're going to get upset?"

Sophia stared at Melissa, who stared at her cup of tea and took a few more sips. The cup was still steaming. It was starting to get dark outside. The leaves that had been brilliant in the sunlight were beginning to take on a gray, muted tone.

"I should probably go home soon," said Melissa. "Feed Momo."

"Really? You're going to be that way?"

"I'm not being any way."

"Well, I'm heading to Ruth's place for wine and a movie later tonight. You can join us after you tend to the cat."

"Thanks for the invitation, but I guess I'm just not very interested in being around people tonight."

Sophia let out a bitter scoff and pulled out her phone. Melissa stood up and brought her teacup to Sophia's sink. The cup was still nearly full, so she poured the rest down the drain. The kitchen was meticulously clean, so Melissa washed the cup, but she slammed it a bit too hard in the dish rack. She walked back into the living room and toward the door.

"Okay, I guess I'll see you at work tomorrow."

Sophia didn't look up from her phone. "Sure, bye."

Melissa bent down to put on her shoes. When she got up, she turned back to face Sophia. "By the way, I think Ruth's cat is a snobby bitch."

Sophia finally looked up. "What–"

"Every time I've gone over, she climbs onto my lap, but if I do anything she doesn't like, even shift my body a little, she scratches my arms and draws blood. I can't even get angry or react because she'll attack again. And Ruth doesn't do anything about it, she just sits there like some fucking princess. The last time it happened, you literally laughed and didn't even care that I was hurt. Why would I want to go over to Ruth's when that nightmare cat is there?"

"What the hell are you going on about?"

"I'm telling you Ruth's cat is a monster."

"You're being ridiculously sensitive. That cat barely did anything to you."

"Sure, make excuses for her. And feel free to tell Ruth what I said about her cat. I know you want to."

The two women stared at each other.

If one were to walk into the room at that moment, silently and without disturbing the scene, one might notice the intensity in both women's postures, how their necks were pitched forward as though each might strike the other. One might also notice how taut the air was between these women, though one might wonder what combination of emotions was causing this sensation–was it the currents of anger or love or jealousy or pain? There was a knowing silence between them, but an outsider would not be in touch with this knowing, would not understand how the many years of their relationship acted as the live ingredients to this one moment. A spectator would, however, note the weird kind of quiet in the room, the only sounds the occasional swish of tires against pavement coming through the open window by where Sophia sat or the lone leaf that fell and tapped gently against the door where Melissa now stood. The sound was enough to snap the women out of their posturing.

"Maybe your little theory about cats is true," Melissa said, putting her hand on the doorknob. "And you know what? I think it's really great that your cats are finally able to relax. I bet it was super-unhealthy for them to be around you all the time. Sounds like it must have taken a huge toll on them, and it's for the best that they can now lead lovely, calm lives away from you."

Sophia stood up from the couch, hackles totally raised. "You're such a—"

"Tell Ruth's cat I said hello," Melissa said, cutting Sophia off as she walked out.

Sophia went to the door and was about to yell out at Melissa that her cat was the opposite of friendly, that he was, in fact, an incredibly rude and bad and cruel friend, but then Sophia saw that her next-door neighbor was watering plants in his front yard, and she grew anxious that he might see and hear her, so she scurried back into her apartment, where it was safe.

OTHER PEOPLE

I REMIND PEOPLE OF OTHER PEOPLE. I GET QUESTIONS LIKE, "Are you related to so-and-so?" or "How's it going, [insert name not mine]?" It doesn't surprise me. I get it. When I was a child, I came back to the States after two years away in Shanghai, and I couldn't tell my white classmates apart. It took many anxious months for me to notice the differences between them, to honestly distinguish one from another. It's based in science, this inability to decode faces across race—way back in 1914, Harvard psychologist Gustave Feingold studied this perceptual illusion. Which was why, when I got off the bus coming home the other day and heard a man's voice ask from behind, "Excuse me, do you know Alice Lim," my instinct was to ignore and continue walking.

But then he tapped my shoulder.

"Hey, look, I'm not anyone—" I snapped, then stopped.

He was Asian, like me.

(If I wasn't clear earlier, those kinds of questions typically come from white people. What surprises me is that most of them aren't nervous about making mistakes with me or people who look like me. "Oh well, you *do* all look *similar.*" As if it has nothing to do with who's doing the seeing. As if it's a simple truth.)

The man's name was Jack. I guessed he was older than I was,

not by much, maybe in his early thirties. He was profusely apologetic. He knew why a mistake like that might hurt. He told me I looked like a friend of his, someone he'd lost touch with, and that he thought we might be related. He repeated her name: Alice Lim.

I apologized, too. One, for not knowing the woman, and two, for snapping at him—in this case, I might truly resemble this Alice. Jack swore that I did, then he asked if I had plans. Typically, I would have lied and said that I was busy, but by then we had been standing together for some time, and I had grown comfortable enough in the interaction to tell the truth. I thought of my parents, how they were always reminding me to work on my people skills. "Don't be so worried. Try harder. You have to live without us now," they'd say on the phone, from across a huge ocean. Jack seemed so eager and apologetic, I thought maybe we'd get along and become friends, or something more. So when he invited me to dinner, I said yes.

He worked downtown at a boutique ad agency as a group account director and lived in the Inner Sunset a few blocks down the hill from me. He'd moved from Los Angeles four years earlier for the job. All of his family still lived in L.A., in a predominantly Thai immigrant community. (Earlier, I had simply thought he was Chinese, since that's what I am, along with most of the Asians in the neighborhood. Another kind of mistake, another kind of erasure, for which I felt incredibly guilty.) He was a fast talker, somebody with something to prove. I tried to ask him more questions about his family, his life, but after formalities, he wanted only to tell me about Alice, the woman whose face was like mine.

He and Alice had met at a rebranding launch party for an account of his, a healthy-snack-bar company. (I can't remember the name, only that it involved a bad pun.) The owners—a married couple from Boston who had quit their finance jobs to work on their "passion project"—were standing in a large group of people. Alice was among them. That must have been when Jack first saw her. Jack swooped in and started shaking hands, congratulating the snack owners and executives on the new branding. Their image had been wholesome, boring, and reminiscent of Grandma in a bad way—but they had successfully transitioned to hip with a twist of wholesome, reminiscent of Grandma in a cool way. Jack had personally come up with the idea that the snack company begin donating a percentage of their profits to a charitable cause—the latest white papers had indicated that this sort of program increased brand awareness without cutting into profits, especially when charitable giving was displayed prominently on packaging and in targeted ad campaigns. Plus, it didn't cost the company much when the donation percentage was undisclosed and very small.

The husband-owner praised Jack's excellent work and brought him in for an aggressive hug and pat on the back. He turned to the woman next to him and said, "Alice is our first hire for the brilliant new Entrepreneurship in the Community program you came up with." That's when Jack first really noticed her. There was nothing especially striking about Alice: nothing offensive but nothing particularly attractive, either. She had a face that seemed almost blank. (I tried not to take offense when Jack said this.) The only thing he remembered thinking in their first encounter was that Alice looked young. ("But you know how it is," Jack said, prematurely laughing at his own joke, "Asians don't age.")

The owners went on to describe Alice's life and their new Entrepreneurship program. The two of them held each other around the waist, talking in tandem. The sun was setting behind the couple, casting them in a pinkish glow, and they both looked perfectly high, high on the new brand, the one that the agency had helped to create, the brand that gave back, inspired, educated, nourished, nurtured, and ideally, fingers crossed, sold better than its earlier incarnation. They seemed to have memorized and rehearsed many of Alice's life details and shared them all with Jack and the rest of the group, each person wearing the kind of polite, strained look one wears while having to endure a story for the second or third time.

Alice was an orphan. She had bounced from foster home to foster home, then been homeless as a teenager, after having escaped a terrible, horrific, frightening living situation—unimaginable, really. At seventeen, she'd landed a job stocking at Rus's Community Market, a local organic food store, become a cashier at eighteen, assistant manager at twenty, and had been there for the last few years. The owners had met her back when they were just starting out, going door-to-door looking for vendors to stock their snack bars. Alice had been incredibly helpful and sweet and endearing. The owners already attributed some of their local success to Rus's, whose aging hippie and punk clientele had been eroded by the growing population of young, wealthy techies gentrifying the area—so sad, truly, but can you guess who buys more snack bars? Alice was incredibly bright and had been through *so* much, who better to be the first fellow for their Entrepreneurship program than her? With just a little push, she could be like them, starting her own business. She could be better than they were. An inspiration to us all. The owners were so, so happy to play even a small role in helping her achieve success.

Alice seemed unfazed by the story. She reminded Jack of a

small, compact statue. Solid and immovable. He, on the other hand, *had* been moved by the story. Here was a girl who was making something out of nothing. It reminded him of his parents' journey in America.

(At this point in Jack's story, I finally interjected and mentioned that Alice's life sounded a lot like something sad and sappy you'd see on *Oprah* or *Dr. Phil* or *Law & Order*. I asked him if he'd heard about the white American woman who had adopted a child from Cambodia and then tried to return him on a one-way flight back when he got "harder to manage." Jack looked at me, somewhat irritated, then immediately smoothed his face over into a calm, peaceful look. The effect was so mastered and seamless, I wouldn't have even noticed his initial irritation if I hadn't been so anxious; I hadn't eaten dinner alone with a man in a long time. He was clearly an expert people pleaser. It was, after all, what he was paid to do.

"No, I haven't," he said. "Why do you bring that up?"

"I don't know. It just reminded me of that crazy story, like almost too sad to be real."

"Well," he said, "there are plenty of very real, very sad stories." He smiled at me.

"Okay," I said.

"If you let me finish, you'll see."

We were sitting at a salvaged wooden table inside a nearby Asian-fusion tapas place of his choosing, waiting for the food to arrive. I began to worry I'd made a mistake in agreeing to eat with him. My earlier vision of him being a possible friend or romantic interest was fading quickly. Why did he so badly want to tell me about a woman I didn't know? Why was I still sitting there listening? My sense of what was appropriate and not hadn't been functioning well since I'd moved to the city alone. But then a bowl of tom kha gai arrived at the table, and Jack offered it to me first, and I felt a bit more at ease. I remembered what my parents said. I should worry less. When you think about it, there are strangers eating together all over the city, all the time, and nothing terrible happens. This stranger before me was wearing a crisp button-down shirt and buffed leather oxfords. He seemed harmless. Even in the dim lighting, his hair had a pretty sheen.)

Alice was also well dressed the evening Jack met her. She looked so well groomed that Jack wondered if the snack-bar couple had already done some charitable giving. Soon after telling Alice's little story, the owners flitted away. Jack lingered by her until it was just the two of them alone. But when he tried to talk with her, Alice gave short, cold answers. Jack was disappointed. He was weighing whether to disengage or try harder, with a different tactic, when Alice received a call, said sorry, and walked away to answer her phone. Whatever happened on the call changed Alice's whole demeanor. Though she'd been away only a few minutes, Alice returned invigorated, practically shaking. Her face had changed. The blankness of earlier was now colored in, flushed and churning.

Again, he said, he was reminded of his childhood, the way his parents' moods would shift so randomly, instantly, he never could identify the inciting event. And though Alice was not his mother, he knew how to respond. He waited silently—allowed the other person to take the lead. (Jack paused and eyed me a little too long when he said this. I focused on a dish of fried Brussels sprouts covered in five-spice, picking at it to avoid his stare. I thought this might be a good opportunity to share something about myself, the fact that my own parents let me talk all I wanted, that they talked a lot in response. But when I looked at

Jack, he didn't seem to want me to interrupt his story with any of my own, so I didn't.)

"Do you want to get out of here?" Alice asked.

"Sure," he said. ("Don't look like that," he told me. "I'm a good guy. Nothing like that happened, it's not that kind of story.")

The two walked to a pseudo dive bar a couple blocks away, the kind of place that looks worn and unclean but serves eighteen-dollar cocktails, and they sat at a table not unlike the one Jack and I were sitting at. "My treat," Jack said; he had been lucky, his parents were naturalized soon after his birth thanks to his uncle, who had married an American. They worked extra-hard, opened up a salon in L.A., bought a few rental properties for passive income, and made a comfortable life for him and his brother. ("I'm proof of the American dream," Jack said to me. I tried not to move my face in response—perhaps having a blank face was a compliment after all.) Thanks to his parents, Jack went on to a Stanford education and a mid-six-figure salary and owning a Bay Area apartment—he could afford to buy Alice at least a few drinks. That's when Alice relaxed a little and started to talk.

Jack didn't learn everything he knew about Alice in one night. It took a handful of meetings. Alice often became agitated by her own stories and would get up and leave. But she would eventually reach out to Jack and ask to get a drink at the bar again.

That first night, Alice asked Jack if he had siblings.

She didn't seem to care about Jack's answer. She wished only to be asked the same in return. Like when you return to the office on a Monday and your coworker asks about your weekend only to immediately talk about their own. Your friend asks how your relationship is going because they want to vent. A neighbor asks about your lawn, wanting to brag about theirs.

Jack said he was an only child, how about her?

Alice said she had a sister, and that was who had called at the snack bar's party. Alice was folding into herself, her sweater wrapped tightly around her curled torso. But something inside her was expanding, reaching out toward Jack.

"The thing is, I'm not an orphan," she said. "As far as I know, at least. I have a family. I did run away from home. But the orphan thing and the foster homes . . . well, those aren't real." She looked up at Jack, embarrassed and apologetic. "I haven't spoken to my family since I was a teenager, not even my sister. She's persistent. She always has been, even after all these years. She's not much younger than me, but I still think of her as my baby sister. It's weird, she's probably graduated from college already . . ."

"I was right, it wasn't real," I interjected, feeling like I'd won some game or predicted the end of a movie.

"I'm not done yet," he snapped. He looked at me across the table, now covered in strange Asian-fusion dishes—pork belly sushi, spaghetti with some sort of "Thai" sauce, fried chicken drumettes over chana masala. Then he softened. "You really have the same mouth as her," he said.

It occurred to me then that Jack could be angling for something sexual, and for a moment I was excited. But then he asked if I had ever used an ancestry or genetic testing service and been matched with anyone in the area.

"No, I haven't done one of those," I said.

"You should consider it.")

Rebecca. That was her sister's name. She'd been fifteen when Alice left home, not very far away, in San Jose. She was energetic and outgoing but also very subservient, eager to please. Sure, they fought. What sisters didn't? They'd grown up in the same room, slept in two twin beds with only two stacked milk crates between them. They'd had a routine since girlhood where one of them would scratch the surface of her bed three times, and if the other person was awake, she was to respond with three scratches in return. Alice was always the last person to scratch, waiting for a response, only to listen to her sister's deep breathing.

They lived in East San Jose, what people called the armpit. Their family rented a house with a little yard, a functioning roof and refrigerator, and windows that actually opened, without bars, which is more than a lot of other people could say. Her parents worked for another Chinese family who owned a few restaurants in the South Bay. For a small weekly pay cut, the family allowed the Lims to list the address of one of the restaurants on school forms, making it possible for the sisters to attend schools in a better district.

Alice and Rebecca were both top students, fighting against other extremely bright, studious kids who all wanted to end up at the best universities. Alice said it was like being in China, how competitive all those kids were. (I doubt Alice knew what school was really like in China, but she was right that it's insanely competitive. The teachers used to make those of us with the lowest test scores stand up at our desks and apologize for our failures in front of the entire class of fifty kids. Not that I ever had to stand like that—I was American, there temporarily, so treated with care. But I didn't tell Jack any of this.) Alice built the academic trail that her sister followed. But Rebecca had something on Alice: charisma and confidence. Rebecca made friends easily, whereas Alice had few and always considered Rebecca her best. By the time Alice started to think more seriously about college, her envy and bitterness toward her sister had become something dense and impenetrable. She attributed all of Rebecca's good nature and uncomplicated spirit to one specific difference between the two of them: Rebecca was a citizen. Alice was not.

"I always thought we were the same because we grew up the same, with the same parents in the same places. We were sisters, with the same blood," Alice said. "But that was naive."

Alice's parents were undocumented, too. They'd brought Alice, at age one, from China with them on a tourist visa and stayed. It was simple, in a way. Rebecca was born in a sterile room on September 12, 1991, at the Regional Medical Center. There was a photo album filled with images taken by a disposable camera from her birth date and the days after, her parents holding her, Alice reaching as a toddler to touch her sister's sleeping face. Only once had Alice seen a photo of herself as a baby. It was an image of a baby alone, tightly wrapped in a yellow blanket, skin splotched and red, mouth open as though screaming. The baby was lying on an indistinct brown surface that could have been in a hospital room or someplace else entirely.

It was understood in their family that Rebecca would save them all. But it would be a long wait until she turned twenty-one and could sponsor first their parents, then Alice. And Alice wouldn't be a priority; she'd be a "fourth-preference relative," according to Homeland Security.

"That's the lowest preference," said Alice. "And do you know how much money you have to make to sponsor somebody?"

Jack shook his head. He didn't know anything about any of it, really.

"Well, neither did Rebecca," said Alice. "None of them, not her or my parents, knew how hard it was going to be. *I* knew it was going to be practically impossible. Rebecca was always a good student, but she was scatterbrained. She could barely keep track of her house keys. How could I live waiting for somebody like that to save me?"

Rebecca was your typical last-born child, she didn't understand responsibility. But in the end, it didn't matter. Alice figured that out as she walked in and out of those required college-and-career sessions with counselors her junior year. Everything hit her. She was different, she was foreign, she was illegal. She couldn't qualify for the loans and scholarships to afford college. What had been the point of following the rules? Of doing well in school? Of obeying everyone when, technically, her existence itself was illegitimate?

Jack wanted to be a good guy. He wanted to be a kind, sympathetic ear, but he wasn't sure what he was getting into, the more he talked with Alice. Was this another lie? And if it wasn't, how did her status affect the snack-bar company, which was Jack's *actual* job to be concerned about? Did the owners know? Of course not. They believed another story. They had told it, glowing and proud. Should he tell them that they had hired an undocumented person? Snitching would be terrible, honestly, and it defeated the whole purpose of the charitable move. But . . . it was illegal. No, he wouldn't tell. He couldn't.

Each time Jack met with Alice, he felt like he was truly seeing another person, raw and whole. Surely she recognized their kinship, too, or else why keep meeting and sharing with him? (*Yes, why?* I asked myself. What did she see in him? Perhaps Jack had simply been there for her at the right time with the right kind of face, just as I was then to him.)

By her senior year, Alice felt detached from Rebecca and her family. One time, while the two sisters were doing their homework, Rebecca laughed at something a friend texted her. The sound of her laugh grated Alice's insides.

"Could you stop," Alice said.

"It's just my coworker saying that the blender broke and spat up fruit all over her," said Rebecca. "Isn't that funny?"

Alice had never been able to find work. Anywhere legitimate wouldn't take her. She'd asked about working at the restaurant where her parents worked, but the owners didn't want a teenager who could come only after school. Hearing Rebecca talk about her job so cheerfully unscrewed something inside Alice. She grabbed the lamp on her desk and threw it. Still attached to the wall socket, all it did was thump against the carpet not far from Alice's own feet. But Rebecca looked at her sister in a way that had been reserved previously for their parents, for those times their mother would drive so fast and recklessly that it seemed she wanted to kill them all, or when their father would return home and scream in his room for minutes at a time, wailing into some dark void.

Alice picked up the lamp. "Just stop," she said, quieter this time.

Rebecca treated her sister with extreme care after that. She moved around Alice as though she were a volatile substance whose effects and reactions to outside stimuli were highly unpredictable.

"I was terrible to be around. I don't entirely blame her. Anymore, at least," Alice said.

Weeks before her high school graduation, Alice left. There wasn't much to say about that. It had been easy enough. She gave herself a new life, she rewrote her backstory, and in it, she was somebody who deserved help instead of somebody who didn't exist enough to be noticed. Before she left, she'd tried to talk to Rebecca, to have a sort of goodbye. Rebecca would get back from the smoothie shop around ten at night, so tired that she'd slump into bed in her weird orange and purple uniform and fall right asleep. Maybe her sister had been struggling, too. Alice crouched next to Rebecca, where she was curled in bed, and scratched the surface next to her face. Rebecca didn't wake up.

Alice never contacted Rebecca again. It was better that way. One less person for Rebecca to save. Alice knew they wouldn't look for her, and anyway, she'd left a note telling them not to. (In Bowen family systems theory, this is called an *emotional cutoff,* wherein a person manages unresolved emotional issues with family members by reducing or eliminating contact with said members.) Jack wondered aloud if Alice had ever sought outside help, if she'd ever told anybody, besides him, her true story—sure, he was a stable guy with a great job, but he had dealt with some shit, too, and he was working through said issues with a Bowen family systems expert, he told me while tapping his fork incessantly against his plate. Being around all these "new-agey, earthy white people" at work had made him feel like it was more okay—even *brave*—to divulge one's own vulnerabilities. He wished someone could have suggested therapy to Alice; maybe things would have turned out better.

"I doubt it," I said.

Jack looked surprised. "What do you mean?" he said.

"How would Alice have afforded therapy? Not all of us have high-paying jobs with health insurance," I said.

"Oh," he said. "I hadn't thought about that." He eyed me for a moment, and I had a sliver of hope that he might ask me about myself, about my life, and this would turn into a different kind of dinner, the one I'd hoped for. I was surprised to feel a desire to compete with Alice for Jack's attention, despite how turned off I was by our interaction. Still, there was something in the way he talked about her that I envied.

"I work a crappy hourly job, so I know how that feels," I said. "And I'm alone, too. My parents had to move back to China because they couldn't afford to live here anymore."

"Oh, really?" He considered this for a short time, then replied, "Well, you know, there are other people who can't even go back to their home country."

I looked away. What was I trying to prove? "Yeah," I said, shamed. "Like Alice."

He nodded.

"So then what?" I asked.)

Rebecca was twenty-five now. She had found Alice's number somehow. Like Alice said, persistent. Rebecca called and left messages; Alice never answered or returned them. Rebecca said she would put in the papers for their parents as soon as she was allowed. She wanted to do the same for Alice, and she just wanted Alice to get in touch, please, it had been so long. One time, after twentysomething calls, Alice did pick up the phone, only to hear Rebecca breathlessly repeat what she'd said in her messages.

"The system isn't fair," Rebecca said.

Alice hung up, having spoken not a word.

The fourth and last time Jack saw her, Alice drank so much she was sick. She was mumbling about the system, the system, ha ha. "Like I have years to wait." Jack patted her on the back and asked if she was feeling all right. He wanted to help her. He knew some excellent attorneys who could assist. Alice said she could take care of herself, she was fine, she just needed to use the bathroom. It took him half an hour to realize she wasn't coming back. That had been about five months ago.

"Never heard from her again," said Jack. We were almost done with dinner. He had insisted on dessert, basic chocolate cake. (The restaurant seemed to have given up on the Asian-fusion theme in the last act).

"She straight-up disappeared," he said. In all the time he had talked with Alice, he never learned where she lived. "Nobody could find her. Phone disconnected. The owners were pissed. They asked me if I knew of anybody else who might be a good fit, given my background, not sure what the hell they meant by that." He paused to pick at the cake. "I just want to know that Alice is okay. You know?"

The thought crossed my mind that this man had just made up an entire life story to endear me to him and possibly end up spending the night with him, but then he asked me again if I was sure I wasn't at all related to Alice in some other way—we were both Chinese in the Bay Area, after all. Did I know any Lims? Think hard—and the desperation in his voice made me believe everything he'd said, or at the very least, I believed that he believed what he was saying.

"There are so many Chinese people here, and we're not all related," I said. "Plus, she could've used a fake name."

"You think so?" He looked disturbed.

"Uh, yes," I said. "Especially given the circumstance."

He was rubbing his hands repeatedly on the cloth napkin on the table, appearing as eager to leave our dinner as he'd been to have it. I saw that he wanted to get home so he could change course in his search for Alice, now that he realized she might not be "Alice" at all. But that could just be me reading into things. He had his credit card ready before the waiter could place the bill on the table.

"My treat," he said, just like he'd said to Alice.

It made me feel a little guilty, but I didn't protest. I had done something for him, I figured, and could at least receive this in return.

Outside, Jack and I hugged awkwardly.

"I'm heading this way," he said, pointing up the hill, and though it was the same direction I needed to go, I pointed the opposite way (and though we had gotten off at the same bus stop, he didn't question me, he just stared at me for a beat, then turned around and left).

I took a walk along Irving, past the old Irish bars, the Asian bakeries and grocers, the new trendy-looking restaurants. Across the street, an old man noisily pushed a cart of what looked to be newspapers and blankets, and behind him, a small girl trailed at his heels as she dragged a heavy-looking plastic bag behind her. I wondered whether I should tell my parents about how I'd met Jack. I didn't think I would. I had a lingering sense of shame, this feeling that the whole exchange didn't reflect well on me. Perhaps that was how he felt after his talks with Alice. I remembered something then, something I wish I could've told Jack. I can still hear him reprimanding me: Other people can't go back. Maybe if I run into him again, maybe I'll get the chance to tell him, maybe by then he will have found Alice, my doppelgänger, and maybe I'll tell her, too . . .

One of my elementary school teachers in China—she taught all the fitness classes—once told me about a woman she knew in Boston. She asked me if I'd ever been. I had not, but I told her that my grandfather lived there, though I didn't say I'd also never met him. (I never did end up meeting him.) She wrote a note to give to my parents, requesting a favor—could they please have my grandfather ask around about this woman and possibly get a phone number and address? I didn't have the ability to tell her no. I kept the note in my backpack for months and threw it away before we moved back to the States. The woman was an old friend of hers. They used to live in the same longdhang as kids; they were on a ribbon dance team together. They hadn't spoken in decades. My teacher knew only her friend's Chinese name but assumed that her friend had an American name by then, too. She told me her friend's American name might be Julie, because her friend once met a nice American woman at a restaurant named Julie. Then my teacher held me by the shoulders and said, "You are lucky. You don't know how many people wish they could be you."

ACKNOWLEDGMENTS

The stories in this collection were written and edited over the course of nine years, in multiple cities across three states, and during several different phases of life. There are many people—too many to name—who helped and influenced me along the way. I'm especially grateful to those who read and offered feedback on early drafts. I also cannot thank enough the friends, family, and readers who have supported my writing throughout the years.

Thank you to editors and journals that published and polished versions of the following stories:

"Li Fan"—Hestia Peppe at *3:AM Magazine*

"Tomb Sweeping"—Susan and Linda Davies at *Glimmer Train*

"To Get Rich Is Glorious"—Michael Ray at *Zoetrope: All Story*

"Klara"—Meakin Armstrong at *Guernica*

"Flies"—Miciah Bay Gault and Christina Thompson at *Harvard Review*

Special thanks to Sara Birmingham, Alexa Stark, Vivian Rowe, TJ Calhoun, Cordelia Calvert, Nina Leopold, Sonya Cheuse, and everyone at Ecco who helped bring this book into the world.